Praise for Katie Porter's *Double Down*

"The writing duo that is Katie Porter knows erotica. From the first sentence, you'll be drawn into the glamour and sleaze of Las Vegas and the wonderful, yet sensitive, world of Ryan and Cassandra."

~ *RT Book Reviews*

"With steamy romance set in the sultry desert of Vegas, this book takes costumes and performance to an all-time high. Readers who are looking for handsome pilots and long, fun-filled nights will love this sassy read, sure to get your jets off!"

~ *Library Journal*

"The story grips you by the neck and doesn't let go, while you watch the lovers dance."

~ *Limecello*

"Faithful reader, if you are looking for a sizzling contemporary and like men in (or out of) uniform, you should definitely check out this new series."

~ *The Good, The Bad and The Unread*

"Run, don't walk to pick up the first book in this new series. *Double Down* is a touching, humorous story about accepting what makes you happy and doing it."

~ *Sizzling Hot Book Reviews*

"I loved the alternation between fun and lighthearted on one hand and scorching heat and carnal passion on the other. Katie Porter is new in the erotic romance ranks and with *Double Down* went straight to the top of my list."

~ *Pearl's World of Romance*

Look for these titles by
Katie Porter

Now Available:

Came Upon a Midnight Clear

Vegas Top Guns
Double Down
Inside Bet
Hold 'Em
Hard Way

Club Devant
Lead and Follow
Chains and Canes

Double Down

Katie Porter

SAMHAIN
PUBLISHING

Samhain Publishing, Ltd.
11821 Mason Montgomery Road, 4B
Cincinnati, OH 45249
www.samhainpublishing.com

Double Down

Print ISBN: 978-1-61921-245-9
Digital ISBN: 978-1-61921-085-1

Editing by Sasha Knight
Cover by Scott Carpenter

First Samhain Publishing, Ltd. electronic publication: July 2012
First Samhain Publishing, Ltd. print publication: June 2013

Dedication

To JD & AA
Saving puppies

Acknowledgments

We deeply appreciate our families' unflagging support. Credit for much of our sanity is owed to the Group That Shall Not Be Named. The feedback Rhianna Schoonover offered on an early draft was invaluable. Thank you for your time and input! In addition, we offer thanks to Sarah Frantz, Rowan Larke, Zoe Archer, Andrea Hodapp, Patti Ann Colt and Kelly Schaub for their friendship, and to Kevan Lyon and Sasha Knight for their amazing enthusiasm.

Chapter One

Seamed stockings. The waitress was wearing seamed stockings.

Major Ryan Haverty groped blindly for his glass since he couldn't seem to drag his gaze away from those long, slender legs and the stockings clinging to every sleek inch. The cool wash of beer didn't do much to clear his head. When the woman's legs slipped out of view behind another table, he still pictured that sheer black and the darker line tracing up the back of each calf. Christ, maybe they were even silk.

She'd been cute as hell even before he realized the bonus she wore. Pixie-like features were topped with huge blue eyes and strawberry-blonde hair twisted along her nape. Something about the quirk of her mouth said she wasn't as innocent as some might think.

"Yo, Fang." Captain Jonathan Carlisle waved a hand in front of Ryan's eyes. "You with us?"

Ryan blinked at the use of his call sign. He'd unconsciously shifted forward in his seat, the better to watch the waitress walk away. He stretched an arm across the leather bench, trying to focus on his friends.

Jon smirked at him before flicking a glance in the direction the woman had gone. "Really, man? A waitress? Hasn't anyone told you they're practically paid to flirt with the customers? Tips and all."

Jon's words came out rounded in some places and clipped in others—the high-class affect of Massachusetts. No surprise since the guy came from money. Buckets of it. He didn't play up the fact, but he was the reason they were sitting in Blakely's Steakhouse, a tiny family-owned joint. If not for Jon, neither Ryan nor their third friend, Captain Leah Girardi, would have ever heard of it.

The dining area was barely bigger than Ryan's small apartment, but it was lux. Light shone from frosted-glass wall sconces, and every table was blanketed by white linen. Were it not for formal Air Force events, he wouldn't have known what to do with the multiple heavy silver forks at each setting. The atmosphere had a softened white-noise effect, muting conversations from the other diners.

The meal itself had been amazing, as evidenced by the scatter of plates between them, which had been all but licked clean of food. Hell, there'd been a time in his childhood when Ryan wouldn't have hesitated to swipe up the last bits of rib-eye juices with his bare fingers. He hadn't eaten a steak that tender and flavorful until his twenty-fourth birthday, home from his first deployment and living large in New York.

"Wait, the waitress? Fang has a thing for her?" Leah twisted around in her seat. "Where'd she go?"

Ryan quirked his brows. "What are you going to do? Pass her a note that says I like her?"

Leah flipped around and flashed a manic smile. Her hair was pulled straight back in a slick ponytail. "So you *do* like her."

He couldn't help but roll his eyes, but just a minute amount. Any more and he might have to give up his balls. "Princess," he said, using her call sign, "sometimes you sound more like a ninth grader than a fighter pilot."

She stuck her tongue out at him.

Jon laughed. "Careful, little girl, or someone'll put that tongue where you aren't expecting."

Leah slugged him in the shoulder. Despite being scrappy and wiry, the other pilot didn't even budge, and Ryan knew from experience that Leah could hit hard when she wanted. "Ryan and I have already been there, done that. Wasn't worth T-shirts."

"Never say," Jon mocked, turning his pretty-boy features into a caricature of surprise. "Our waitress is going to be disappointed?"

"The problem wasn't the sex," Leah said. The woman had barely even a promise of tact. "We were too wound tight for each other. Two type-A's in a relationship is a very bad thing."

"Anyway, she's no one's waitress anyhow." Ryan stretched his legs to the side as cover for searching her out again. The booth really was too small for him—one of the perils of being a couple inches over six feet tall.

There she was, near the swinging wooden doors to the kitchen. Though clad in the same charcoal-gray skirt as the other waitress, she wore it with entirely more grace over her sleek curves. The plain white blouse did him a huge favor and clung to her small breasts.

Some short, rat-faced man had taken her by the elbow, and neither of them looked too happy. Red flushed across her rounded cheeks. Her pretty pink mouth twisted.

Ryan's hands fisted below the table. Those lips were meant for much more fun tasks than spitting words at a pinched asshole.

When she walked back toward Ryan's table, she smoothed her features into the genial friendliness required of servers. The skin around her eyes remained tight.

A hard swallow contorted her graceful throat as she set the leather check-holder on the table. Somehow she still managed to dredge up a smile. "Here you go."

Ryan grabbed the rectangular folder and flipped it open. His eyes bulged. For God's sake, the bill was almost a third what he spent on rent, and more than the monthly mortgage his mom had paid for their trailer when he was growing up.

With a fast display of dimples, Jon snagged it from Ryan's grip. "My choice. My treat. Go back to chatting her up."

Ryan resisted the urge to tell him to shove it. "Fine, but I'll get the tip."

"I hope you were happy with your meal," the waitress said.

"Everything was wonderful." The smile he flashed was the same one that had talked his seventh-grade gym teacher, Miss Pavers, into ignoring the fact he hadn't dressed out for a week. It was difficult to find clean gym clothes when his mom hadn't gotten off the couch in almost a month. He ignored the kick Leah aimed at his shins beneath the tablecloth. "Especially the service."

The woman's eyebrows went up. "Does that line work for you often?"

"See now, there's no way I can answer that," he said with a laugh. "If I tell you no, it'll just confirm what you think. If I tell you the truth, that I've never tried it before, you'll never believe me."

She gave a mock pout and shook her head. "That certainly is a difficult dilemma. I'm not sure you can recover at this point."

"Be careful," Jon said as he took the check and slipped a credit card inside. "At this rate you're going to make yourself a challenge. There's nothing Ryan here likes more than a challenge."

Leah smothered a laugh, making it Ryan's turn to kick at her.

"Ryan? That's your name?"

"Ryan Haverty." He stuck his hand out and nodded to her name tag. "And you're Cassandra, right?"

She put her hand in his with a curt nod. An electric tingle worked its way up to his shoulder. Her fingers were slender and graceful and so smooth that he could imagine them wrapped around his cock. He practically twitched in his slacks.

Cassandra nibbled at her bottom lip. The blue of her eyes shifted darker. "Any relationship to Joseph Patrick Haverty?"

"Not a clue who that is."

She pulled her hand back as she chuckled. "It was a joke. Mostly. He was a painter." She gave an abbreviated wave, as if to brush away her words. She picked up the check. "It's no big deal."

"Cass," said a voice with a distinct whine. The man Cassandra had been talking with near the kitchen doors approached the table. He wore a suit coat that did nothing to conceal his narrow shoulders. His eyes were amazingly beady. Ryan was surprised he could see at all. "Excuse me, gentlemen," he said to Ryan and patted Jon on the shoulder.

Ryan was surprised he didn't draw back a stump. Jon, call sign Tin Tin, might be something of a pretty boy—especially with his goddamn dimples and faux-innocent smirk. The guy had a ruthless side that was only more intimidating for its coldly mechanical streak. Ryan was willing to have him on his wing anywhere, anytime.

After a quick glance over Leah that spent entirely too long on her rack, the man tagged on a, “Miss.”

Leah only raised her eyebrows, thank God. She could be a bit reckless at times.

The guy Ryan presumed was the manager returned his attention to Cassandra and tugged her to the back of the room. There was no mistaking their antagonistic body language. The guy hovered over Cassandra while she kept her face averted. Ryan probably shouldn’t have been able to listen in, but he’d always had excellent hearing. And he was very interested in the conversation’s outcome.

“Why are we out of napkins, Cass?”

“I don’t know, Tommy.” She rolled her eyes before facing her menace. “Probably because it’s not my job to order them.”

“You’ve been taking care of it for the last six months.”

Her smile only got bigger, but it took on a brittle edge. “Let’s not do this in the front of the diners.”

“I tried, but you’re the one who leaves the prep area every time I walk in.”

“Fine,” Cassandra said in a saccharine tone. “I stopped ordering the napkins when you dumped me and took up with Cynthia. How about you ask her to take on that duty?”

After gesturing to the dishwater blonde taking an order at the other end of the room, she stalked back to Ryan. Her eyes sparkled with an amusement that invited him to join in. She wiggled the black leather case with Jon’s credit card inside. “I’ll be back in a minute with this.”

The dickweed followed her to the back of the restaurant, unfortunately obscuring Ryan’s view of both her sweet ass and those sexy stockings.

Jon laughed and shook his head. “It’s my card in there, but she tells you that she’ll be back. Maybe you’ve got a shot after all.”

Leah took a healthy swallow of her red wine. “Nah, that’s a hot mess. You don’t wanna get mixed up in all that drama.”

For the privilege of holding those thighs, still wrapped in silk while he fucked her, Ryan would put up with a lot of drama. The last time he'd had an up-close encounter with a girl who liked fancy stockings had been in college with his ex-fiancée, Ashleigh.

Just look at how that had ended.

He shoved the past back where it belonged. "If anyone would know hot messes, Princess, it'd be you."

"No way. That's Tin Tin and his stream of women. All the way."

"They're not a stream." Jon ran a hand over his dark hair, which was buzzed to a quarter inch like he were some Army grunt freak. "They're a select assortment."

Leah laughed. "That's not what it looks like from here."

"Don't tell me you're jealous."

"Right," she replied with a look of disgust. "Just like I'd be jealous of the girls who make out with my brothers."

Ryan let their patter fade into the background, knowing exactly how their sibling-style bickering would continue. Instead he watched the kitchen doors. A blur of reddish hair zipped past but didn't return.

He tapped his fingers across the white tablecloth. It was way too long since he'd been with a woman who liked wearing rare bonuses like the stockings, because he certainly wasn't about to ask for them. This was an opportunity too good to pass up.

He needed an in. Something that would give him an edge. Make a date with him a challenge. If it was also a way to snub her nose at that cocksucker, so much the better. Cassandra was way out of that guy's league, and Ryan wasn't above rubbing it in the other man's nose.

He sat up straighter when she finally popped out the doors.

She plunked the credit-card holder down in front of Jon. "I'm sure you know the drill," she said with laughter lurking in her voice. She turned to Ryan. "I hope you guys didn't hear too much. Things have been strained around here lately."

Leah knocked back the rest of her wine. "Why do you put up with that crap?"

She shrugged. Slight embarrassment flickered across her features, temporarily turning her lush mouth down. "It's complicated." She plastered a grin on. "Besides, the tips are great here. You have my permission to take that as a hint."

Ryan laughed. "You've got more patience than the three of us combined."

"That wouldn't surprise me in the least."

Jon and Leah slid out of the booth and headed toward the door. Knowing when to make an exit was only one of the things that made them such good friends.

Ryan dug his wallet out of his back pocket. "What time do you get off?"

She checked her watch. "About fifteen minutes, thank the sweet baby Jesus. You asking for a reason?" Her hip cocked saucily, that slim gray skirt clinging. Beneath it the black stockings made his palms itch with curiosity.

He pulled two fifty-dollar bills out of his leather wallet. "I tell you what. This is your tip, no matter what."

Her lips parted on a quiet gasp. "That's thirty percent."

"You say the word and I'll leave it on the table."

"Or?"

He stood. Even in her slingback heels, she only came to his shoulder. Fuckin' A, he liked that. He'd never been into the macho thing, but there was something about her that brought out his protective streak.

The fact that she was hot as hell in an apple-pie kind of way didn't hurt at all.

"Or," he echoed, dragging out the word. "You come with me and we'll turn them into chips up on the Strip. Just to see what kind of trouble we can get into."

Chapter Two

Cassandra Whitman did not fall for cheap lines. Or All-American smiles. Or biceps that strained against black cotton.

Nope. But being sainthood good for longer than she could remember made a girl greedy.

It didn't help that she was still boiling mad at Tommy—make that General Manager Thomas Blakely. She deserved medals and commendations for not mouthing off even worse in front of Ryan and his friends. Choice remarks about Tommy's allergy to foreplay and his Rogaine obsession had remained caged inside her seething brain.

She grinned at Ryan. "Your friend says you like a challenge. That true?"

"Yes, ma'am."

Oh, shoot. She went briefly weak in the knees. It wasn't just the automatic "ma'am", but how he made it earnest. A real Southern gentleman.

"Good," she said. "Then here's one for you."

"I'm listening."

He was. Completely. Dark eyes fixed on hers. He'd leaned closer. His intimate posture suggested confidences and sordid secrets. Crossed arms on another man might seem defensive, but Cass could only admire how his black button-down stretched smooth over the caps of his shoulders.

He took care of himself. She wanted him to take care of her.

A night out. It was about time.

"Tommy," she said. "My manager."

"And ex?"

"Definitely ex." She matched his intimate posture, just the angle of her hips. "He never liked public displays of affection."

"Guys who can't perform generally don't. Too many

witnesses." His voice was huskier now, going from good to wet-undies sexy.

Cass licked her bottom lip and smiled when he noticed. "But I don't want to get fired. Can you meet me in about ten minutes?" She gestured back to the swinging doors that led to the kitchen. "Through there, take a right, and you'll find the employee locker room."

Something about this guy Ryan had her thinking words beginning with B. Brazen. Bold. Balls. If anyone had the balls to stride into the kitchen and kiss her in front of Tommy, it might be Ryan. If they both managed to go through with it...

Well, then the night had turned golden.

"How do I know this isn't a plot to get rid of me? Ten minutes is a long time. Slip out the back door. I'd never see you again."

He made that sound like a tragedy. Cass definitely approved.

"Consider it a show of faith. Just like I'll assume you aren't some weirdo murderer maniac."

Oh, he had a great smile. She loved guys who smiled. Tall, built, *interested* guys who smiled were like big-time Vegas jackpots. You heard about them, but you never imagined seeing one in person.

Some sex demon took possession of her hand. That studly arm was too tempting. She ran the tip of her finger down the firm curve of muscle. The breath Ryan quietly sucked in was almost as exciting as his body.

"I'll be there," she said. "And I'll clean up. I hate smelling like I've been hauling steak for six hours."

Before he could reply, before she lost her nerve, Cass turned and walked toward the kitchen. When she reached the door, she couldn't help but look back over her shoulder. Ryan stood in the same spot. Arms still crossed. Expression still intense. He was staring at her, but not at a guy's usual T&A choices. Cass glanced down at her calves, half thinking she'd find a splatter or stain. Wouldn't have been surprising at all. After six hours on the floor, she felt like a filthy dishrag.

She only found her stockings, the seamed ones she wore

when she wanted to feel like a woman, not an overworked waitress and gallery lackey.

Ryan met her eyes. His frank sexual interest was one thing. The naughty grin sent a shiver up her spine.

She barged into the kitchen. The doors clanged against the inside wall. She laughed to herself when the staff looked up from their preparation tables and sizzling grills. Pulsing excitement made her giddy, even reckless.

After shutting the locker-room door, she stripped out of her disgusting uniform. The only thing she had to change into was the spare set she kept for emergencies—yet another gray pencil skirt and white shirt. Her plans for the evening had involved staggering home exhausted, with a shower and pajamas optional as she collapsed. Now she had the energy of a nuclear reactor.

Gillian Flores, an MFA candidate who studied sculpture, shut her locker. "You outta here?"

"Yup. You just getting here?" Cass ran hot water in the sink.

"Tommy's gonna give me shit for being late again."

"I wouldn't worry about him tonight."

Gilly doubled a rubber band around her thick black ponytail. "Oh?"

"Yeah, I got him covered."

"Now I'm intrigued. You plan on giving him the kicking he deserves?"

After running a washcloth over her skin, Cass toweled off. "Just don't be out on the floor in about four minutes. I've found someone intriguing."

She wiggled into her spare uniform. The skirt wasn't the flashiest in the world, but she appreciated how it fit. Like the stockings, it made her feel curvy and feminine. She undid her hair and combed it with water, then braided two pigtails that trailed over her shoulders. Splash of perfume. Powder and clear lip gloss. She didn't have time for anything else.

Cass had just slipped back into her heels—her tired feet protesting like whoa damn—when she heard the commotion in the kitchen. Perhaps the sound of a certain customer venturing where he didn't belong? A glance at the wall clock made her smile.

Tall. Built. And punctual.

She'd almost been second-guessing herself. He was right in saying ten minutes was a long time—not for getting ready, but for letting the doubts creep in.

"So show me the money, missy." Gilly, wearing the world's most fantastic shit-eating grin, pulled opened the locker-room door with a flourish.

Ryan was right there, standing in the doorway. His hand was poised to knock. Backlit by the much brighter lights of the kitchen, he filled the space. Owned it. "There you are, Cassandra."

Shivers that were becoming more familiar by the second climbed up Cass's back. He said her name like the low harmony of a song, making love to each syllable.

She gulped back the last of her nerves and met him in the doorway. He offered his arm like the Southern gentleman she'd imagined. His forearm was solid beneath her fingertips.

Fluorescent lighting generally did no one any favors. Not so with Ryan. Now she could see the exact sun-tea shade of his short, neat hair. His skin was smooth and lightly tanned, with only the slightest hint of scruff. His eyes weren't as dark as when the dining room's tasteful low-watt atmosphere had obscured their color. In truth they were a perfect blend of brown and green, a true hazel, full of mischief and blatant, panty-dropping desire.

Cass snuggled deeper, with her palm curled flat around that miraculous biceps.

"You ready?" he asked.

She looked around the kitchen. Tommy was nowhere to be found. A flicker of disappointment seemed ridiculous considering the man she stood next to.

It seemed the fates and the gods and the whole damn universe were on her side that night. Tommy walked through the swinging doors. He stopped dead. Pinched eyes swerved from Ryan to Cass, then back to Ryan again. If a man could bristle, Tommy did.

"Can I help you?"

"No, sir." Ryan glanced down at Cass, his humor like an aphrodisiac. "I'm good."

"You can't be in here."

Lordy, how had she put up with that for six months? Being sensible wasn't worth that level of compromise. What did it say about Tommy that his customer was the one who used "sir" while he mislaid that courtesy?

"Don't worry," Ryan said. "We were just leaving."

Tommy smoothed a hand down his suit, that telltale nervous habit of his. "Cass, you said you'd close tonight."

Shoot. She had.

"That was probably because you thought I was a no-show," Gilly said. She stood against the notice wall where schedules and time cards were the only decoration. All the finery in Blakely's was saved for the dining room. "I'm here now. I'll close."

Cass mouthed a silent *thank you* to her friend. Knowing Gilly, she'd want to be repaid in details. Maybe for once Cass would have a few to share.

"I can't believe you," Tommy said.

The flush was high on his cheeks. He was handsome. He really was, no matter his squint and his lanky thinness. Yet he could look downright rodentlike when he turned mean. Cass suppressed a shiver of a different kind. Their last argument—the Big One, as she'd dubbed it—had revealed his true colors. Being called desert trash wasn't something she'd ever forgive, let alone how he'd wet his wiener between Cynthia's rail-thin thighs.

"You're just going to go with this guy? This guy you met an hour ago?"

"Now hold up there." Ryan's voice sounded gruff and confrontational, but Cass caught the teasing glint in his eyes. "I was a *customer* an hour ago. We only met about, what, fifteen minutes ago?"

"Maybe twenty," Cass said. "Not long."

"Yeah, not long."

She'd been expecting a grand, passionate grope—the kind that would roast the innards of any still-clingy, still-possessive ex. That didn't seem to be Ryan's style. He leaned down, taking his time, inviting the tiny world of Blakely's kitchen to watch. He nudged one pigtail aside with his nose. His kiss, when it came, was the gentlest touch of skin to skin. Warm lips pressed against the hollow behind her jaw, just below her earlobe.

Much better. She forced herself to hold still, to soak in his deliberate restraint. Let 'em wonder what went on behind closed doors. They'd get no wild mauling from this gentleman.

Only his exhalation gave him away, hot against her cheek. Too fast. Too erratic. *Good.* She liked the idea that he was raring to go, no matter this slow pantomime.

Ryan straightened to his full height. He nodded once to Tommy, then to Gillian. "Sir, ma'am, have a good evening."

Cass helped make their in-your-face exit perfect by guiding him back through the kitchen toward the door to the employee parking lot. Her knees were mush. Her feet felt a hundred yards away. Every time she thought her strength would fail—out of sheer, unbelievable excitement—she gripped his rock-solid arm.

The air outside was no relief. Vegas in April may as well be a cool day in hell, and it wasn't even summer yet. The exit door closed behind them. Compared to the din in the kitchen and the throb in Cass's head, the city noises were almost peaceful.

Ryan chuckled. "Hot damn, that was fun."

The tension in her chest burst out in laughter to match. She collapsed against the restaurant's stucco outer wall. "Oh, yeah. Best time I've had in months."

"We're not done yet."

"Good." And she meant it. She wanted more and more, like a kid at a fair gorging on cotton candy and too many rides.

He stalked closer. Hard body. Hard wall. Cass was caught in between. Only the grin clinging to his fine mouth kept the moment from becoming intimidating.

"Can I kiss you?" he asked.

"You just did."

"For real this time."

"That one cost you, didn't it?"

"You have no idea." Ryan ran his tongue over his lower lip, almost bashful. "Especially with those braids."

Again she caught that intensity in his eyes—the same he'd shown when staring after her stockings. Okay, that was hot.

She touched the place where his shirt opened at the throat. The tiniest hint of chest hair brushed beneath her fingertip. "Can I tell you a secret?"

"Sure."

"My stockings?"

He swallowed audibly. "Yeah?"

"They're old-fashioned," she whispered. "Lace tops. Garters. The works."

She shoved gently against his chest. He was built like a goddamn Mack truck, but she had a clear advantage. He staggered back just a bit, his expression slack, then followed as she walked toward her tiny Honda. She clicked her key fob and made for the driver's side door.

"You assume I'm a magician if you think I can fit in that tin can," he said.

"Your choice. Give it a try or don't." She raked a long look up and down his body. "You're cute, but I'm not letting you drive."

Rather than press or make another joke, he returned her deliberate perusal, inch for inch. Cass wiggled in her own skin. She'd let him kiss her, all right. If she admitted the whole truth, she was probably going to let him do a lot more. The night was young, and she hadn't been to the Strip in ages.

It was time to play.

Chapter Three

Even with a small stack of chips sitting in front of him at the blackjack table, Ryan couldn't concentrate on a damn thing other than Cassandra's legs. As if the old-fashioned seamed stockings hadn't been enough, she'd gone and told him about the garters. With lace tops. He'd like to drag them down using only his teeth.

Ever since, he'd been sporting a bit of a chubby, even when he'd needed to fold himself into her ridiculously compact car.

More proof Ashleigh had been right all those years ago. They'd dated through his entire senior year of college, long enough for him to propose when he'd started making plans to join the Air Force after graduation. Long enough that he'd risked confiding his secret wants and needs.

She'd been disgusted with his confession. He still recalled the look of pinched condescension on a face that had once shone with respect, even love. Their engagement ended the same night. He hadn't made that mistake again, instead swearing off giving in to those urges.

It wasn't like he'd *asked* Cassandra to wear the stockings or do her hair in pigtails. That was all her own initiative.

Tossing a chip into play, he couldn't take his gaze off her. She deliberated carefully, worrying at her pink bottom lip, flashing a glimpse of white, even teeth.

Then she crossed her legs. Christ, he even liked her knees.

The air went thin in his lungs, as if he'd stripped his oxygen mask at thirty thousand feet. He coughed. "So," he said, without any idea of what he would follow up with. Anything that would get his thoughts back in line.

Of course, thinking about the way she'd pulled her strawberry-blonde hair into two pigtails wasn't much better. He could wrap them around his fists while she did delicious things with that lush mouth.

She glanced at him out the corners of her eyes. A knowing smile curved her lips. "So," she echoed.

"Haverty. What did you say? John Patrick?"

She nodded, then tapped her cards so the dealer would hit her with another. "He's obscure, but I like his work. He's most known for a painting of a piper. It was one of the most famous lithographs in the eighteenth century. Morose, perhaps, but the textures and the colors are memorable."

"You know a lot about art."

A bright pink flush spread over her cheeks. "Sorry, I shouldn't go on like that."

He couldn't help but reach for the pigtail nearest him. A lock of hair like raw silk slipped between his thumb and forefinger. "I don't mind."

"That makes you a rare man indeed. No one's been able to listen to me babble about paintings."

"There aren't many men like me, but that's probably a good thing."

He tapped his cards. Cassandra lifted her eyebrows as the middle-aged dealer flicked him another. Ryan made himself look down and saw why. He'd hit when he'd already been on eighteen.

An older woman, the dealer wore a red vest over the white long-sleeved shirt of the Bellagio uniform. She scooped away his chips. Her dark eyes twinkled, but all she said was, "House wins."

A laugh burst from him. "Yeah, I should think so."

Cassandra leaned an elbow on the padded, green table edge. "You're not much of a gambler, are you?"

Her blouse wasn't low cut, but her angle plumped the soft inside of her breast, bringing it barely into view. "You're not great for my gambling," he said.

"Ah. Your head's not in the game."

His gaze dropped back to her legs. He could almost swear her slow uncrossing and re-crossing was deliberate. "Can you blame me?"

Something hot and sexy flashed in her already bright eyes. She gathered up her chips, then his, and shoved them in his pocket. Her slender fingers brushed his hipbone through the thin fabric lining, sending a full-body shiver out from the base of his spine.

The mischievous look she angled at him didn't help calm him much. Her lashes were thick but pale, almost glimmering with blonde at the tips. Absurd to think, but he'd like to feel them against his skin.

Cassandra hopped off her stool and looped her fingers beneath his black leather belt. "Come on. I've got an idea."

Ryan followed her blindly as she wove through the casino floor. Banks of brightly lit slot machines chinged and dinged with electric recreations of the waterfalls of the coins they'd once spit out. Voices rose and fell, a loud cheer going up from the far side of the room. Someone must have hit a jackpot.

A virtual conga-line worth of drunk people streamed in the opposite direction. A few of them wore three-foot-tall paper hats with absurd sayings. Ryan remembered with crystal clarity why he didn't spend too much time on the Strip, despite living a stone's throw away. The idiot quotient was way too high.

Two brunettes wearing short-as-hell miniskirts and carrying yard-long margaritas stumbled at them, giving Ryan an excuse to fold his arm around Cassandra and pull her near. She fit there perfectly. She was neither too lush nor too skinny. Her curves pressed against his hip, and she wrapped a hand around his biceps, just as she had in the steakhouse.

Combined with how she looked up at him, her eyes shining like he was some bloody hero for pulling her away from drunks, he felt like the king of the hill.

"Over here," she said, abruptly veering them to the right.

In only a few steps, they stood in a relatively quiet, dim corridor. Signs pointed to the elevator at the back. To their left was a bank of payphones. Vegas was probably the only place in the world where the relics could still be easily found. All for the tourists. The clang and noise of the casino floor sounded miles away.

"What are we doing back here, Miss—?" He broke off, surprised and chagrined. "I don't even know your last name."

Considering what he'd been imagining doing with her, he felt pretty shitty about that. She pulled away to lean against the wall—unsurprising when he'd revealed himself quite the jackass.

She only smiled. "We can't have that, not with what I'm about to do for you, Mr. Haverty."

The low, sultry way she used his last name sent him into overdrive. With the naughty librarian skirt, the pigtails and musical voice, he was surprised that he hadn't all-out mauled her yet. He braced a hand against the wall beside her head. Jackass wasn't even close. He was way worse.

"Give me your name." He couldn't keep the growl out of his words, even though he hoped like hell he didn't scare her away. "I should know more about you, considering that I'm going to kiss the hell out of you."

"My name is Cassandra Whitman." Her eyelids drooped with desire. "I have a degree in art history, I'm twenty-six, and I've lived in Nevada all my life."

"And you like old-fashioned garters."

Her throat worked over a swallow. "I do."

The rapid-fire flutter of her pulse at the base of her throat drew him. He bent his head, giving her plenty of time to get away, but he needed another taste of her skin. That moment in the restaurant kitchen had been for the benefit of her ex, but Ryan craved another go. Her skin had been soft, the tickle of her hair across his nose even softer.

She was everything he'd remembered. Just spicy enough. His fingers clenched against the cool wall. He brushed his lips over her neck, then forced himself to pull back. "Apparently, you like dragging men into secluded corridors too."

"Only certain men and only for certain purposes."

He chuckled, but it was strained by his choppy breath. "Should I be afraid?"

She pushed him back to arm's distance with a few fingertips against his chest. "I don't think so. This is for your benefit, after all."

"Is that right?"

"Certainly. I'm altruistic. Practically a saint. You can't keep your head on the cards because you keep thinking of my stockings. So..." She drew the word out. Blood surged down Ryan's body before he even knew what she was up to.

Her hands slid down her torso. Down farther, down, from her hips to the hem of her skirt. Slim fingers curled around the dark gray material and tugged. So fucking languid.

First came inches of sheer black, made even hotter because he knew they were backed with the seams. Then came a wide band of black lace, topped by tiny silk bows with even tinier pink rosettes in the center. The skinny straps that disappeared under her skirt were pink as well.

That was as far as she went, but it was more than enough. His chest practically shook with the force of his violent breathing. His only saving grace was that she breathed just as quickly, which pressed her breasts against the plain white of her blouse.

Ryan caged her head with his hands. Either that or he'd palm the creamy length of thigh peeking out between the stockings and her skirt. If he gave in to that impulse, he'd be inside her as soon as he could kiss her into agreeing. They'd be booted out of the casino for indecent behavior—which would catch him hell from his CO.

He swiped his tongue across his bottom lip, but it didn't do much good. His mouth had gone as dry as the desert outside. "I'm going to kiss you now. If that's not what you want, you better duck and run. Right now."

She tilted her head back against the wall. "This is me, not running."

"Good."

He forced himself to lower his head by degrees, in case she panicked. He wasn't sure how he'd get himself under control if that happened. Thank Christ she didn't. She even surged up on her toes, meeting him halfway.

Her mouth was ten times sweeter than her skin. She tasted like crème brûlée—candied, rich and a hint of burnt sugar. Her lips readily opened under his. He dipped his tongue inside, first to taste the plump vulnerability of her bottom lip, then to stroke over hers.

She gave a quiet moan in the back of her throat, and he hungrily drew it into his mouth. Her breath rushed hot over his cheek. Feminine hands curled into the muscles over his ribs, under his arms. He wanted to touch her but couldn't risk removing his palms from the cool wall. If he touched her, even to cup her face, he might lose his tenuous patience.

Shit, he could be in real trouble with this woman. She had a sense of adventure that seemed woven through with naughty good humor, threatening to turn him inside out.

He tried to pull back, but even that was harder than he'd expected. He swooped back in for another kiss that was no less of a turn-on for its speed.

"Do you...?" He hesitated and tried to swallow the hot lust that hamstrung his body. He hadn't moved this fast since he'd been an idiotic teenager living in the trailer park. He'd thought joining the Air Force and going through officer training and flight school would beat some sense into his head.

Apparently not.

"Do you want to get out of here?" he asked.

Pale lashes fluttered, clearing the haze from her pretty blue eyes. Her fingers trailed down his ribs then danced over his belt. Nibbling on her bottom lip, which was still wet and slick from their kiss, she stroked over his cock. He hissed in a breath, hoping that was more manly than the moan he'd needed to choke down. Her touch was a fascinating mix of bold and tentative, which did nothing to calm him.

"More than anything. But..." She shifted her hand to the pocket that held their stash of chips. "We've got some gambling to do."

Chapter Four

The temptation to say "shove it" to the whole farce and just drag Ryan up to a Bellagio suite was one of the strongest Cass had ever denied. The teasing was foreplay now. She knew it. Admitted it.

So she guided him back to the blackjack table. They didn't hold hands this time, as if they both knew that fresh contact would only strike sparks. Instead he followed, two careful paces behind. Cass felt pursued. Stalked. She couldn't help an extra shimmy, wiggling her ass as she walked. He was sure to notice. That fact had her near to melting.

Erotic. That was the only word slamming through her mind. Every move, every look, every slight caress—all of it led back to what they hadn't yet done. That potential.

She curled her fingers into her palm and squeezed, the nails digging deep. He had potential, all right. Huge, hot, throbbing potential, wedged firmly against the seam of his fly. It was well beyond ladylike to grope a man's cock in a casino hallway, but curiosity had ruled the moment. Had Ryan been a *little* disappointing in that department, she wanted to know in advance.

No need for worries on that score.

She nodded to the dealer who, at this table, was a South Asian man with a heavy black mustache. He had a smooth way with the cards, not showy, just quick and competent. Quick was good.

Ryan sat down first, then pulled her onto his lap. The sudden jostle—going from standing to sitting—was more disconcerting than it should've been. Or maybe it was the hot pipe of his erection against her ass. He groaned softly, right along her nape, and nuzzled his forehead there.

Now who was having trouble concentrating?

Cass gulped in a breath of air, trying to ignore the possessive way his hands settled on her hips. He had big hands. Big and strong. He splayed his fingers so wide that the tips of his thumbs brushed her underwires.

"Gimme the chips." She was more than breathless now.

Ryan groaned again. He shifted on the seat, which pressed his hard-on against her lower back. Cass giggled.

The dealer lifted a stern eyebrow. "Are you in, ma'am?"

"I am." She grabbed half the chips from Ryan's hand, slipping one inside her purse. A souvenir. She plunked the rest on the green felt. "All of this on the next hand."

"You're not a very good gambler, either." Ryan's voice was a low purr behind her ear.

"Hush. I'm doing this my way."

"Really fast?"

"Exactly."

The dealer only shrugged and dealt the cards. Another couple sat to their right, but they were in their seventies at least. The man's thick bifocals didn't seem to help as he squinted at his hand. Two businessmen who looked Korean occupied the other two seats.

Before Cass picked up her cards, she turned her upper body to whisper in Ryan's ear. "If I win big, we leave right away. We can spend the rest tomorrow."

"Where would we go?"

"Don't know yet." She chanced looking into his eyes. That same intoxicating mix of humor and passion waited for her there. So damn sexy. She forced her lungs to work. "But I don't want this to end."

"Then play."

She turned back to the table, doing the best to ignore how Ryan's pinkies had snaked beneath the fitted waistband of her skirt. He tried to peek over her shoulder, but she clutched the cards to her chest. "No way, Jose. You'll give something away."

"You think I'm indiscreet?"

She wiggled on his lap. "I have proof."

Taking a steadying breath, she peered down at her cards.

Damn. A ten and a six. Nothing to do but stick and wait. She'd lived too long in Vegas to know there was no way around shitty hands. She waved off the dealer and eased back. Ryan's chest was warm and solid against her spine.

The first Korean man asked for another card and bust with twenty-three. He slumped in defeat, signaling the nearest cocktail waitress for another beer. The old woman also bust, hitting a fourteen and receiving a nine.

Everyone else stayed, including the dealer. When it came time to reveal the hands, Cass didn't have a chance. Her sixteen fell victim to the dealer's nine and queen.

"Shoot," she muttered as he swiped away her chips.

Ryan squeezed her waist. "I thought you wanted fast."

"Sure, but..."

"But that was forty dollars. I know."

The odd note in his voice made her turn, but whatever it was couldn't be seen on his face. She forced a shrug. "Your turn, Mr. Haverty."

"Why, thank you, Miss Whitman."

He plunked the rest of his chips on the table.

The dealer slid card after card out of the plastic sleeve. Zip. Zip. Zip. Fortunes won and lost. Cass had never been much of a gambler. She'd seen too many tourists disappointed, fortunes squandered, and souls ruined by that lust for another chance. It could hook people and not let go. That didn't mean she was blind to the allure—the urge to have one more shot at the bigs.

Maybe being raised in Vegas had been a sort of inoculation. Her family lived there, making their way by catering to the vacation scene. Bus trips to the Grand Canyon didn't seem flashy when compared to that magnificent casino floor. Glitz and excess made the fact she was sitting on a near-stranger's lap a trifle less crazy. She was just getting her kicks another way.

Giving herself a mental shake, she felt the exact moment when Ryan let her go. It was only one hand, as he reached out for the pair he'd been dealt. The other still claimed her waist. She'd only just gotten used to being held that way. She didn't want to be released.

"Close your eyes," he said.

"Why?"

"You didn't let me look at your cards."

"Spoilsport."

"Close 'em."

Cass only pretended to obey. She angled her lashes to see when he revealed a scant corner of each card. A seven and a five.

"Dang," she whispered.

"Hey." He tickled his fingers up her ribs, making her laugh. "I said no peeking."

"Sorry. And for the hand."

"Shhh."

The dealer went around the table, offering additional cards to each gambler. Ryan had slid his hand up her back, bypassing her bra. He snagged one of her pigtails and toyed with its uneven end.

"Where would you have gone?" he asked against her throat. "Did you decide?"

Oh, yes. She'd thought of the perfect place. Tommy had thought the idea repulsive, but she had a sneaking suspicion that Ryan would love it. That wholesome, handsome All-American grin would falter. He'd barely stagger, as if she'd jerked out all his bones.

"I did, but it's too late now."

"Never say never."

When the dealer asked, Ryan requested another card. Without enough money to double down and bet again, he had to hope he didn't bust with a ten or a face card. Twenty-one was a winning hand. Twenty-two meant the dealer grabbed another fistful of chips.

She couldn't look. She pinched her eyes shut when he checked out what he'd received.

Then he hit again. And again.

Cass had to bite her tongue. Was he nuts? Was his brain still in his pants?

She squeezed his thigh, showing her displeasure without

words. He yanked her pigtail in reply. The sharp tug almost hurt. He applied pressure until she was forced to angle her head backward. "I know what you're thinking, but I'm not crazy."

"No?"

"I just go for what I want."

"Maybe not crazy, then," she said. "Reckless."

He huffed a tiny laugh. The hot breath sent steaming pleasure across her skin. "If I win, we go where *I* want."

A stronger shiver made her shoulders shake. This was going beyond crazy or reckless. The possibility of giving up control reinforced the fact she'd only met him a few hours earlier.

"Sure," she said at last. She put more faith in his losing than winning.

The old lady had bust again, this time with a jack to spoil her queen and three. The Korean man on the right gave a pleased smile when he revealed his nineteen. Around the table they went until only Ryan remained. He turned over his cards, one at a time. First the seven. Then the five. A six. A three.

Cass squealed in surprise. "Twenty-one!"

The dealer revealed his pair of kings. "The gentleman wins."

The older couple laughed quietly, and the Koreans raised their glasses in toast. Only the dealer seemed perplexed as he paid out the winnings, at which point Cass realized the order of the cards. "You hit on eighteen? Eighteen is a great hand."

Ryan shrugged. "Sure, but in this case it was a losing hand."

Cass felt dizzy as he scooted her off his lap. Solid ground didn't seem solid anymore. She gripped the lip of the blackjack table as Ryan stacked a hefty pile of chips then slipped them in his trouser pocket. A quick glance revealed he was just as ready to go as he had been in the hallway.

She swallowed. He could talk her into just about anything, especially if his kisses joined in on the persuasion, but the idea of going wherever he wanted was too much. His nerve was intimidating. Frankly, she didn't know if she could keep up, no matter how provocative she'd already behaved.

Ryan tipped the dealer and offered his arm. Rather than collapse where she stood, Cass took hold. He was slow and considerate as he led her back to the money-changing windows. Part of her didn't want slow. She wanted an end to the mystery. Was what he proposed something she could live with? Or would it mean the end of their games, as good sense trumped her barely reacquainted sense of adventure?

"This is for you," he said.

Her hands numb, Cass found herself holding two fifty-dollar bills. "Hm?"

"Your tip, remember?"

"How much did you net?"

"Another hundred. Not bad."

"I should think not. So," she said, tucking the money in her tiny black clutch. "Where to?"

"You can tell me now." He laced his fingers with hers. "Where would you have gone?"

"Why?"

His grin was back. He was so much less intimidating when he was the boy next door. Less intimidating, but no less dangerous. Her heart flipped over when she noticed the tiny laugh lines that edged his mouth. He made it a habit, smiling. She could fall for a guy who enjoyed life as much as he seemed to.

"Here's the deal," he said, absently toying with the end of her pigtail again. "I'm game for anything, okay? It's a Friday night. I have nowhere to be. No obligations until Monday morning. No one waiting at home for me." He shrugged. "I'm also well-trained in self-defense. There's absolutely nothing you can do to me where I won't beg for more."

She chuckled at that. The tension that had momentarily reclaimed familiar territory slunk back into the corners.

"Cassandra?"

"Yeah?"

"I'm thinking that's not the same for you." One large hand cupped her cheek. Hazel eyes had turned somber. "I want you to call the shots. Only what you're comfortable with. I know…I know this is fast."

"Fast." She huffed out another laugh. "You could say that."

She remembered his kiss, his hands on her waist, his growling purr against her neck. His stubble would feel amazing against her skin. Her nipples puckered at just the thought. Then there was the promise of that cock. Dear God, she'd turned shallow. After half a year of polite and frankly inadequate lovemaking, Cass wanted to go for it. She wanted to have sex with the man who'd hit on an eighteen. Something hot and daring.

A memory in the making.

"Tonight I like fast," she whispered.

He let out a breath, sounding relieved. "Good. So where to?"

Chapter Five

Ryan shifted in the passenger seat, trying to find enough room. He'd even jacked the seat back as far as it would go, but some things were unavoidable. A six-year-old Honda Civic hadn't been designed for him.

He twisted his shoulders, both maneuvering for more room and catching a better view of Cassandra. She drove well. There was nothing flashy or showy about the way she shifted, staying precisely at the speed limit. Sometimes he forgot that not all people challenged the barriers of speed—unlike every combat pilot he'd ever known. Her profile was freaking adorable, with a button nose and dainty pixie jawline. At a stoplight, she turned to grin at him.

She still hadn't told him where they were headed, and he wasn't familiar with this side of town. They'd traveled all the way across the city from Nellis Air Force Base, where he kept an apartment just outside. The shopfronts and signs marked this area as a commercial district, but most of the plate-glass windows were dark.

Signaling her intention, Cassandra turned left into an alley that spit out to a blacktopped parking lot. She smoothly pulled into a spot then shut off the engine.

Her hands were unsteady as she stuffed the keys into her purse. "Well, here we are."

Ryan managed to unfold himself from the seat, but he didn't have time to stretch the kinks in his lower back. He hustled around the nose of the car to open her door, grabbing the smallest glimpse down her cleavage to a pale bra. The orange glow of the parking-lot lights made the color difficult to pick out, but he imagined it might be pink to match the rosettes on her stockings.

He clenched the warm metal of the car door and cleared his

throat. "I'm not even sure where here is."

That seemed enough to reawaken her smile. Probably the reminder that he was at her mercy, as satisfying as it was. "You'll see in a second."

Ryan was happy to let her lead the way across the parking lot, mostly for the chance to watch her ass swivel. He also kept a sharp eye out, watching for anyone lurking in dark corners. Vegas thrived on its nightlife, but that meant the potential for criminals too—especially in a part of town he didn't know or trust.

They made it to a plain door without any bogeymen popping out from the shadows. When he reached around Cassandra to push it open, Ryan found painted steel that still carried the warmth of the day. A small plaque read *Anna's Boudoir.*

He lifted an eyebrow, but she only shook her head with a constrained smile. The door opened and red light spilled out, hiding what he thought might be a blush across her cheeks. A pounding bass beat swirled around them, delving his brain two or three levels down toward sex. As if he hadn't already been headed that way. Maybe it was one of the off-Strip cabarets that catered to locals with risqué shows.

The narrow hallway didn't spill into a small club.

It was a store. A sex store.

His pulse faltered. "Holy hell," he breathed.

Ryan took the blow straight to his gut. His cock, which had barely stopped throbbing on the drive over, perked up.

The shelves and racks were filled with quality stuff. Gleaming leather floggers. A colorful array of dildos and vibrators. Gold and silver jewelry to adorn intimate piercings. This was no Walmart adult novelties aisle but a high-class kind of place.

Cassandra cast a sultry look over her shoulder. Something in his gobsmacked expression must have pleased her because she grinned. "Too weird?"

"Not at all."

"I've known about this place forever," she said, trailing her fingers over a rack of clothing. "I never got up the courage to actually come in."

A hot rush of something primal made his chest feel even wider. "But you brought me here."

She shrugged. "What can I say? You make me feel dangerous and...safe? It's kind of weird, all things considered."

Weird, sure, but he liked it. He wrapped a hand around her waist and drew her backward until her pert ass snugged up against his groin. He bent his head over hers and drew in a slow breath, letting his lips coast over that tender place behind her ear. "So what did you have in mind?"

He'd go along with absolutely anything. Some massage oil. Maybe that honey-dust stuff that he could lick off every inch of her.

Cassandra lifted a hanger off the rack. "Maybe this?" She twisted out of his grip and held the outfit in front of her. Adventurous mirth sparkled across her face. "I'd have to try it on, wouldn't I?"

Jesus. If Ryan were any less of a man, his knees might have gone out from under him. The outfit she held up was miles from the innocuous things he'd allowed himself to imagine. Red lace laid over a tiny black corset. The skirt pinned underneath was about as long as his hand. The perfect getup for a dirty Goth girl.

It had been so fucking long. For so many years, he'd barely allowed himself to think about the possibilities. About a woman dressing up. For him. The games they could play.

That perversion flat-out didn't fit with the life he'd made.

He cleared his throat, but his voice still came out hoarse. Over the blaring metal track he asked, "You're going to try that on?"

Her gaze slid over him, hot as a touch. A slow, dark smile bloomed across her moistened lips. "Yeah. I think I might."

"Do I get to see?"

"Of course."

That was it. He grabbed her by the wrist and dragged her pell-mell across the store toward the blue neon sign that read *Dressing Rooms*. The giggle that furled out behind them like a jet's contrail said she didn't mind.

The door to the dressing stall was full, going all the way to the floor. He shoved back the disappointment. Maybe she'd open the door a crack once she was dressed.

When Ryan held it open for her, she slipped in and froze. "Well? You coming in?"

"You sure?"

Her grin dimmed for a second and she smoothed a loose lock of strawberry-blonde hair back behind her ear. "I think so. That is..." She pushed up on her toes, then kissed him hard and fast. "Yeah. I'm sure."

He shot a quick glance behind him. One clerk with a shock of purple hair sat behind a waist-high counter, but she had turned away, rustling through a bin of something that looked like mini French ticklers. Ryan entered the tiny dressing room and clicked the door shut behind him.

Cassandra pointed to a seat in the corner. It had no back and a black leather cushion that gleamed beneath a glare of blood-red light. "Sit."

"Yes, ma'am," he said on a laugh. He stretched out in that small space.

She stepped carefully over his knees, between his thighs, then hooked her purse and the padded hanger over the back of the door. "You take up a lot of room, don't you?"

"Can't help it. Accident of birth and all."

Her hands lifted to the top buttons of her shirt. Ryan hitched a knee, hoping to hide his hard-on. It was pretty much a losing cause.

She unbuttoned her plain white uniform shirt, revealing skin that was nearly translucent. He'd been right about the paleness of her bra, although the sex shop's red haze made it impossible to tell the real color. The effect of seeing it in person was so powerful. The lacy cups held her breasts like a lover's hand. His palms itched. The soft mound of her cleavage was prime territory for tasting.

Ryan shoved his hands under his arms. No touching. Not yet. He'd promised they would only go as far as she wanted, and at her choice. This was all her show.

What a show it was. Christ, the inward curve of her waist

was long and sleek. When she shucked off her skirt, her tiny panties made him groan. They matched her bra, both trimmed with black lace.

"Anyone told you lately that you're fucking gorgeous?"

She laughed quietly, which was nearly drowned out by the loud soundtrack. "Not recently enough."

Turing around, she shimmied into the itty-bitty skirt, which hugged her hips and barely covered the curve of her ass where it met her creamy thighs. That she kept the garter belt on was even hotter.

She snapped off her bra and slid it down her arms.

Naturally Ryan leaned to the side for a glimpse in the mirror. Her breasts were beautiful, tipped with pale nipples that almost matched the bra she'd dropped to the floor. His look wasn't near long enough. He'd love to spend hours on her, licking and sucking and nibbling.

A bit at a time. Just enough to make her gasp his name.

She tugged the corset over her head. "Do me up?"

His hands shook slightly as he gathered the silk strings. He pulled and they ran through the eyelets, closing over her band of sleek skin. A flick and a twist left her with a knot rather than a bow, but he wasn't a bow kind of guy. His dexterity was nearing nil.

He turned her by the hips, letting his fingers slide over the two inches of skin displayed between the bottom of the corset and the skimpy skirt. His mouth dropped open, unable to help it.

The corset plumped her breasts up into delectable mounds. Her skin looked even smoother and creamier wrapped in the naughty costume.

Hands fluttering for a moment, she let them rest on his shoulders. "Well?"

Ryan stroked her hips, then up her ribs and over the lace border edging the top of the corset. "I don't think I've seen anything sexier in my entire life."

"I can't be that sexy if you haven't kissed me yet."

With a quick look at the door, he reminded himself that he'd closed it securely. "Here?"

Cassandra sank to her knees. Every bone in his body locked. Even his cock felt as hard as bone. With the costume and the stockings and the twin braids, she was a full-on fuck fantasy. A sinful rocker chick who loved living on the wild side—and was dragging him with her.

"Yeah. Here." She ducked her chin even as her hands slid up his biceps. "I want something...exciting. Something memorable."

"Oh, sweetheart," he said on a rough chuckle. "That much I can promise you."

He tipped her chin up and took her mouth. All of his finesse was gone, ripped away by such blatant, exotic provocation. The kiss went incendiary in about zero point two seconds. Her hands twined behind his neck and her nails dug into that tender skin. He shuddered.

Ryan filled his palms with the tight curve of her ass, then hooked his fingertips under the strings of her garters. Holy Jesus, she was everything responsive. Her mouth drank in his excitement. Her body arched toward him at the same time that he curled over her.

It wasn't enough. He hooked a grip underneath her arms and yanked her onto his lap. His erection fit perfectly along the notch between her legs. She moaned when he pulled her tight down over him, and his hips jerked up on their own.

Touching her all over, he couldn't get enough. Soft skin and scratchy lace. The wet heat of her mouth was a mimic to the heat pressing down over his dick. He caressed her ass and traced the gusset of her panties. She was already dripping wet. Proud, hot satisfaction made his cock ache.

She dove between their bodies and tugged at his belt. Cool, slim fingers undid his fly and wrapped around him. He kissed her harder, groaning into her mouth—loud enough to hear it over an earsplitting track by Tool. She didn't stop there. She opened up his slacks to bring his cock out into the warm, sultry air.

Pulling away from the kiss, she skated her lips over his jaw, up to his ear. "Are you man enough to fuck me right here?"

He looked into her eyes. Her words had been bold, but deep

in the blue flickered something uncertain. She wasn't quite as wicked as the costume made her act, not way down inside. That was what he liked about sexy costumes and the games that went along with them—the chance to step outside himself. Ashleigh, however, had made it crystal clear he ought to be happy with the woman he had.

Cassandra... All he kept repeating was that she'd started this.

Just one time. One special time. An extra something he'd never asked for.

"Are you sure?"

She dropped her forehead to his in a soft press. Her graceful throat worked over a swallow. "Do you have a condom?"

He nodded. He always carried one, even if he hadn't been laid in months and had seen no chance on the horizon. Like the Boy Scout he'd never gotten to be, he stayed prepared.

She closed around his dick and pulled up until her fingertips danced over his head. "Then I'm sure."

He kissed her again. It was depraved. That she wore such a slutty outfit, though it was obviously not her normal style. That he was fully dressed, with only his dick thrusting up to brush against her lace-covered stomach. Ryan knew he was a sick fuck, but man did it work for him.

He fished the condom out of his wallet. They put it on him together with assorted whispers and one choked giggle from her. He stripped her panties down over her legs, which forced a regrettable space between them. Before he had time to miss the exciting press of her thighs over his, he welcomed her back onto his lap.

His hard-on slipped through her drenched pussy. He lifted his knees and planted his feet to provide her a stable surface. Cassandra leaned back and wrapped a grip around his thighs. Her wild blue gaze seared him as she looked down the length of her body. He was teasing her clit with the head of his cock.

She bit her lip as she shuddered. "Now," she whispered. "I don't think I've ever been hotter."

Neither had he. He strapped one arm around her lower

back, his wrist brushing both lace and silken skin. He clamped his mouth over hers in a fierce kiss.

And took her.

His cock drove into her with one cruel thrust, then he froze. She was so fucking tight. Unbelievably so. He wrenched on her hips but forced himself to ease up. He didn't want to leave bruises. "You okay?"

She shoved her hand under his shirt collar. "Oh, God yes," she breathed. "More than okay. Wonderful. Fabulous. Give me more."

That he could certainly do. With abandon. He cupped her ass and pulled her down onto his thrusts. Their mouths came together again in a pinching clench of a kiss. Her pussy clung to him on every withdraw and welcomed him in with every push. Her ankles hooked behind his lower back.

Ryan shoved away the hot tingle of his orgasm, which already gathered at the base of his spine. He slipped fingers between the wet smack of their bodies, searching for her clit. He had to make this good for her.

It was already the best he'd ever had.

Chapter Six

At the start of the night, it had been about getting back at Tommy. Even an hour ago, it had been about playing games. Kissing. Flirting. Feeling like a desirable woman.

Now it was about the best damn sex of her life.

Lordy, what had prompted her to grab that costume off the rack? Maybe the way he kept toying with her braids, and how he practically drooled when gaping at her stockings. Or maybe because she knew, without a doubt, that she'd never be riding Ryan Haverty in a sex-shop dressing room if she were dressed as herself. Plain ol' Cass Whitman was responsible, timid and far too anxious about what people thought.

The black lace and the pinch of the corset made it almost...easy. To give in to what she desired. To be as depraved and greedy as he made her feel.

She moaned. Each drive shoved harder, pushed deeper. Ryan's thumb hooked between her pussy lips. He didn't even have to circle against her clit, just held still. Pressed. The motion of her body was enough as she rubbed and thrust.

Fingers wide, she grabbed as much of his lean, hard bulk as she could—the power in his shoulders and the sinewy grace of his upper back. Needing more of him, more of this gorgeous man, she tugged open his shirt. The top two buttons pinged away.

"Oh, look at you," she breathed.

He had the most delicious thatch of chest hair. It whorled over flat nipples, shadowing the strong curve of his pectorals. Fine brown hair tapered down to a point that bisected a taut, defined six-pack. His abs contracted and relaxed with each grind, accentuating his power.

It was too much. *Too much.*

Cass wanted more.

She fitted her mouth against his throat and sucked hard. He jerked beneath her, his rhythm faltering.

"Goddamn," he groaned. "Do it, baby. Suck me."

Cass shuddered. Hearing rough talk from such a polite gentleman set her insides on fire. She nibbled, teasing, tasting his salty sweat, before delving in for another deep, sucking kiss. Already the marks showed on his chest, no matter the bizarre red-haze lighting. A thrill surged through her. She'd never intentionally left marks on a man's skin. She did it again, then again, as she bit the hard curve of his pectoral.

Ryan grunted. "Goddamn, that's good."

Sweat trickled down his throat. Cass licked it away.

"Your turn," she panted against his shoulder.

He leaned her back, arching her cleavage out before him like a buffet. His thrusts slowed just enough for him to concentrate. The intensity of his expression might have made her giggle earlier in the night, but her laughter had fizzled away when he pushed into her pussy.

His hands back on her ass, he used only his mouth. With tongue and teeth and lips, he feasted on the swells of her breasts. The corset held them up to be worshiped.

He'd reached his limit. She could tell the moment it happened, when taut muscles began to tremble. Ryan laid his cheek against her breast. Wrapping her arms around his head, Cass held him close. Locked together.

She glanced to the left where the dressing-room mirror detailed their entwined pose. Oh, God. That wasn't her at all. No, some naughty slut was riding a stranger in a dressing room. She watched as his body fucked up into her, each stroke tighter, more truncated now. The sight of his tense hands, so dark against the white flesh of her upper thighs, was the last push she needed.

Her orgasm became a guarantee, a promise she could feel *just there*. She didn't have to fight for it anymore.

Cass nuzzled her mouth up to his ear. "Ryan, your body is magnificent," she whispered. "Do you know that? Fucking *gorgeous*."

He growled something low and obscene against her neck. "Don't stop."

"The dirty talk?" She was dizzy, strung so tight, breathless. Cass fixed her eyes on their mirror image. The filthy words spilled out of her as her orgasm built and built. "Slam that cock into me. I need it. Harder. Fuck me, Ryan. All you can give me. Oh—"

A wall of sensation crashed over her. The shuddering force of her climax was more than she could control, more than she could stand. Big hands that smelled of her own arousal clamped over her mouth. Her scream vibrated against his palm.

Ryan followed right after her. That glorious cock jammed all the way in, pressed tight, straining. He made a choking sound in his throat as his body went rigid. A hard shake racked his big shoulders. They were still so close that she felt it deep in her bones.

They sat there for hazy, lightheaded minutes. Cass couldn't catch her breath, while beneath her hands, Ryan's wide back expanded with every shallow inhalation.

Slowly, the world began to make sense again. The heavy bass of a Nine Inch Nails track climbed her backbone.

The edge was gone. The primal urge sated.

For now.

She looked down to where Ryan kept his face between her breasts. Almost tenderly, she smoothed the damp hair back from his temples. One stroke, then another, soothing them both to reality.

She kissed his slick forehead. "You okay?"

A very contented masculine chuckle reverberated off her breastbone. "Hell yeah."

He untangled their upper bodies and leaned back against the corner of the dressing room. Only then did Cass get a good look at the damage she'd done.

"Oh, shoot."

"What?"

She reached out to touch the bruises and teeth marks, but her courage failed. After all they'd just done, she didn't have the guts to touch him there.

Ryan sat up slightly, his hips still joined with hers. He leaned toward the mirror. "Whoa. Remind me not to tick you off."

"I'm sorry. I—"

"Hey," he said softly. Both hands came up now, cupping her face. "I was right here, remember? I could've stopped you, but I don't think that's what I asked for."

"I've never..." She couldn't find the words. She'd never done *any* of this. It seemed silly to fixate on the proof of her aggression, but it was easier than looking all of it in the face.

"Cassandra?"

Oh, that wasn't fair.

"What?"

"I've never either, okay?" Almost primly, he kissed her on the nose. "Not ever. Not like this. Believe me, I'll be pinching myself in the morning."

She found a wobbling grin. "You'll only give yourself more bruises."

"Nah, I'll leave that to you."

Cass took comfort in the return of his smile. It was going to be all right. That's what his smile said. Mindless storm of passion gone. Resume being funny and flirty. She knew what the flirting led to, but she needed that break to regain her footing.

Speaking of which, she edged off his lap before her sudden self-consciousness made movement impossible. She couldn't look at him as she got dressed.

A finger along the back of her thigh made her jump. "I ripped your stocking," he said. "I'm sorry."

"You can buy me a new pair with your winnings."

"Done."

He touched her again, this time helping to undo the ties of the corset. She would've expected another man to cop a feel while she was vulnerable, but Ryan didn't press. He watched. Of course he watched, yet he gave her space enough to return to herself—as if he really was as considerate as she'd first imagined.

When she finally felt put back together, at least half-assed, Cass turned to face him. He'd done up his slacks, and the condom was nowhere to be seen. She didn't want to know. The missing buttons on his shirt were a lost cause, which meant it would gape open for the rest of the night.

Great. Might as well put a neon sign over his head. *Yup, got fucked.*

But she couldn't leave his hair that way. Bits of it stuck up where she'd tangled and twisted. She grabbed a comb from her clutch. "Don't move."

With efficient movements, she sleeked his hair back into place. Only when she finished did he take gentle hold of her wrists.

"Hey," he said gruffly. Cass could barely hear him over the steady thrum of a Stone Temple Pilots riff. "Thank you."

She opened her mouth to speak but couldn't find the words. What did one say in such a situation? "You're welcome" didn't seem appropriate. That made it sound too one-sided.

The tenderness in his eyes, the wonder that lit his expression… She couldn't leave him hanging. What they'd shared, no matter what else they ever had, was something she'd never forget.

Cass bent at the waist until her mouth was level with his. Their calmer breaths mingled. She pressed a kiss against his lips, filling it with all the amazement and satisfaction she felt.

"Thank you," she whispered there.

The song ended. Maybe the whole CD needed changing because silence blanketed the shop. It was like the lights coming up for a bar's last call.

Ryan grinned. "You don't have to go home, but you can't stay here."

"We're gonna get busted."

"It would've happened already."

Cass's ears still rang in the abrupt quiet. As she strung the costume back on its hanger, she said, "I'm buying this."

"I suppose it's only fair. Though if you don't want to keep it, I'll have it."

"Not your size."

"I could get off on the memories for years."

"You don't seem the type to take trophies."

He lifted his brows. "That's just my wholesome looks. I had you fooled."

"Not at all, Mr. Haverty."

Resolved to keep her backbone, Cass pulled open the dressing-room door. The strangest thing happened as she stepped out. She didn't feel ashamed. Her dignity was all there, strong as ever. Instead she felt almost...arrogant.

Fucked in a sex shop? Been there, done that. Bought the naughty Goth costume souvenir.

She swallowed a giddy bubble of sound as she walked to the counter. "I'll take this."

The clerk shoved a hunk of bright purple hair out of her eyes. "Took you long enough to decide."

"Wanted to make sure," Cass said, proud of how even her voice was.

Ryan came up behind her, warming the length of her back. The clerk's eyes went wide. Cass could just imagine what she saw. Buttons missing. Chest scratched all to hell.

"I'm going to have to charge you extra." The clerk smirked.

"What for?" Ryan asked.

"Discretion charge. Twenty bucks."

Cass laughed. Ryan, however, appeared surprisingly embarrassed. She hadn't expected that at all, not from such a hard-charging guy.

"I don't think that's necessary," he said.

"Not *necessary*." The clerk shrugged. "But I didn't have to let you finish, buddy. Believe me, the police come pretty quick when I call. They generally get a good laugh out of what they bust up."

Ryan looked eager to dissolve. The sideways slant of his shoulders and the loose set of his knees made him seem like an animal preparing to flee. Again Cass was surprised. He came across as such a confident man that this hesitation stood out big time.

She laid the money on the counter. “Would you bag that up for me?”

“Sure thing.” The clerk smiled as she slipped the extra twenty in her pocket.

Cass took the opportunity to sort out Ryan. She pulled him off to the side. “Hey, you okay?”

“Fine.”

“All in good fun, right? She’s just teasing us. Now she gets a bottle of wine at the end of the night—everyone’s happy.”

“Yeah, sure.”

She couldn’t help her frown. He wasn’t the same now. Something darker had come up from behind them both. She didn’t care for it, and she didn’t know what was wrong.

Fatigue was starting to get to her. She felt it behind her eyes and in her joints. Lucky thing it was the weekend because she’d need the next forty-eight hours to recover.

One more glance at Ryan revealed the truth. She didn’t want this to be it. Not yet, and she really didn’t want it to end on such an oddly sour note. They both deserved better after what they’d already shared. The potential she’d sensed earlier in the evening was only partly realized.

She took his hand and petted the back of it. “I have an idea, if you’re willing to hear it.”

“Lay it on me.”

“Smile first. Smile like you’ve just had the best fuck of your life.”

That got to him. He grinned around a huffing laugh, ducking those beautiful hazel eyes away. “Guilty as charged.”

“Good. Then let’s get out of here.”

“Where to?”

“Don’t know.” She shrugged. “You got any ideas?”

“Tons.”

“I knew you seemed resourceful.”

Ryan kissed her forehead. Some of his teasing was back, but with that darker edge she couldn’t pin down. Maybe he was just what she’d assumed from the start—a gentleman. He didn’t seem to mind getting his grind on, but being caught was a different matter. Cass should've sympathized. Instead, she wanted him to be as brazen as she unexpectedly felt.

She shook away the impulse. They were damn lucky to be getting along as well as they did. They didn't *know* each other—other than carnally, she thought with a private grin.

Give him time. Let it go.

"How about I go wait in the car. You pick something out for me. A surprise."

"Oh? Like what?"

Moment of truth time. She'd trusted him this far. He could very well do a one-eighty and pick a sex toy she couldn't go through with using. Despite the brief dip in his mood, he was still the same guy.

"Your choice, Ryan. Anything you want."

Chapter Seven

In the tiny hallway that led to the parking lot, Ryan took a half second to gather his thoughts. A red-striped bag dangled from his grip. The sound system kicked back on—System of a Down this time, and of course the song was "Violent Pornography". He shot a glare at the clerk, but she only crossed her arms on the counter and smirked.

He shook it off. Everybody fucks, indeed.

Not everybody lucked into an amazing one. That it had been so...*out there* was only an accident. A lightning-fast twist of fate—not the type of thing a guy kept up for a lifetime. If it weren't for the black-and-white outfit wrapped in tissue paper, Ryan might believe that.

Do it or don't, Fang.

Cassandra grinned at him as he opened the car door. "Where to?"

He tossed the bag in the back and wedged himself into the passenger seat. "First, the steakhouse."

"Oh." Her smile faltered, but she turned the ignition anyway.

"Hey," he said, curling a hand around her jaw and forcing her to look at him. He made himself grin. She seemed to like it when he was friendly and funny. Not that he could blame her. This was a night outside reality. She didn't need to know how indulging in something so sordid and carnal went against his every carefully hoarded scruple.

He'd worked damned hard to make a life that wasn't trashy. Getting busted by some smirk-faced sex-shop clerk didn't figure in the picture.

"I said 'first', didn't I?"

She huffed out a laugh, but it was enough to blow away the

tension. “Yes, you did.”

The ride back to her work was filled with quiet teasing. As if by agreement, neither of them said anything about the red-striped bag on the rear seat. Ryan didn’t miss how her gaze flicked to the rearview mirror as if she were trying to see inside. Hell, he knew what was in there and he felt like turning around to poke, if only to make sure he hadn’t lost his mind. He’d actually, really bought that for a woman he’d just met.

In a way, that made it easier. If Cassandra assumed he was a freak, he had less to lose. Not nothing, because he already found her fascinating. The chance she’d think badly of him wouldn’t ever be as bad as losing Ashleigh. The disgust in her voice... All of her respect and love, simply *gone*.

Finally Cassandra pulled into the lot, and he pointed at his extended cab F-150. It was one of the only vehicles left in the lot, except for what looked to be a catering van at the far end and a shiny BMW two spots down.

She giggled as she put the car in park. “You know, I’m not surprised you drive a big truck. It fits.”

He took a hold of the end of one of her braids. She was raggedy, with reddish locks slipping out to frame her face, but it only added to her appeal. She looked like she’d been screwed to the high heavens. He couldn’t help but feel damn proud of that.

“What do you mean?”

“You’re so All-American. The guy next door. Suburbia and tailgate parties.”

That was sort of what he’d been shooting for. All his life—everything he’d grown up without. Everything he still worked so hard to protect.

“Except for where I bang dirty Goth girls in dressing rooms,” he said tightly.

“Except for that.”

Her smile went so wide that he had to taste it. Just like that, all the air stripped out of the compact, replaced with their hot panting. A tiny halo of condensation circled the windshield.

Ryan pulled back. “If I don’t get out of here immediately, you’re going to get fired. Here, give me your phone.”

Cassandra handed it over, and he plugged in his phone

number.

"Here's the deal," he said. "If you like what's in the bag, you're going to go get a hotel room. One on the Strip, I think. You choose. Then you're going to text me with where and the number. Nothing more, nothing less."

Her eyes went dark as her pupils widened. "Yes, sir," she breathed.

Oh shit, did he like that or what? He was turning out to be more of a sicko than he'd thought. He ignored it in order to steal a last kiss with his hand wrapped around the nape of her neck where her skin was softer than down.

When he got out of the car, he paused in the open door and leaned back in. She looked at him with anticipation, but her hand was already on the gearshift—as if she was ready to zip away. Where she'd go remained a mystery.

"If you don't like it…" He gripped the edge of the door, letting the warm metal bite into his palm as he attempted to order his words. "If you don't, just text me that you got home safe, okay?"

She nodded. An indulgent smile curved her mouth. "I will."

He watched her pull away. At almost the exact moment she turned left out of the lot—in the direction of the Strip—the back door to the restaurant banged open. Cassandra's ex charged out, head down as if he were going into battle. Ryan didn't figure the guy would know a war zone if he were dropped in by parachute. Not to mention, it must be freaking boring to head into battle when he was the only one around.

Might as well help him out.

"Evening, sir," he called.

The other guy drew up short. His eyes narrowed as he scanned Ryan over from head to toe. "What are you doing here?"

Ryan knew how he must appear. He deliberately scratched a hand over his chest, edging under his open collar. His nail grazed against a sore spot, sending a perverted rush of excitement through him. He grinned. "Just had to pick up my ride."

The ex's mouth opened and closed. Maybe he wasn't as

dumb as he seemed. On second thought, if the man had chosen someone else over Cassandra, he shouldn't have been able to manage even simple breathing. He thumbed his key fob. The Beemer's lights flashed.

"Have a nice night," Ryan called as the manager got in the car. "I know I have."

The guy—Tommy, if he remembered right—pulled up even behind Ryan's Ford. "You better get out of here or I'll call the cops on you for trespassing."

As usual, guys with small dicks grew big balls when they were safely ensconced in their expensive cars. However, Cassandra still had to work with her manager. Ryan tipped two fingers to his brow in a mock salute. "I'll be gone."

The Beemer's tires spun up a cloud of desert dust.

Smiling, Ryan jumped into his truck and debated his options. Stay put until he knew for sure? Nah, that wasn't his style. He keyed the ignition and headed toward the Strip, determined to be optimistic.

About halfway there, he heard his phone chirp. He pulled it out at the next red light. A text message read, *The Paris, Room 1419.* He wanted to pump his fist in the air, but that meant she'd looked inside the bag. A niggling worry settled into his stomach, a heady combo of nerves and hot anticipation.

His phone went off again, but this time with a ring. He thumbed the answer button without looking at the display. If Cassandra had changed her mind, he'd...do nothing. Wish her a good night and thank his lucky stars if she agreed—possibly, maybe—to see him again.

"Hello?"

A smash of voices and music came across the line. "Yo, that you, Fang?" Jon was nearly yelling.

Ryan held the phone away from his ear. "Duh. You called me, didn't you?"

"Smartass." The background noise faded for a moment. "What are you doing? Or should I ask *who*?"

Keeping his gaze firmly on the traffic, he tried to figure out how to answer that one. Jon was a notorious kinkster. Knowledge of what Ryan had been up to would probably earn a few high-fives, but he wanted to keep the details private. He'd blurred the boundaries of what he'd considered acceptable for himself. Messing around with roleplaying to spice up a marriage? Fine. Maybe one day. Needing it the way he'd started to in those final weeks with Ashleigh? Not okay.

Plus part of him wanted to protect Cassandra and her infectious sense of fun.

Finally he answered, "Nothing."

"You lucky dog." He should have known Jon would pick up on the hesitation. "I was going to ask if you wanted to meet me at the club. Princess is too busy drinking herself into a stupor to give me the attention I so richly deserve."

"Gee, that sounds like such a fun time. I don't see how I can ever pass up an invitation like that."

"Yeah, yeah." Jon laughed. "Go back to your waitress. I'll try to keep Her Worship out of a fight. *Again.* You've totally got next time."

"Agreed."

After they signed off, Ryan tossed his phone into the center console. A dark worry chewed at the back of his brain. Jon was too fucking perceptive. He'd take one look at Ryan on Monday and know he hadn't had a random one-night stand.

He could only imagine what hell he'd get then.

He didn't think he was that unusual, wanting to keep his business to himself. Growing up, he hadn't had a private inch in the world to call his own. When his mom hadn't been passed out on the couch, she would stagger into his room, sobbing on his bed about how she was a shit mother—or pawing through his drawers in search of proof that he was up to no good.

He'd learned early that part of the simple, respectable life he wanted was privacy. Regular people didn't sit on their trailers' front porches and laugh about how well they'd gotten laid, at a volume loud enough for the whole park to hear. Regular people shut the doors and turned down the lights. Good, regular men didn't ask women to dress up and play stupid sex games. He wanted to at least make the attempt, no matter what turned him on.

After this one risky night, he'd go back to being sane.

Normal.

When he pulled into the parking deck behind The Paris, he shoved all the memories away. Cassandra liked funny. She liked charming. So that's what she'd get.

Even if it killed him.

He was already asking her for a lot if she actually wore what was in the bag.

Thank God his spare dress uniform was hanging from the oh-shit handle in the back. He'd picked it up from the cleaners earlier in the afternoon. No way could he walk through a casino floor looking the way he did, even if it had been fun to rub in her ex's face.

He grabbed his flight bag from the Ford's backseat and fought his way into the uniform, watching out for security cameras the whole time like he was some sort of punk.

Oh wait, he was.

Getting changed in the cab wasn't easy, but he managed with a minimum of cussing. Eventually he emerged and tugged the blue sleeves, using the silver braid band at the cuffs that marked his rank.

The entire inside of The Paris casino had been decorated to look like Parisian streets. Ceilings painted sky blue, complete with fluffy clouds, soared over white marble balustrades. He wondered for half a second what it would've been like to swarm through Paris as one of the WWII allied forces after the occupation.

He earned fewer looks than he might have expected as he walked through the banks of slots toward the elevators. Thank Christ for the craziness that was Vegas. He'd have to be fully decked out in Elvis regalia to garner attention.

It wasn't until he punched the button in the elevator that his heartbeat surged to Mach one. Was he really doing this? With a woman he'd just met?

Their sex in the dressing room had been mind-blowing. Explosive. He rubbed a hand over his dress shirt, pressing carefully at the teeth marks she'd left at the edge of his pecs.

Cassandra was...amazing. He was sounding like a broken record even in his own head, but his body was so tightly wound it was hard—pun intended—to think of another word. She'd taken what she wanted of him in greedy, grasping fistfuls, but she'd given back in full measure. Watching her slight, curvy body working over his lap, wrapped in that microscopic costume, had been one of the most epic moments of his life.

And he flew fighter jets for a living.

If he'd pushed too far... Shit, he'd be pissed at himself. No two ways about it. Not everyone appreciated his hard-charging, full-throttle attitude, just like no sensible woman would appreciate his ridiculous fetish.

The elevator spit him out on the fourteenth floor. He had to force his feet to march down the thickly carpeted hallway. Eventually the moment of truth arrived. Even if backing out and leaving Cassandra hanging had been within his capacity, his cock wouldn't have allowed it.

He raised his hand to knock.

Chapter Eight

"Yeah, I'm fine," Cass said to Gilly for the fourth time. "Honest. I told you where we're staying, gave you his name and cell number. If anything happens, you can play cavalry for me." She smoothed her hands down the sides of the skimpy black skirt and its prim white lace. "You're not going to talk me out of this. We're having a fun time."

Understatement of her year, by far.

Gilly made a grumbling noise, after she'd finally turned down the volume of her stereo. "Fine. Just be safe, okay?"

"Promise. I'll call you when I'm up and about tomorrow."

"Lucky girl. It'll probably be noon."

"At least," Cass said with a grin. "Night, honey. Thanks for caring."

"Got no choice. Nighty-night."

Cass closed her cell phone with a smile. She'd only known Gilly for about eight months, since the other woman had moved to town to pursue her MFA. Not since her days in college had Cass found someone who appreciated her love of art.

Memories of conversation became mere background noise in her mind as she assessed her appearance in the bathroom's full-length mirror. For the hundredth time. No change. She still looked like a naughty fantasy.

A French maid. She should've guessed.

Her grin took on a distinctly sexual edge, which she didn't mind at all. The blush too felt right—a little self-conscious, a little anxious. Already the temperature in her blood upped toward scalding.

"You greedy slut," she whispered to her reflection, the grin broadening. "One great time wasn't enough."

Her nerves stretched and stretched as she waited. She'd

ordered room service and managed to take a quick shower. Her hair was still wet, but she'd bound it in a sleek bun at the base of her neck. A light application of the cosmetics she'd snagged during a two-minute run through a store in The Paris's lobby had done wonders to hold back the look of fatigue.

She was tired, nearly exhausted after a long week, and yet so wonderfully charged up.

Ryan's knock, when it came, sped her heartbeat. If she played the French maid, she wondered what he would be. A bedraggled traveler who'd had the buttons yanked off his shirt? A down-on-his-luck gambler?

And just how far would she push this? Cass had spent the last hour trying to get inside his head. There was a huge gulf between a bit of dress-up and full roleplaying. She was almost surprised at how much she wanted it to be the latter. Something that tipped over, deep inside. Something had *unlocked.* She could be anything, say anything, do anything. The right set of clothes adjusted her attitude, helping her step outside of the ordinary.

Don't doubt it. Just do it.

The worst he would do is laugh, maybe flash that pulse-pounding smile and tell her to drop the act. He might merely be a guy after something different to look at, but that didn't feel right, not for Ryan. She had a guess as to what he liked, and she was willing to give it a shot.

His knock was more insistent the second time. Good. She didn't like to think that he'd give up on her.

Cass took a deep breath and opened the door.

Ryan stood at the threshold wearing a fantastic dress uniform. The dark blue did marvelous things for his healthy tan, and the braided silver trim looked impressively realistic. Navy? No, that wasn't right. Air Force, maybe?

More than the color and the authenticity of the costume, she loved how it was exactly tailored to his body—tall and lean, long and strong. Only a slack, bewildered expression gave away his response to her maid's outfit. Otherwise he embodied everything impressive and sexy about a man in uniform.

"Oh! *Monsieur* Haverty," she said in her best French accent.

A year spent studying art in Paris would finally prove good for something. "I hadn't expected you so soon. *Merci*, come in."

He hesitated for only a second. Then the reality of what she'd done and said—how she sounded—seemed to click in his brain. "Thank you. I didn't expect to be kept waiting."

"My apologies, *monsieur*. I was only just finishing up."

"I don't appreciate sloppy service."

She nibbled her bottom lip, daring to glance up from beneath lowered lashes. He surveyed the hotel room with the air of a man who expected perfection and found it lacking. A curious heat bloomed in her stomach, reveling in his command of the moment.

She'd been right. The man wanted to play.

"Your room-service order is waiting for you in the bedroom," she said, pitching her voice toward conciliatory. "As you requested."

"Oh?" He lifted his brows. "I'm curious if you managed to get that right, at least."

"This way, *s'il vous plaît*."

She ushered him into the bedroom where a rolling silver-tone cart was topped with a plate of fresh fruit and a bottle of champagne on ice. She'd ordered the items no matter the sticker shock, figuring they'd sort out paying for it later. Tonight was about living a fantasy.

Ryan strolled to the cart. His expression verged on haughty as he surveyed the assortment. "Good enough."

"I'm pleased, *Monsieur* Haverty."

"It's Major Haverty, actually."

"Major?"

"I don't stand on ceremony with civilians. Please, call me Ryan." He held out his hand. "And you are?"

"Cassandra," she said, briefly shaking hands. That same electric zap they'd shared from the first moment reappeared, only stronger. She almost dropped character. Ryan's teasing grin made a brief reappearance, as if he too was tempted to laugh.

Then it was gone. He was Major Haverty again.

"Where are you from, Cassandra?"

"Montparnasse, in Paris."

"Beautiful place."

Cass tipped her head. "You've been there, *monsieur*?"

"A few years back, yes."

"Oh, but of course. A man in the military. You must have seen many ports of call."

"I have."

Dear Lord, he was unbelievably handsome in that uniform. She wondered again where he'd picked it up. Had he returned to the sex shop? Or someplace else? He stood with his shoulders back, his posture firm and solid. The thought turned her on in funny, unpredictable ways. The roleplaying was easy to indulge when he fit the part so perfectly.

"What do you do in the military? Is it the Air Force?"

"That's right. I fly fighter jets. F-16s."

Cass's jaw dropped. He could do that all day, adding facts to his character that would've seriously jeopardized the absorbency of her panties—had she been wearing any.

No matter how fabulous Ryan looked, her hands were restless for wanting to see him stripped. Something about his expression, however, told her he'd be the one giving orders.

Yes, sir.

"Well, I should finish up my duties." So breathless now, she heard her accent slipping.

She turned to leave the bedroom, but he called out, "Miss? Could you help me first?"

"My pleasure, *monsie*—I mean, Ryan."

He seemed to stifle a private smile. "This coat." He began undoing the buttons. "It's too hot in here for it. I won't be able to get comfortable."

"I should think not." She crossed the floor, her knees shaky. "Here, let me help."

He dropped his arms to his sides as she undid the remaining buttons. Her breath was coming in fitful gulps, but she forced herself to concentrate.

Calm down.

By the looks of how they were playing this hand, they would take their time. She needed to get herself under control or she'd wind up begging for a quickie down on the carpet to cut the tension. What she loved about their game was what would rip her up inside. The waiting. The deliberate buildup.

She pressed her hands flat against his body, right above his ribs. Slowly, slowly, she smoothed them up the inside of his coat, making love to his chest with her palms and her fingertips. His shoulders were tense. Corded ropes of muscles bunched and relaxed beneath her touch. She eased the dress coat over his shoulders then down his brawny arms.

Through it all he held his tense stance, chin thrust out. She liked to think she had all of him at attention, but she didn't dare go for his crotch. Not yet.

The coat dropped to the floor behind him. Ryan seemed to snap out of his trance. "Thank you," he said curtly. "You can hang that up now."

Cass hid her smile. She angled her backside in such a way that he would get the choicest view as she bent at the waist. She took her time, first retrieving the coat, then strolling to the closet where she found a hanger. Every action felt bathed in molasses, so achingly slow. In that hotel room, time had ceased to have the same properties.

A *pop* sound yanked her heart into her throat. She turned to find Ryan pouring champagne. The pale blue dress shirt did even better things for his tan than the dark coat. Muscles pulled and shifted with every movement. Her mouth watered at the prospect of seeing him fully nude. They'd shared so much so quickly, but damn did they have a long way to go.

"Come," he said.

"So soon?"

His gaze jumped to hers. His expression told her she was naughty to risk ruining their charade. "Cut the impertinence, miss. Come here."

She toyed with the lace edge of her skirt as she approached. His eyes jumped and danced, as if trying to take in everything.

"My apologies again. It's… I'm new here in *les États-Unis*. I wasn't trained in cleaning. Not really."

"What did you study?"

"The history of art."

"Paris is a lovely city for that."

"It is."

Ryan handed her a full champagne flute before downing a big gulp from his. Maybe he wasn't as controlled as he managed to appear. "Then what are you doing here, working such a menial job?"

Something about his eyes, the way he regarded her so intensely, transcended their game. They'd met in a restaurant, after all, where she bided her time waiting tables.

"One must have money," she said.

"Then why not earn it doing what you love?"

Cass glanced down at his uniform, wondering for the first time what he did for a living. "Not all of us can be so exotic, Major, in following our passions."

"No? Seems if you want something bad enough, you go for it." He nodded to her champagne. "Now, drink."

"Oh, but I cannot. I'm still on duty. My manager would be very displeased."

"Your manager has a nasal whine and beady eyes. I've already taken care of him."

Cass hid her giggle behind her glass then dove in for a healthy sip. The bubbles went straight to her oxygen-starved brain. Ryan made her half-drunk already. The alcohol didn't stand a chance when compared to his blatant sex appeal.

"I want you to do something for me," he said, his voice tight and low. He wasn't a man about to ask for a hotel-issued toothbrush.

"Anything. Anything you need."

He finished the last of his champagne then refilled them both. "Go sit on that loveseat."

Cass willed her feet to move. She crossed away from the serving cart and sat primly on the edge of the loveseat's stiff cushion.

"No, no." Ryan wore the look of a man who was on the

verge of losing his temper—or his control. "Not like that."

He set his glass aside and met her there. The window behind her allowed the lights of the Strip to shine in, bathing his face and his crisp, pale blue shirt in color. His hands taut with tension, he grabbed Cass beneath her arms. Roughly he lifted her until she sat on the arm of the loveseat, her feet turned to rest on the seat cushion. A wall was at her back, about a foot away. She could lean against it if she needed to. For now she just waited, perched there, loving the way he touched her everywhere with his hot gaze.

"Cassandra," he said softly.

"*Oui*?"

"I'm going to go down on you."

"Oh! *Monsieur*, I cannot permit that."

He sat on the cushion, right between her legs. "Why not? You deserve a reward for such diligent work."

"I was sloppy. Impertinent."

"Well, consider it a punishment, if you want. I won't be deterred in this."

He eased nearer, one hand on each of her thighs. The bag from the sex shop had contained a replacement pair of stockings. His expression was tense, serious, until he caught sight of that new black silk. Now playfulness and stark, powerful arousal fought for control.

Without warning he pulled her thighs apart. The skirt dipped into the valley between her legs, concealing her naked pussy. His fingertips trembled slightly as he lifted the lace hem. Cool air washed over her bare skin.

Ryan sucked in a breath. "Jesus."

"Major?"

"Hmm?"

"I will let you do what you want."

He looked up. She'd never seen a man so caught up in his desire. Cass felt powerful, feminine and so damn hot. "Good," he rasped.

He ducked his head and licked, starting at the top of one stocking. He stopped just short of her neatly trimmed bush. A breath. A second of hesitation. Then he licked dead center, just one quick swipe of his tongue.

She shuddered.

Against that wet, sensitive skin, he whispered, "Just out of curiosity, why did you change your mind?"

He licked her again. Cass could hardly breathe, let alone form words. She swallowed and tried again. "Because after you're finished, I'm going to return the favor."

"Not if I don't turn you over and fuck you first."

"We'll just have to wait and see, won't we, *monsieur*?"

"Seems like. But, Cassandra?"

"*Oui*?"

Ryan hooked his arms beneath her knees. "That's gonna be a long time from now."

Chapter Nine

Ryan was pretty sure he'd died and gone to heaven somewhere during the drive to The Paris.

Naturally, heaven was centered right between Cassandra's sleek legs, wrapped in sexy packaging.

He'd thought her kisses tasted like crème brûlée, but he'd been insane. The taste of her pussy was even more delicious than her mouth. Creamy with just enough spice. Even better, she'd been soaking wet before his first lick.

He swiped his tongue flat over her center then curled one hand over her hipbone. He scraped his nails through her neatly trimmed curls. When he spread her lips open, he was rewarded with another shudder that worked down her legs. She dug her feet into his back. Even the bite of the heels she still wore worked for him.

Absolutely everything about this worked for him.

When the door had swung open and he'd seen her completely decked out in the French maid costume, his brain cells quit firing. The tiny straps of the bodice curled over her shoulders, and the skirt... The skirt had been barely there. The white underskirt flounced around her thighs as she'd turned away.

When she'd spoken in a French accent—the final straw. His mind had just been...blown. It had been everything he could do not to throw her onto the bed and bang the hell out of her.

Ryan had to make this right, to thank her for her willingness to humor him in this fantasy. He hadn't indulged for so long, only lived it in his head more times than he could count. So the fact that she was ready to go along made the night even more amazing.

He licked and sipped at her pussy, pouring every ounce of

gratitude into giving her pleasure. Her hands curled under the collar of his dress shirt and spread wide over the tops of his shoulders. Sucking, he set the barest edge of teeth against her clit—just enough to make her stomach jump. A quiet moan purred in her throat.

Ryan dragged the nubs of his nails back around her thighs, playing with the lace border of the new stockings. If he kept up, he was likely to ruin this pair too. He didn't think she'd mind if he kept buying replacements. Maybe if he promised to make her come every time.

The stiff white petticoat brushed against his forehead. He pushed back the pulse in his balls that said his orgasm was entirely too close. He was *not* going to come in his dress slacks. Absolutely not. If that happened, she'd know exactly how nuts the entire scenario made him.

He circled the opening to her cunt with two fingers. Her juices spilled over his tongue.

"Oh, *monsieur.*" She kept up the act, but the accent seemed too much to maintain. Her trembling, restless hands said she was right on the verge of an orgasm. "God that's good. Your mouth, sir. Lick me."

Oh fuck, yeah. He loved it—loved the pretending, loved the step they'd taken outside of themselves.

Not like there was any chance he would stop. He wouldn't end this until his sexy maid came so hard she saw stars.

He pushed both fingers into her tight channel then curled his fingertips toward him, searching for that certain spot. He knew he'd found the right place when her nails dug into his neck and her entire body jerked.

She dropped backward, her upper back hitting the wall with a soft plunk. "Oh, God, sir. *Yes.* Right there. Don't stop. Your mouth—" She broke off with a keening wail that signaled she'd come and come hard. Her sheathe clenched on his fingers.

Ryan was unbelievably glad he didn't have to cut off her scream like he'd needed to at the sex shop. Heavy satisfaction almost let him forget about the way his cock throbbed against his uniform pants.

Though he drew his fingers away, he kept licking until her shakes eased and she pushed gently at his forehead.

He swiped the back of his hand across his wet mouth, unable to hold back his grin as he looked up at her. "Do you think your punishment was appropriate, Cassandra?"

The sigh that lifted her chest was rife with contentment. "I'm not sure, *monsieur.* Perhaps you should try another application."

He pinched her hip underneath the fluff that barely imitated a skirt. "Is that how you speak to your employer?"

"No, sir," she said with a swift smile. "I should never dare be so bold. *Merci*, do forgive me."

"I think you might have to make it up to me."

She pressed her skirt between her thighs, hiding the beautiful view of her wet pussy. "Right away, sir. First I believe we must take off this uniform. Your superior officers would be quite disappointed should you show up all...mussed."

Would they ever. Ryan shoved back thoughts of the outside world and let her pull him to a standing position.

Cassandra stripped him methodically, starting with his uniform shirt before moving down to his belt and slacks. Along the way she stole caresses and strokes across his skin. He forced himself to stand at attention as if he wasn't totally eating up the way she adored his body.

She folded each piece of his uniform and placed them in a dresser drawer—the bottom one of course, so she was forced to bend at the waist. The pale curve of her ass had likely never seen the sun. She treated him to a prime view.

When Ryan was finally stripped, she pushed on his chest until he walked backward toward the bed. The mattress hit the backs of his knees and he let himself sprawl.

"Oh, *monsieur*," she breathed, her hand wrapping around his cock. He was so eager that a drip of precome dotted the head. Her fingers cooled his hot skin but offered no relief. She sank onto the mattress with one smooth move. "It appears that you have a problem."

"I think that would depend on your point of view." From his position, flat on his back and staring at Cassandra where she knelt between his knees, life looked damned good. The black bodice of the outfit cupped her breasts. He trailed a touch over the bare slope of her shoulder. “Perhaps you should do something about it.”

“I should hate to be told I give bad service.”

He had to choke back a snicker at that. Instead he coughed. “I would hate to give you a bad review.”

Cassandra’s stretch, reaching behind her, turned her body into a long sinew of beauty. The skirt flirted around the tops of her thighs, hinting at the sweetness he’d just tasted. She snagged her half-drunk glass of champagne, then looked up at him as she deliberately tipped it over his cock.

The cold splash sent a shiver through him and made his balls draw up. He loved it anyway.

“Oops. I seem to have caused a terrible mess.”

He schooled his voice to a modicum of sternness. “You better clean it up then, hadn’t you? You wouldn’t like to see me displeased.”

“Of course not, *monsieur*,” she cooed, still using that perky hint of an accent. Then she bent her head. Her tongue dragged up the full length of his cock.

His head fell back for a second before he yanked it up again. He didn’t want to miss a single second of this show.

She licked and sucked at his flesh, opening her mouth over the heavy curve of his sac. Her tongue danced wet fire over his swollen head. When she took him in her mouth, she looked up at him. Wicked amusement danced in her blue eyes.

Ryan ran a hand over her head. He almost wished she still had the braids, but the prim twisted bun fit the scenario much better. Still, he’d like to be able to wrap his hand in her hair. He gave in to the impulse and drew out the pins and elastic tie holding the bun in place.

He tugged the red-gold locks forward over her shoulders until they tumbled across the top of her chest. On one level, he hoped the distraction of her hair would hold off the orgasm steadily building at the base of his spine. It didn’t work.

If anything, it contributed to the entire picture: Cassandra kneeling in front of him, worshiping his cock with licks and a strong suck. The mess he'd made of her hair only contributed to her appeal. Now she wasn't just a French maid; she was a French maid he'd tempted into depravity.

She set her teeth behind the ridge of his head and rocked ever so slightly.

Ryan hissed in a breath then grabbed her chin to draw her forward. He couldn't let her keep that up. Their time would be over much too soon.

"*Monsieur*," she said. Her mouth glistened almost as brightly as her eyes. "You didn't allow me to finish my task. You'll think me quite negligent."

He choked on something that was half laugh, half chagrin. That she was keeping up the game was almost enough to make him come. "Go get the condoms out of my inside jacket pocket."

"Yes, sir," she breathed. She hopped to her feet to obey.

Watching her sashay across the room was a gift in itself. Her ass peeked out now and then below the fluff of her skirt. She reached unnecessarily high into the closet, as if she'd somehow mislaid his jacket on the shelf. Then she came back with a strip of condoms dangling from her fist.

"So many, *monsieur*? You were quite sure of yourself, weren't you?"

Not nearly. He'd been merely hopeful when snagging them from a convenience store. He took them and ripped one off the end. He held it out to her. "You know what to do."

Fuck, he was sick. The sight of Cassandra's slender fingers unfurling the latex over his dick was almost as affecting as the strokes. Pulling her up his body along the bed, he framed her face for a kiss that flared hot about as fast as humanly possible. She eased onto his lap, sitting sideways across his legs. Her hands dove into his hair and wrenched. The small pain wasn't enough to ground him. He didn't know if there was anything that would bring him back to earth after this night.

He scooped her into his arms, only to deposit her against the pile of white pillows. She let go of his hair and stretched her arms over her head. Ryan settled onto his front between her outstretched legs.

She had the best pout on the planet. "Have I made up for

my…transgressions? Whatever shall you do with me next?”

Using just one finger, he traced the edge of the bodice. The top curves of her breasts were pinked with arousal, and her chest lifted and fell with fast breaths. The outfit had a miniature apron made of sheer lace. Directly beneath it was her pussy. When he cupped his hand over the spot and pressed firmly, he flicked his gaze up to take in her expression.

Pleasure. Sugary pleasure slackened her mouth and made her eyelids droop. Good. He didn’t want anything for her but flat-out enjoyment.

He looped his fingers around her ankle, then stroked all the way up to her thighs, over the sheer material of her stockings. He couldn’t help a grin. “My dear Cassandra, I’m going to do anything I like with you.”

Chapter Ten

Cass had lost sight of almost everything she'd known about herself. All she wanted was mindless, obliterating sex with Ryan Haverty. Nothing else mattered. Nothing else came close.

She looked down, soaking in the sight of his body. He was the fittest, most luscious man she'd ever been with. That wasn't even taking into account his long, thick cock—a fabulous bonus. Those beautiful muscles along his ribs were tense with the strain of holding himself in check. His abs quirked and quivered. Even the hard bulge of his quadriceps shivered with the effort.

"Up on your knees, Cassandra. Face the headboard."

She almost felt like resisting. Just for a moment. How long could he go without completely losing control?

That was an experiment for another day. She wanted him. Now.

With deliberate care, she levered off the pillows. He allowed her enough space but hovered over her the whole time. Only when she turned toward the wall did he touch her. Both of his hands took hold of hers, forcing them up to the elaborate wrought-iron headboard.

"You like when I tell you what to do, don't you?"

Cass dipped her chin to her chest, dragging a long breath into her lungs. She'd experienced flickers of this feeling before, but never for long. Her boyfriends hadn't been the most competent stream of clowns. Taking control of her own orgasm, no matter a lover's failings, had been a sign of strength and independence. Worst case, she could always get off on her own.

This was different—this night, this stranger. She wasn't the only one working toward her pleasure. That made her submission practically freeing. So good. So much easier to admit in the guise of her French character.

"Only because I trust you to make it good. For both of us."

"Cassandra," he whispered, his lips brushing her bare shoulder blade. "You are a wonder."

"Major?"

"Hm?"

"I'm waiting."

"Indeed you are. Hold on to that headboard and don't you dare let go. Understand?"

"*Oui, monsieur.*"

"Good girl." He nestled against her backside, his palms flat on her outer thighs. "Such a good girl."

Ryan's thumbs circled the flesh of her ass, kneading, squeezing. Arching back, Cass let her body beg for what it needed. She was strung out on the rack of another climax just waiting to happen. Palms beginning to sweat, she gripped the headboard until her knuckles turned white.

Their first time had been so fast, his cock thrusting deep with one smooth push. Not so now. Those clever, blunt fingers found the entrance to her pussy. He teased in and out, each tickling flick of movement ratcheting her higher.

"So mean," she whispered.

"You love it."

"God, yes."

"You want more, don't you?"

"*Oui.*"

He curled over her, holding his balance with those powerful thighs. His body bent to match the arch of her spine. Big hands slid around to scoop her breasts out of the bodice, teasing and tugging her nipples until they stood as hard points, her flesh hanging heavy and full. All the while he nipped biting kisses along her nape and down the bumps of her spine.

Cass couldn't breathe, couldn't see straight. She let her head dangle uselessly between her upraised arms, dragging gulp after gulp into her lungs.

Only when his hands returned to her clit did she hope for an end to the exquisite torture. He was so good. Damn good.

But she needed to come or she'd start begging.

Maybe that might do the trick.

"Please, *monsieur. Merci.* I need you."

"Tell me what you need." He sounded like another man altogether, so gruff and clamped down. He positioned the head of his prick at her entrance, still teasing, still driving her crazy.

"I need your cock inside me," she said, enjoying the freedom of giving voice to her depraved thoughts. She flipped her hair so she could look back over her shoulder. "I need you to fuck me. *S'il vous plaît.*"

This time he gave her what she wanted. Each inch, each maddening inch, spread her wider, filling her. Her shuddering moan matched his when his pelvis finally snuggled flush against her ass, his cock buried to the hilt.

"Goddamn," he choked out.

Then he started to move, dragging out the moment. They were suspended between wanting it *now* and wanting it never to end. Cass was already fighting the orgasm that gathered where he filled her so completely.

Ryan too had human limits. His rhythm picked up, as did his ragged breathing. He grabbed a fistful of Cass's unbound hair, tugging her head back. The sharp pain made her smile—just enough sting. She was caught there, held captive by his body. That thought alone made her shake.

Faster now, pounding now, Ryan hit his stride. God, he was huge. Huge and strong and fucking her deeper with every thrust. The headboard clattered against the wall, but Cass was ready to make some noise. Wake the neighbors. Wake the whole damn Strip. Her orgasm built and built, so strong that when she finally came, she let a gasping scream go free.

Ryan had grabbed the headboard too, using it for leverage. Up and up, deeper now, he thrust into her slick, quivering pussy. His guttural grunt and a low, groaned, "Fuck," signaled his potent release.

Coming down from such a high was like the most euphoric morning after. All Cass could do was laugh. The giddy, bubbling laughter wouldn't be contained. Her mind had gone dark except for how incredible it had been.

Disengaging, Ryan ditched his condom and flopped back on the bed. Still clinging to the headboard, her body a wreck of overused muscles and adrenaline, she looked down at him. He wore the expression of a man who'd been ushered into heaven. Her bite marks had bruised his skin, but the dressing room seemed so long ago.

He opened his arms. "C'mon," he said softly. "Lie down."

Cass forced herself to move, but she didn't join him on the bed. First she stripped out of her costume. Though the naughty beauty had served its purpose, she wanted to sleep skin to skin. Preferrably for a week.

Ryan's eyes were all over her again, but not with the intensity of lust. He wore a crooked smile. "I like how you think."

"Haven't been doing much of that lately." Her voice sounded odd without the accent. She was Cass again. That could be good too—as if the costume and the character had served their purposes.

She snuggled in close beside him, both of them wiggling under the covers. Only when she rested against his chest, their breathing returning to normal, did she ask the big mystery question of the night.

"Where did you get your costume? It's amazing."

Ryan froze. "My dress uniform?"

"Yeah? I mean, where...?"

He was the one laughing now. "Oh, that's too much. You thought... Huh, I'm kinda glad."

Cass raised up on her elbow. "What are you talking about?"

Laughter still danced in his eyes and shaped his mouth into a smile. "I am Major Ryan Haverty, US Air Force."

"For real?"

"For real."

"No way."

"Here, hold on."

He slipped out of bed and crossed to the closet where she'd hung his coat. She got a fabulous view of his naked backside. Taut, defined muscle flexed as he walked. Absolutely glorious.

Ryan returned to the bed with the easy walk of a self-assured man. The penis she'd enjoyed so much was much less intimidating now. Seeing him this way, now, only hours after their first introduction, struck her as almost unbearably intimate.

"Here," he said. "My flight wings and name tag. I was so worked up that I didn't trust myself to pin them on."

Cass ran a finger over the metal wings. The name tag said *HAVERTY.* These were no costume shop doodads.

Her snort was *not* attractive. She buried her face in the pillows. "Oh, *God.* How embarrassing."

"No way. It was perfect." He sat on the edge of the mattress, which dipped under his weight. Again, just that simple detail was more intimate than she could've imagined. He touched her shoulder, tracing slow circles over her skin. "I'm glad you didn't know. Too real. You know?"

She turned to face him. "I think so. It might've been harder to pretend had I known you were telling the truth."

He was back in bed before the rest of his story caught up with her.

"Wait, so you really do fly…what plane was it?"

"F-16s. That's right."

"And you've been to Paris?"

"Best leave of my career," he said with a grin. "But I won't go into that."

"Probably explains the French-maid thing."

His expression sobered, almost as it had in the sex shop. "I don't know what explains that, Cassandra."

He blinked and looked away. The vulnerability was gone in a flash.

"You always call me Cassandra. Why?"

"Because Cass doesn't fit you."

"No?"

Rolling onto his side, Ryan faced her while she reclined on her back. "You have the best curves. So damn sexy." As if to accentuate the thought, he petted and smoothed with those big, broad hands. "Cassandra," he whispered against her collarbone, "fits you much better."

She shivered and grabbed his hair, dragging his mouth back for a deep, tender kiss.

Ryan only got up again to turn off the lights. She noticed how he checked the locks on the hotel-room door, securing the chain. It didn't surprise her at all. Somehow that nod toward their safety was in keeping with how protected he'd made her feel all night. Such a bizarre thing to imagine about a near-stranger.

She had to stop thinking of him that way. Two people didn't do what they'd done and still regard one another as strangers. They were lovers. Even if they never shared another night together, Cass would always think of him that way.

With the room in darkness, the lights of the Strip seemed all the brighter. He walked back to the bed bathed in dots of color. Together they snuggled under the covers. Warm and contented, still fizzy and giddy and thoroughly worn out, Cass liked how his arms curved her more snugly against his hard length.

"Fighter pilot," she said in the dark. "No wonder you're in such good shape."

"I'll take that as a compliment."

"Meant it that way. So those two you were with at dinner?"

"More pilots."

"Wow." She wouldn't have pictured the wiry young man or the vaguely ditzy woman as pilots. Then again, she hadn't even guessed it of Ryan, no matter how right that knowledge seemed now. "Do you have call signs, like in *Top Gun*?"

He sighed.

"What?"

"Everyone always mentions *Top Gun*," he said. "Navy schmoes."

Cass giggled.

"My call sign's Fang."

"Fang? That's fairly badass, Major Haverty."

It was his turn to chuckle. "It wasn't when I started. It stands for 'Fuck...another new guy'."

"Priceless."

"Yeah, but don't tell my students. 'Fang' is wonderful for intimidation."

"You're an instructor?"

"That's right." He sounded sleepy now but proud at the same time. Obviously, some years ago, he'd wanted to be a pilot and he'd gone for it. That much determination was humbling. "I'm stationed at Nellis with the 64th Aggressor Squadron."

"Again with the badass."

"Damn straight. I fly like the bad guys to teach other pilots how not to die. Love it."

A few seconds later, he was snoring softly. The possessive way he'd been holding her began to ease. Cass couldn't sleep, not for a long time. She watched the lights of the Strip, heard drunken voices out in the hallway, and felt the rhythmic beat of Ryan's heart beneath her cheek.

Events from the evening became a repeating movie in her mind—all they'd said and done and revealed. Ryan Haverty was too good to be true. But for the moment, on that amazing night, he was hers.

Chapter Eleven

Ryan quietly eased onto the bed then brushed the hair off Cassandra's face. He'd closed the curtains a couple hours earlier so she could sleep longer, but a single sneaking finger of sunlight lay across her cheek. She'd curled into a half-moon with one hand under the pillow. She looked like some sort of woodland fairy.

He glanced at the costume she'd dropped to the floor. Maybe not a fairy. A nymph. That seemed more like her. Wicked but a lot fun-loving.

He traced the delicate hollow of her temple where the skin was tissue thin.

She shifted and blinked up at him. A sleepy smile curved her lips. "Good morning, Major Haverty."

He wasn't surprised she was the type to wake up cheery. "It's the afternoon, Miss Whitman."

"Is it really?" She stretched her arms up over her head. The sheet slipped a few inches, but unfortunately not enough to drop below her nipples. After scrubbing at her eyes, she twisted to look at the glowing display of the alarm clock. "Wow, you're right. How long have you been up?"

"A couple hours."

He'd always been an early riser, and then his Air Force training had finished him off. He could rarely get more than six hours of sleep anymore.

This time he'd been able to indulge in watching her sleep. Not that he'd ever tell her, but when she was really racked out, she made a noise that wasn't quite a snore and wasn't quite a snort. A snuffle, he'd call it. Probably a sign he was already pretty far gone that he'd found it sort of cute. Adorable in a geeky way.

She rubbed the base of her palms over her eyes again and her jaw cracked on a yawn. "What is that I smell?"

"Coffee and pastries. I also picked up a toiletry kit in one of the gift shops. It's in the bathroom."

His first stop, though, had been a clothing store. That had been quite the walk of shame, entering in his bedraggled dress uniform shirt and slacks, then leaving in a pair of cargo shorts and T-shirt. Once again he was lucky to have lost his mind in Vegas. No one gave him a second look.

He'd also had reception extend their stay for another day, switching the room to his credit card. The thought of her paying for their good time rubbed him very, very wrong. Now, even if they didn't stay over, he had guaranteed that she could sleep as long as she needed. Not to mention that he didn't want to be rushed out by housekeeping at an inopportune moment.

She grinned at him. "Are you implying my breath stinks?"

"I wouldn't dare."

He'd been aware that something would change by morning. The shiny would have worn off, or they wouldn't get along as well in the daylight. Or it would finally dawn on her exactly how broken he was. They'd been high on the rush of excitement and adventure, but it seemed like they were still on the same page. That realization unfurled some of the tension in his limbs.

"I love a smart man," she said. "They're so rare that they should be appreciated as the fine works of art they are."

She slipped out of the bed and stretched. Her hands rose to scratch through her hair, which lifted her breasts. The dim light clung to her and outlined every beautiful curve—from the soft line of her stomach, down to the small fluff of strawberry-blonde curls.

Ryan's chest clenched on a silent *guh*. He leaned back onto his palms, intent on enjoying the view. She was beautiful. That was for damned sure.

She tossed a small smirk over her shoulder as she walked away, apparently completely aware of the power she had over him.

The spell dissipated with the click of the bathroom door. He managed to make it to his feet and reach the small table in the other room where he'd dropped their breakfast. The coffee was nearly scalding, but he sucked it down anyway. He needed something to get his mind out of the gutter.

She might not be ready to go again. Last night they'd fucked twice—but that didn't feel right either. It hadn't *quite* been making love, but it had been something more than a mindless fuck. Special. A gift.

The shower hissed on. He wiped a hand over his face as if that could wipe out the image of her soaking wet standing under the showerhead as water poured over her curves and dips.

The door cracked open. "Hey," she called. "You getting in here with me?"

Oh, hell yeah. He slammed down his coffee and was off like a shot, stripping his T-shirt as he went. His shoes toed off somewhere at the halfway mark. He kicked off his shorts at the threshold to the marble bathroom, right after he snagged another condom from his pocket.

She held her arms out to him. Soaking wet, she was everything he'd imagined. Just as sexy as she'd been in the outfits. Even hotter with an inviting smile on her face.

He was kissing her before he'd even stepped beneath the spray, his fingers delving into the wet mass of her hair. With her arms around his shoulders and one leg hitched over his hip, she wrapped around him like some sort of sex monkey. He loved her enthusiasm. He filled his hands with her ass and lifted her up against the wall.

They crashed and slid together, then apart. Ryan wedged her into the corner to hold her in position for his thrusts. She curled up into every push. When her toes slipped off their perch on the soap dish, she giggled.

The sex was no less powerful for being filled with smiles and laughs. Another nice reassurance. He'd worried their night of debauchery and costumes would make him incapable of finding her sexy for just being Cassandra. But the orgasm that weakened his bones and turned his knees to Jell-O, right after she moaned in his ear that she was coming, was equally intense.

They toweled off together amid plenty more laughter and teasing. She found the only ticklish spot on his body, right at the top of his ribs, then exploited it mercilessly. He chased her out of the bathroom with a snap of his towel to her ass.

She fell back into the tumbled mess of bedding. "Peace," she cried. "Treaty. Whatever you military guys call it."

He laughed one more time as he scrubbed the towel over his damp hair. "Baby, you can say anything you want as long as you're naked in my bed."

She twisted around until she was on her stomach and propped her head on her fists. The long line of her back curving into the gentle swell of her ass was a thing of beauty. "Is that all it takes? Then fetch me my coffee."

"Yes, ma'am." He snapped a full salute.

"Ooh," she breathed, "now you're just playing dirty."

"I was under the impression that's what you liked."

He ducked into the other room to grab the coffee and pastries, then hurried back. She'd shifted to the head of the bed. To Ryan's deepest regret, she'd drawn the sheet up over her perfect body and was speaking to someone on her cell phone. After reassuring whoever it was that she had not, in fact, been murdered by a sex pervert, she hung up with a smile.

"There," she said. "Gilly's happy. We can proceed with our day."

He handed her one of the cups and plunked the white bag of pastries on the comforter. Because Cassandra had covered up, he grabbed his shorts and pulled them on.

"I wasn't sure what you liked, so I got a selection. There's creamer and sugar in there too."

"Thanks."

"Who's Gilly?"

"My friend. The dark-haired woman last night at Blakely's, the one who said she'd close for me." She snagged two small cups of cream and three packs of sugar to doctor her drink. When she dug further in the sack, her blue eyes lit up. Her hand reemerged with a sugar-dusted croissant. "Oh, my. You've made me very happy."

Ryan grinned. He shifted onto the bed and reached into the

bag. He pulled out the first thing his fingers touched, a glazed donut. "That's good since I've decided to make it my goal for the day."

"Do you always achieve your goals, Major Haverty?" Something flickered across her face and darkened her eyes.

A tiny sugar crystal clung to her top lip. He couldn't resist leaning forward to kiss it away. "Always. Don't you?"

She shrugged. "Most of the time, I guess."

"What do you mean?"

She took another bite of her croissant, as if to delay answering, but he waited patiently. "I want to be the director of an art gallery. For now I'm interning. It'll get me there. Eventually."

"What's holding you back?" To be truthful, he couldn't understand someone who didn't go full force after their dreams. It had taken him long enough to figure out what he wanted and to find the opportunity to pursue that better future. He hadn't had time to screw around after that.

"It's not that easy. There's politics in galleries. You have to prove you have that special eye for art." She shrugged again then plastered on a smile. "But I'm not at the gallery today."

"No, you're not," he said, consciously letting the subject drop. "So what do you want to do? We're on the Strip. We've got the room 'til tomorrow."

"We do?"

He nodded. "Yep. I took care of it. So the itinerary is all yours."

"An itinerary." She took a deep sip of her coffee. "That sounds so formal."

"It kind of does, doesn't it?"

He put the bag of pastries on the nightstand, followed by Cassandra's coffee cup. Her wrists, so slender, were easily wrapped in his hands. Enjoying the buttery taste on her lips, he kissed her until she was breathless.

Finally he needed to draw back, or they'd never make it out of bed. "So let's call it a vacation. Let's play tourist."

"Tourists are so boring. If you grow up here, you get tired of their antics."

"What do you have in mind?"

She angled her lips over his and took one more kiss. "Something darker. What if we'd snuck away? We're two people hiding from the world. Like we were having an affair or something."

"Definitely darker." The skin of her throat was so soft. He brushed another kiss in the hollow below her collarbone.

"Mmm." She bent her head to give him more access. "We're wicked cheaters."

He drew his head back abruptly. "I wouldn't, you know."

"What?"

"Have an affair. Ever."

It was of vital importance that she understand that. He wasn't sure why since they were just having fun. He'd known from a very early age that if he were ever lucky enough to find someone to build a future with, he'd do everything in his power not to fuck it up. Keeping his dick appropriately in his pants seemed the easiest part of that puzzle. Resisting the temptation to beg her to dress up in sexy scraps of lace would be much harder.

One of the first things he'd learned about her was that her ex cheated. He didn't want to be anything like that toady schmuck.

Cassandra curved her palm around the back of his neck. Her gaze flickered over him for a second before her smile returned. "Of course you wouldn't. We're just playing here. Right?"

"Right." He spread his hand over the curve of her waist, nestling his thumb against the bottom of her ribs. "So a getaway. Mini vacation with anything in the city. What would you do?"

Her lashes dipped as she dropped her gaze. "Anything?"

"Anything that's in my power to arrange."

The pretty pink that swept over her round cheeks was damned cute. "There's a showing of Impressionists at the Bellagio. I've been so busy that I haven't had a chance to get over there. If you think you'll be bored, though, we can go somewhere else."

He stole another kiss. "Baby, as long as I'm with you, I don't think anything could bore me."

Chapter Twelve

The heat wasn't so bad that afternoon as they crossed Las Vegas Boulevard. A fine mist from Bellagio's tremendous fountains had Cass in mind of the shower they'd shared. She smiled to herself and snuggled against Ryan's body as they walked.

April in Vegas meant spring-break vacations. The Strip was thick with a trillion tourists. The inconvenience of so many self-centered pleasure seekers didn't bother her that afternoon. She was one too. Intentionally, she looked at the chaotic excess with new eyes. What if she were seeing all this glitz and adult fantasy for the first time? Her imagination wasn't quite that good. At least the effort made squeezing through a tour group of two dozen retirement community members easier to endure.

When they stood in line at the Bellagio Gallery of Fine Art, stuck like complacent cattle between the velvet ropes, Cass took Ryan's hand and kissed the back of it.

"What was that for?"

"I don't know," she said. "Maybe just thankful the spell hasn't worn off yet."

"I was thinking the same thing this morning."

"Oh, yeah?"

He looked fantastic in his white cotton T-shirt. The soft cloth clung to his broad back, the solid caps of his shoulders, the flat ridges of his stomach. He probably wouldn't like her to point it out, but his cargo shorts did fantastic things for his ass. Dark hair dusted his calves. The loafers he wore were brand new, reminding her that this escape was costing him a fortune.

It was their turn to buy tickets. Cassandra almost groaned at the price. The expense didn't seem to faze Ryan, who dragged a credit card out of his wallet.

"Please, please tell me you aren't going into debt for this weekend," she whispered.

He shrugged. "I'd been saving for a hiking trip this summer with Jon and Leah—my friends from at the restaurant. We thought heading into the mountains might be a nice break from the heat come July."

"Camping's not so expensive."

"Not with normal people. Jon comes from money, and Leah has expensive tastes. I'm sure a spa or a villa would be involved eventually. It takes a bit of prep to keep up with them."

"You're giving that up for me?"

He signed the receipt then grabbed the tickets and her hand. "If I'd bought you diamonds, you could argue it was for you alone." He eased in close to her ear. "Unless you wore *only* diamonds. And you were on top. That would be for me too."

Cass kissed him before swatting him away. The gallery seemed too intellectual, too exotic for their teasing. She loved it. Everything was golden. The lighting, the walls, the gilded chandeliers. Huge colorful Persian rugs covered floors polished to a gleaming shine. She'd never been able to decide if the effect was elegant or gaudy. Probably both—the best of Vegas. The gallery was the only reason she ever came down to the Strip.

They presented their tickets and waited to enter the main exhibit. "Are Jon and Leah a couple?"

Ryan snorted. "Hell no. They'd cannibalize each other first."

Hesitating, knowing it was probably against the unspoken rules of their weekend, Cass asked, "You and Leah? Maybe before?"

"Yeah, for a while." His expression had sobered slightly, his gaze intent. "That was a long time ago."

"What happened?"

Shoot. Shut up, Cass.

"It was like two wolverines in a burlap sack. You can't have a relationship based on a constant game of chicken. We couldn't even compromise on our choice of bottled water."

"Generic all the way, baby," Cass said, trying for levity.

He winked. "Now stop asking questions. We're having a

torrid affair, remember?"

"While edifying ourselves. Multitasking!"

They had just reached the threshold of the exhibit when Cass's cell phone chirped. The guard on duty gave her a stern look. "Not in the gallery, please, ma'am."

She checked the caller ID. "Dang. It's my mom. I have to take this."

Ducking out of the queue, with Ryan shooting the evil eye at the guard, Leah answered. "Hey, Mom. What's up?"

"Oh, it's just terrible, honey."

Her mother's reedy voice was higher pitched than usual. She was in full-fledged panic mode. Already the hairs on Cass's arms had prickled. This wasn't going to be fun.

"I need you to take a tour tomorrow. Your father's arthritis is bad this month, and Emily has some family thing with Robert's parents."

"Mom, why didn't you tell me in advance? You know I can't do last minute."

"It wasn't my fault. You know how flighty Robert can be. I'm not knocking him, really. He's a great son-in-law and he loves little Claire something fierce. But he forgets."

Cass ground her back teeth together. Emily, her sister, had married a geology Ph.D who led tours for their family business. He knew the Grand Canyon like the back of his hand, but remembering to put important events on the company calendar always slipped his mind.

"Honey, where are you? It sounds busy there."

"Grocery store. Hold on. I'm just buying my stuff." She hit mute and leaned against the wall.

"Trouble?" Ryan asked.

"What are we doing tomorrow?"

He shrugged those godlike shoulders as if the fate of future relations with her family didn't hang in the balance. "Building houses for the homeless?"

"Not exactly what I had in mind," she said. "Yet very noble of us."

"How about eating breakfast off one another?"

"Much better."

"Spending hours by the pool until I need to drag you back to the room and strip off your bikini?"

Cass grinned. "You assume I have a bikini."

"With a body like yours, *not* owning a bikini is a crime against mankind."

"Mmm." She shifted her legs, loving the sudden rush of arousal. "You're merciless."

"Cassandra, I really don't care. I'm having too much fun to stop now." He nodded to the phone in her hand. "If you need to do family things, I'll understand. Honest. This isn't the only weekend ever."

Oh, she liked the sound of that. It was the first time either of them had suggested that their good time might not end come Sunday evening.

She wasn't going to bank on that. Maybe this was all they'd have. Cass didn't want to give it up before she absolutely had to.

"Hey, Mom?"

"I'm here, honey."

"I'm really sorry, but I can't. I have plans."

A telling silence hissed over the line. Cass never had plans. She either had work or she was in a gallery. That had been especially true since breaking up with Tommy.

"Plans?"

"That's right," she said, reaching out to grab Ryan's hand. She needed to stay strong. Her mom, no matter how wonderful, could wield guilt like a medieval knight swinging a sword. Cass wasn't still living in her bizarre hometown by accident. "You know I don't duck out on you often. This is...this is important."

"It's not that guy Tommy, is it? I thought you broke up."

"No, not Tommy. Mom, I gotta go. My ice cream's starting to melt. Call Phillip. You know he's always ready to take a tour."

"He just about pushed a couple into the Canyon last time, trying to take their picture. Dad doesn't like how much of a liability he is."

"That's what insurance is for, which you have plenty of. I

really gotta go. Talk to you later."

She barely heard her mom's "I love you" before closing the phone.

Ryan had crossed his arms, leaning against the wall next to her. "You okay?"

"Yeah." She let out a heavy breath, feeling as if she'd dodged a bullet. "My parents run a small company, Vision Tours."

"I've heard of it. Some of the guys on base have used them. Tours out to the Hoover Dam and the Grand Canyon, right?"

"That's right. I've been a tour guide since I was about fifteen. My sister and her husband practically run it now, but I still fill in when they have emergencies." She forced herself to stop nibbling at a rough cuticle. A short laugh escaped her. "I think that's the first time I've ever told her no when I wasn't scheduled to work."

"Feel selfish?"

"Yeah."

He kissed her neck. "Naughty?"

She giggled as he found a ticklish spot. "You're hopeless." Blinking, straightening, she put the phone back in her purse. "I guess sometimes you just need to say no to family. It's not something I've ever been good at."

A frown pinched between his strong brows. "I wouldn't know."

"No?"

Despite the subtlety of Cass's prompting, he'd already gone into lockdown. She was getting to know his smiles better now. Most were genuine. This one was forced. "Not from experience, no," he said. "C'mon. That guard keeps giving me the evil eye."

"Then quit trying to stare him down."

The atmosphere between them, however, took time to ease, even after they'd joined the gallery throng. Cass couldn't concentrate. The gilt looked gauche, the lighting artificially posh. Her affair with Ryan wasn't even twenty-four hours old and already they'd hit pesky barriers. Dratted human beings with their *feelings*. They'd be having a much better time if they could just turn off all that squishy nonsense. She was hanging out with a piece of one hundred percent prime All-American beef, but her brain wouldn't be quiet.

She knew so little about him, and maybe that was part of the problem. She wanted to know everything. *Now.* Even if that might end their fascination with one another. In a bizarre way she envied his friends, those other pilots. They probably knew what he wasn't saying about his family. Maybe they could navigate around the weird wall he threw up at a moment's notice. Cass didn't have anything like that inside knowledge at her disposal.

She swallowed a sinking feeling. What if she'd done a terrible thing by indulging, even encouraging his roleplaying? What if that set them up for disappointment? After all she hadn't been, until very recently, the kind of daredevil who had sex in public and donned frilly costumes. She was a waitress without the slightest speck of ambition, one who spent her free time studying art books and browsing the internet for gallery jobs she never applied for. He'd figure that out eventually, and that would be the end of them.

"Hey," he called softly.

Cass shook free of her doubts, only to have them redouble when she grabbed another glance at Ryan. The golden lighting made him into a modern-day bronze sculpture, all jagged angles and curved muscle. Short sunny brown locks curled onto his forehead. Bright hazel eyes regarded her with his full attention. He always did that, as if he couldn't look at her closely enough.

A *fighter pilot*, for gosh sake.

Whereas Cass Whitman was about as exotic as a shrub. He made her want to keep up, but she didn't have any practice at hard-charging. It sounded worse than difficult. It sounded scary.

He held out his hand. "Come tell me about this one."

Taking a deep breath, she joined him in front of a painting of an isolated French commune. He didn't hold her hand for long, instead cupping her hip, fingers slightly splayed.

"It's by Corot," she said. "He was the leading painter at the French Barbizon school in the mid-19th century." She pointed to the buildings in the background nestled behind a clear blue stream. "See here? His structures are almost classical, but the trees and the grasses use early impressionistic techniques. He was the bridge between those two styles. People like Monet, Degas, Van Gogh—none of them would've been the same without Corot to come first."

Only after speaking did she realize that Ryan was no longer looking at her, but at the painting. That frown was back—his expression of concentration. "It's great. I like how cool it looks. Me and a couple guys, during that leave in France, we took a train from Paris to Marseilles. The countryside was just like this."

"I remember that, how strange and lush it was compared to here in the desert."

"Ah," he said. "So you were telling the truth last night too."

She smiled softly. "A little."

"You had the nerve to head off to Paris for a year. That's something."

"Once. Years ago. But coming back home... I kind of got out of the habit of taking chances."

He cupped her cheek. She wanted to nibble his lower lip, if only to distract him from being so damn perceptive. "Seems a shame, Cassandra. Being bold looks good on you."

Chapter Thirteen

The parking garage was sweltering. Even the dim shadows didn't help break the warmth. Ryan tossed Cassandra's scant possessions in the trunk of her car then swiped at a trickle of sweat sneaking beyond his hairline.

She already sat in the driver's seat, cranking up the air in order to blow out forty-eight hours worth of heat.

For almost two days, they'd hidden from the world.

It was the best weekend he'd had in a seriously long time. He didn't want it to end, but they both had real lives to get back to. Days to prepare for.

He propped a forearm on the roof of her car and leaned down. "Do you have to work next Friday?"

She wore a light green tank top that left her shoulders bare. He couldn't help but run his knuckles over her soft skin. It was insane to think she'd allowed him to touch her so casually after meeting him just two nights ago. More than that, she'd indulged—no, *welcomed* his weird games Friday night.

Cold slithered over him despite how the parking garage could roast a Thanksgiving turkey. Shutting that part of him down once again would be hard as hell, but he'd manage. He was rapidly starting to suspect Cassandra was a woman worth knowing. That meant treating her with the respect she deserved. No more weird stuff.

Besides, sex had been fantastic no matter what they did. He didn't need seamed stockings and French accents. Wouldn't *let* himself need them.

"I've got a Saturday night shift, but I'm free Friday." Her smile lit up her whole face. "Are you asking for a reason?"

"I sure am," he said. "Would you like to go out with me?"

"Go out? You mean on a real, honest-to-goodness date?"

He kissed away her laugh, taking it into his mouth. Her zest for life had been wonderful all weekend, making it even more odd that what she'd mentioned about her jobs and her goals sounded so stuck. He didn't like thinking of her that way, not after the initiative she'd shown with him.

"Yes. A date. I hear people do that when they like someone of the opposite sex."

"Or the same, if they like."

"Yeah, that too." He sank to balance on the balls of his feet, the better to see her eyes. The concrete beneath him was dark and slick with old oil. Not somewhere he'd like to have this conversation, but he'd take the cards he was dealt.

"Does this mean you like me, Major Haverty?" Her eyes sparkled. She angled her shoulders toward him.

"Yes. Is that surprising at this point?"

"No, not really." She leaned forward to brush a kiss over his lips. "Because I like you too."

"Are you going to write my name with flowers drawn around it?"

"No," she said with a fake sour look. "But I will expect you to call this week. We can firm up details then?"

"Sounds good." He stroked his thumb down the slender column of her throat. She was so goddamned soft. He could barely keep his hands off her, even now, even after two days of being glued to her. He'd touched her at every opportunity, and it still wasn't enough. "Will you do one thing for me before then?"

"Is it sexy? Because then I'm all in."

She made him laugh like hell. "No, not so much. Well, I suppose it *could* be, but I'm feeling kind of greedy. I'd like you to keep your sexy stuff for me, at least for the foreseeable future."

"That seems appropriately vague enough for me to accept."

"I'm trying to be serious here. Vainly, it seems like."

She smoothed her features into mock seriousness. "Okay. What do you need?"

Rocking forward, he pressed his knees against the open car door. "Will you do something bold? Before Friday? Take a risk."

He wasn't even sure why he was asking it of her. Their time together had been great, but part of the magic was because they'd shut out the rest of reality. He hated to see anyone so mired down by life. Cassandra of all people had the energy to take more for herself.

She stared at him for a quiet moment. "I'll make you a deal. I'll do it, but only if you tell me something about yourself first. It's not fair if I'm the only one taking risks."

He shifted backwards a few inches. The air seemed extra steamy in his lungs, even with the cool wash of her A/C. "About me?"

"Something true. That not many people know."

Her lush mouth quirked, as if she was nervous about asking. If anything, that made him more determined to level with her. She wasn't asking for that much.

"When I was in high school, I was the varsity quarterback."

"I bet everyone knows that." She grinned wide. "I bet you were the star of the school. All the girls loved you."

"Hush, you." He curled a lock of her hair around his fingers, grounding himself. "There was an assistant coach, Dan Mackles. He probably saved my life by letting me crash on his couch whenever I wanted."

Her eyes turned dark blue. Her mouth formed an "oh" but no sound came out.

Ryan had to shift his gaze down to her legs, bared by her new jeans shorts. This would be easier to say without seeing that sympathy in her face. He'd gotten his fill of that as a kid.

"Whenever my mom was drunk...Dan let me come over. We didn't tell anyone because it would've sounded skeevy. People would've thought something bad was going on. But he was a good guy. He was there for me."

Her fingers made a tentative foray into his hair, then petted and stroked with more assurance. "I'm glad you had someone."

"Me too. It was because of him that I ended up in the Air Force. He was prior service. Tried to fly, but it didn't work out for him. Medical stuff."

She curled her hands around his jaw and tugged until he was forced to look up at her. "Thank you for telling me."

He made himself smile, since that was how she liked him. "So you'll do it then? Take a risk?"

"I promise." She sealed it with a kiss. "I'm not sure what it is yet, but I'll think of something."

"Good. You're braver than you think, Miss Whitman."

"We'll see, won't we?"

After a few more goodbyes that involved two really lingering kisses, Ryan watched her car pull away. With his flight bag slung over his shoulder, he made his way to his truck.

He drove out of the garage as if on autopilot, not ready to head back to his empty apartment. Instead he wound up on the back forty of Nellis, directly under the flight path. Few planes would be taking off on a Sunday afternoon, but Ryan thought best when he was there. He dropped the tailgate and sat looking up at the sky.

The flight path at Langley was the first place he'd visited on an Air Force base, with a slick recruiter in tow. A C-130 had flown directly overhead. He'd taken a couple flights in Dan's Cessna, but it was then, at that moment, when Ryan had been sure. There was nothing like flying. It was what he'd been born to do.

He'd discovered the same feeling of rightness when he gripped Cassandra's hips.

Once he made decisions, he stuck to them. He picked a road and stayed on it. End of story. With personal decisions, however... He'd never moved so damn fast before. A single weekend seemed so little to spark an obsession. The best he could do was make sure he didn't screw it up by letting his stupid fetish get the better of being with a real woman.

His phone chirped, and he dug it out of his pocket. "Yeah?"

"You come up for air yet?" Jon's voice carried a laugh.

Ryan looked up at the sky. The clear, deepening blue was nice, but he couldn't help wishing for a plane or two. "Yeah. How's Leah?"

"Sleeping off the weekend, last I saw her. Where are you?"

"On the flight line."

Dead air hissed for a few seconds. "I'll be right there."

"You don't have to do that."

"Don't move."

Jon's fancy-assed convertible pulled up bare minutes later. He must have pushed the glossy black Aston Martin to its full capabilities.

"How do you not get a ticket every week?"

The wiry younger man pushed up to sit beside him. "Because I'm the bomb."

"And a jackass."

"That too."

They sat in silence for a good long while, until the chain-link fence circling the flight line threw a long shadow across the ground. It was enough that Jon had showed up. He always did. He might act like he didn't give a crap about anything, but when his friends needed something, he was right there. In an *instant.*

Still, that didn't mean they needed to dissect everything as if they were chicks.

Finally Jon slanted a look at Ryan out the corners of his eyes. "So I guess the weekend with the waitress ended badly?"

"Her name's Cassandra, remember?"

"Ah, I see."

Ryan crossed his arms over his chest. "What's that supposed to mean?"

"It means the waitress has a name."

"Everyone does."

"Yeah, and you want to make sure I use it." Jon grinned. "I've changed my mind. The weekend ended well."

"Damn well," Ryan said with a laugh. "So well that we're hooking up again Friday."

Jon clapped him on the back with surprising force. "Good for you. You could use a steady lay."

Wiping the back of his hand across his mouth, Ryan glanced toward the empty flight line. He wasn't sure what to focus on first: the fact that Cassandra was becoming way more than a fuck, or the implication that his relatively calm sex life had meant he was a freak.

"Don't take it like a bitch," Jon said. The kid—relative only to the age of most members of the Aggressor Squadron—was annoyingly perceptive. "You're wound too tight sometimes. If this Cassandra chick helps you unwind, she must be pretty cool."

Ryan laughed again. Saying Cassandra was pretty cool was one hell of an understatement. What he knew about her was verging on downright perfect.

That was part of the problem. No one was perfect.

Everyone had secrets. Seedy things they kept hidden from the world. People like his mom had one advantage on the rest of the world. Sure they were trashy, but they threw the doors open wide—with very few secrets. One of the first things he'd done when trying to put together a real life was to lock down all his shit. Keep his business to himself.

There had to be something Cassandra hadn't told him yet. Something that would break the spell. Hell, maybe she'd be the one who got sick of him—or he'd give away too many clues about what really turned him on and she'd lose all respect. Ashleigh had, and she'd loved him enough to accept his marriage proposal.

Jon gave his shoulder a shake. "Look, Fang, I'm gonna say this once. Get the hell out of your own head. You think too fucking much. Fuck too much instead."

"Let's get the hell out of here." Ryan slid down off the tailgate. "We've got work tomorrow."

"Any day flying is a good day, my friend."

"Amen."

Ryan rubbed the spot on his chest that was still bruised from her teeth. He wouldn't mind taking Jon's advice, especially if Cassandra was still willing.

Chapter Fourteen

After pulling into the parking lot behind the Hungerford Gallery, Cass killed the ignition. The switch from a blaring Tears for Fears track to complete silence jolted her into focusing. She swiped her damp hands along the driver's seat upholstery. Her dark blue merino wool suit, with its tailored blazer and A-line skirt, was her absolute best set of clothes. No way did she want it ruined by sweaty streaks.

Take a risk, he'd said.

Agreeing to Ryan's request had been much easier in the sweltering parking garage. She'd been high on the excess of their weekend. High on *him*. The realities of the rest of the week had seemed so far off.

He'd phoned on Tuesday afternoon while she got ready for her shift at Blakely's, his timing perfect. Just the right combination of interest and not seeming like a crazy eager stalker. However, to say their conversation had been stilted was generous. Lots of giggles on her part. Tons of silence. They'd managed, even if Cass had needed to close the bathroom door and flip off the light. The darkness had helped her give voice to what she wanted.

They'd made plans for Friday night—her bold plans, actually. Even there in her Honda in the shadow of the gallery, she found breathing more difficult, anticipating what she had finally managed to propose. Ryan's curiosity still made her smile. Wiles and charm had gotten him nowhere as he pried for more detail, but she really liked that he made the attempt. Repeatedly.

There were lunch plans too. It was Thursday now, with about four hours until she'd make her first trip to Nellis. She needed to have good news by the time she saw Ryan again, or at least an affirmation that she'd tried. No matter their new relationship, Cass didn't want to let him down. The idea of his disappointment made her feel like a cowardly speck.

She fiddled with the Bellagio casino chip she'd kept from Friday night, having knotted it on a silk cord to carry in her purse as a good-luck charm. Surely she could do this. It was what she wanted, after all. What she'd wanted for so long.

She pushed in through the rear employee entrance, her knees unsteady. The slender portfolio she carried had been a gift from her parents when she graduated from college. Its leather was warm and soft, and she fought the urge to score its surface with her nails. She'd only ruin it and her fresh manicure.

Get it over with.

Her manager, Pat Talbert, was in his mid-sixties, having taught art history at various universities before turning to private work after his retirement. Though only slightly younger than Mr. Hungerford, the gallery's owner, he carried himself with a sprightly air.

Cass knocked on the open door to his tiny office. "Morning." Instantly she disliked the forced chipper note to her greeting.

He glanced away from his monitor for only a second, still typing something. "Morning, Miss Whitman."

"Could I speak to you, sir?"

"Sure. Now's fine." After pushing his wire rims up his nose, he swiveled his chair to face her wholly. "What's up?"

"Any word on Lisa?"

"I spoke to her yesterday evening," he said, his voice taking on a haggard edge. "The baby's fine, but he'll be in the NICU for at least three weeks—maybe longer. She hasn't left the hospital yet, as far as I can tell."

The gallery's head event planner, Lisa Moyet, had been scheduled to take maternity leave in another six weeks. An expert in photography, she'd been slated to head the July exhibit of E. J. Bellocq's famous nudes. After her preparation, the rest of the staff would've pitched in for the event itself, had she been unable to attend. The premature arrival of her son some ten days earlier had derailed all plans.

Cass sat on the chair facing Mr. Talbert's desk, the portfolio like a shield in her lap. It contained a neatly typed list of all she'd accomplished across her two years at Hungerford, as well as copies of her annual evaluations. If he needed a reminder that she was able and hard-working, he'd have one.

A wild pulse beat in her ears. She swallowed tightly. Then she dove in. "Sir, I wonder if it might be possible for me to take over Lisa's work on the Bellocq exhibit." He lifted his bushy white brows but she pressed on. "I was her assistant for the last two shows. I've worked with her caterers and have fledgling relationships with her best contacts among the patrons. With a lot of work and her assistance, I could step in. I know I can do this."

He leaned back in his chair, which had almost identical wear marks in the cloth armrests. Cass endured his scrutiny. Sweat had gathered under her arms and along the soles of her feet. She forced her bouncy heels to be still.

"I know you can too," he said at last.

She blinked. Her mouth opened. "Sir?"

"You heard me, Miss Whitman. Have at it. Frankly, I'm relieved. I was tearing out what's left of my hair trying to figure how we'd delegate her responsibilities. Now that can be your job." He sat up straighter, hands back on the keyboard. "Let me know if anyone gives you trouble—especially the museums. You know how prickly they can get."

"Yes," she said with a giddy titter. She forced her knees to function as she stood. A really dumb smile made her cheeks hurt, but she couldn't help it. "Thank you, sir. You won't regret this."

As she spun away from his desk, she thought of Ryan. Just like that, she wanted to tell him as soon as possible. Elated wasn't the right word. Her success had transformed her into a divine being. Thoughts of feeling that good sucked her right back to their weekend together.

She'd done it. Not only would she helm her first opening gala, but the subject matter was classic nude photography. If that wasn't the definition of bold, then she needed a remedial session in sex-shop dressing-room misbehavior. Either way,

Ryan was the man to see.

Between now and their one o'clock lunch date, she had a *lot* of work to do.

"I'm meeting Major Ryan Haverty," she said to the guard at Nellis. "He's expecting me."

"Pull your car into the secured lot and sign in."

Cass parked and came around to the squat office building beside the guard's station. After handing over her ID, recording her license and answering a couple official-sounding questions, she waited as the blunt young man behind the plexiglass window phoned Ryan.

"Ma'am, he's wrapping up his a.m. operation, but he's sending Captain Girardi to sign for you."

"Who?"

The airman didn't provide any additional information. Cass sat on a bench to wait. Ten minutes later, her nerves growing tighter, she was amazed by how different Nellis seemed from the whole rest of Vegas. There were townies and tourists. That's all she'd ever imagined of her famous birthplace. The air base proved the existence of a whole separate contingent in Sin City.

The woman who'd dined with Ryan at the restaurant strolled in. Pieces clicked together for Cass. This was the friend he'd slept with. She looked like a ballet dancer who'd suited up for air combat by mistake—an analogy that got her thinking. Had he asked past girlfriends to dress up? The thought of him playing the same sort of games with this woman was, inexplicably, harder to bear than just knowing they'd had sex.

Thrusting her junior-high jealousy aside, Cass offered her hand. "Wow," she said involuntarily, taking in Leah's flight suit.

Grinning, the woman smoothed a tiny wisp of hair at her temple. The rest was twisted into a tight bun at the back of her head. She pushed her ID card through the slot and smiled at Cass while the clerk scanned it. "Hot shit, isn't it? I'm Leah."

"Ryan's mentioned you."

She rolled her eyes. "Oh, great. Probably something about how I'm blind to the virtues of Perrier. C'mon, let's get out of here. See ya, Hanson," she called to the man behind the desk.

"Later, Princess."

"Bite me, Hanson."

"Princess?" Cass asked as they stepped out of the office.

"My name's Leah, so my call sign has always been Princess. *Please* don't give me any shit about it. The guys ration it out pretty thick."

"Won't say a word."

"You know, I can't remember Ryan ever having a girl come out here."

Cass's heart thunked a hard double beat. "I don't know what to make of that."

"Yeah, damn. Guess not. I mean, he could keep a harem on base. Not that he does." Leah shrugged. "Never mind."

They walked for what seemed like an hour, but it wasn't nearly so long—just a lot to take in. Cass couldn't get over the activity. An array of military vehicles and uniforms made it seem as if she'd stepped into an entirely different universe. A ten-foot-tall, camouflage-painted truck rumbled by. She felt terribly conspicuous in her modest business suit, which she'd worn especially for her conversation with Mr. Talbert. There at the gallery, she'd been in her element—no matter her nerves.

Here her element was nowhere to be seen.

For the first time, the reality of what Ryan did for a living hit her square between the eyes. He was a combat pilot. The men and women surrounding her on that busy Air Force base were trained for war. She shivered even under the blazing Nevada sun.

"First time?" Leah asked.

"That's right. It's a little overwhelming."

"Or dull as dirt. I've been here…two years? I'm screaming bored of it." She pointed to various features as she rattled them off. "Mess, clinic, BX, and way over there's the airfield. If Ryan has time, he'll be sure to want to show off his plane, so be prepared."

"Thanks."

"Through here."

Leah led her past an aircraft hangar where, through giant doors, Cass saw technicians working on fighter jets, just as mechanics would work on her cheap Honda. Only these were million-dollar war machines. That Ryan, a guy she'd met at the restaurant, could be so important to such a huge operation was really humbling. Next door was an office building that seemed insignificant by comparision.

Into the foyer and past a chest-high desk, Leah waved to the young airman sitting there. The tiled hallway was practically antiseptic, but it rang with the power of a masculine tirade. The voice was terse, clipped and seriously ticked off.

"Whoa, damn," Leah said, grabbing Cass's arm. "He's not done yet."

"Who?"

"Fang. Ryan. He's ripping some boys a new one. Come on." She motioned for Cass to follow, backing down the hallway to the entryway.

The other man from that first night at Blakely's was leaning casually against a display cabinet filled with military memorabilia. A mortar shell. A model jet. Plus two folded American flags that made Cass's heart clench.

"Here for the show?" the guy asked.

"Shut up, dickweed. I thought he'd be finished by now."

"Just about."

"You remember Cassandra, by the way."

"Hey," Jon said with a nod. "Captain Carlisle. Call me Jon."

Although he seemed to be flipping through a chart on a clipboard, he flicked his eyes back down the hallway. The door to the office was closed, but the thin walls didn't keep sound in well.

Leah had been right. That was Ryan's voice. He was genuinely upset. A shiver skittered down her spine. Who would've thought that the man who'd licked sugar crystals off her lips was capable of such a temper?

No, *temper* wasn't the right word. More like *intensity*. He didn't have an out-of-control mania, like Jack Nicholson in *The Shining*, all batshit crazy. The control in his voice was nearly as intimidating as his anger.

"What happened?" Cass asked, unable to hold back her curiosity.

Leah leaned closer. "They dropped below the hard deck for the flight. It's dangerous and stupid. People get killed that way."

"Bottom line, they broke the rules," Jon said with a naughty smile. "Fang doesn't take too kindly."

Cass didn't know whether to find the guy strangely creepy...or kinda like him. He was probably her age, maybe mid-twenties, which didn't seem to fit his rank and duties. He had a truly disarming smile, complete with matched dimples—not adorable like Ryan's, but the kind that could charm snakes.

"So what's your call sign, then?" she asked.

"Tin Tin."

"What, like the dog? Rin Tin Tin?"

"For my unerring loyalty," he said with a broad smile.

Leah snorted. "You are so full of crap."

Cass couldn't help but grin at the two, but again her attention returned to Ryan. He was standing in the doorway now, his back to the hangar. "If I see any of you before oh six hundred tomorrow, I'll have you lined up and shot. Understood? Now get out of my sight."

Three men in unfamiliar uniforms hurried out of the office, straining to hold on to their composure.

Ryan turned. He stood watching them go, his hands braced on the doorway.

Swallowing hard, Cass couldn't take her eyes off him. The dress uniform had been one thing, so handsome and clean-cut. Plus, she'd assumed it was a costume. This...this was the real deal. Between the rugged utility of the flight suit and the lingering surprise of Ryan's angered tirade, she found herself fighting a surge of mindless arousal.

Good gravy. She was getting turned on by her polite, All-American boy going full-on thug.

"Yo, Fang," Jon called, shoving the clipboard under his arm. He hooked a thumb toward Cass. "Your lady fair."

Ryan's eyes lost their hazy wildness. That tense, tight expression eased. His gaze met Cass's and he smiled. Just like that, he was back to being him.

Wow. Gentleman *and* prize fighter. A rhythmic pulse in her belly expanded. Into her muscles. Through her veins. The tension in her thighs eased and eased again, as if already eager to accept the driving invasion of his body. She was melting into a pool of molten chocolate and craved his tongue there, licking, murmuring how much he adored her sweet taste.

She needed to find a quiet place. A dark corner. A closet. Hell, even a bathroom stall. This wave of desire was too crazy not to indulge.

Cass mustered her nerve and walked down the hallway. Even knowing Leah, Jon and whoever else watched, she met Ryan in the doorway.

"Sorry about that," he said, seeming almost embarrassed at having been caught out. "You look amazing. Very classy."

She was in no mood for small talk. "Is this your office?"

"Yeah."

"Is it private?"

He blinked. "Um, not really."

"Damn."

Realization turned his smile wicked. "My apartment's six and a half minutes away. Let's go."

Chapter Fifteen

Ryan's truck had tinted windows but they weren't dark enough. Not by half. With the sultry smile Cassandra gave him, combined with her heated stare, he wanted black windows. Opaque. Something to give them privacy.

As it was, he helped her into the passenger side and snatched a hard kiss off her pretty mouth. Hand wrapped around the back of her neck, he delved fast and deep with his tongue. She clutched his shoulders then dipped under the open neck of his flight suit to fiddle with his black T-shirt.

"You are not going fast enough, Major Haverty."

The slick business suit looked good on her—all wrapped tight and neat, like she was someone different than the Cassandra he knew. Folding his hands around her hips still felt the same. He kissed her again, leaning into the open passenger door to take more. The parking lot was crammed with cars, and thankfully he'd parked next to a Suburban that was even larger than his F-150. Their odds of being seen were low. Otherwise he would've had to behave.

"I don't know," he said. "Feels like I'm going at just the right speed."

"You promised me six and a half minutes."

He laughed as he shut her door and rounded the nose of the truck, then hopped in. "So to clarify, that's six and a half minutes to get to my place. Longer after we get there. *Much* longer."

She adjusted her skirt with careful, prim movements, but she slanted him a playful glance. His mischievous Cassandra was back. "I should hope so, mister. Otherwise I'll be very disappointed in you."

"Can't have that," he said, even as his foot tried to slam

down on the gas pedal.

His leg vibrated as he did his damnedest to pull back. Blowing through base over the speed limit would be the absolute fastest way to kill the moment. No way he could look at Security Forces and keep a straight face.

The contrast of chewing those three jerk-offs new assholes, only to turn around and find Cassandra watching him, had been too much. He'd been overstrung already. Bitching out foreign pilots meant walking a fine line. Most of the time he wouldn't have done it at all since they'd deal with their liaisons, but they had come to him asking for special tips—even after they'd been so foolish as to put *his* pilots at risk. The sheer hubris had rubbed his nerves raw.

So he'd been riding a rush of adrenaline when Cassandra asked about the privacy of his office. In other words, fuck yeah, he was all over her.

Two red lights in a row meant it took just over seven minutes to reach his front door. Cassandra pressed against his back as he fumbled with the lock. Her hands ran up and down his flight suit. She giggled when her fingers dug into his ribs and he jumped, even though the tickle was muted through the sturdy material.

"Time's a-wasting," she said, her voice full of laughter.

"No way." He found the right key and jammed it in the lock. "Doesn't count yet."

Her hips pushed against his ass in a slow, repetitive nudge. "That's up for debate."

The door finally banged open against the wall. Ryan yanked them both inside, then slammed it shut. He filled his hands with her perky ass as he took her mouth. She wrapped her arms around his neck.

Christ, it was like the first time all over again. Like they couldn't get enough. As if they hadn't spent the entire previous weekend glutting on each other.

He tangled his fingers with her loose bun and angled her neck, seeking soft skin. She tasted as amazing as ever, but a tiny hint of perfume added a spicy note to her scent.

Fuck if it didn't add to the possibilities. Like she'd dressed up for him. Maybe to welcome him home from a deployment. He'd never had that. Never gotten off the plane after three long months in a shithole, all the while knowing someone waited on him, having decorated one of those cheesy banners specifically for him.

He flattened his hand against the wall and kissed her harder. Deeper. Trying to push back the stupid fiction his mind always wanted to create. Cassandra would be enough. *More* than enough.

Then she spread her hands over his back. "Do you know how hot you are in this?"

"What?" He laughed, fueled by the awkwardness pinching the back of his head. "My uniform? It's no big deal."

"I disagree." She nuzzled her face into his neck, chasing shivers down his spine. "Especially after hearing you chew those guys out. Very hot."

His eyes drifted shut. "It's just my job."

"I know. That's why it's hot. The whole hard-charging jet-pilot thing? Works for me."

Her words only cranked up the noise in his brain. More fervently now. He claimed her mouth again, just to keep her from adding to the clamor. He didn't need those sick, stupid bullshit games. She brought him to life, especially when he curved his hands around her ribs, sliding up to the small, lush weight of her breast.

Cassandra hitched her leg around his thigh, pressing her hips against his. He was so goddamn hard. He needed to be in her. *Immediately*. But he never carried condoms when he was in uniform. Being prepared tripped over into stupid territory when he wasn't the type to run home on his lunch break to get some. Never before, at least.

If he'd really been gone on deployment, knowing Cassandra would be waiting when he stepped off the plane, he'd keep an entire string of condoms shoved in his pockets.

He pulled back from her kiss-swollen mouth but couldn't seem to drag his hands away. Her body was too perfect. The smile he dredged up was probably off-kilter. "Bedroom. Now. I'll give you the tour later."

She crossed her wrists behind his neck, her bright blue eyes sparkling as she nibbled her bottom lip. “Nope. I’m good right here.” Up on her toes, she slid along the wall before feathering kisses on his jaw.

Ryan gritted his teeth to hold back the pressure building at the base of his spine. “I don’t have any protection on me.”

Graceful hands flattened over his chest. She pushed him back until his arms extended full length out from the wall, gently caging her there. “I do. In my purse. Though I’m not sure we need them. Yet.”

She curled her fingers into the front placket of his flight suit. Found the zipper. Pulled. Up underneath she caressed his shoulders as she pushed his uniform down off his arms. It pooled around his hips. Her smile bloomed wider as she sank along with it. Ryan’s pulse jerked up another hundred RPMs.

With slow, mouth-watering grace, Cassandra dropped to her knees. Her classy skirt tightened around her thighs, which showed off their sleek length.

“What are you doing?” His voice came out harsh at the edges despite his best efforts.

The look she flicked up at him was all wanton amusement. “If you don’t know, I think we might have some problems.”

Her fingers were cool when she delved behind his boxers and pulled his cock into the air.

Spreading his fingers wide along the wall did nothing to abate his need to grasp her skull. To guide her mouth.

He’d be damned if his head wasn’t still playing games. Now…

Now she wasn’t his girlfriend, happily welcoming him home from overseas. If she were, she’d be climbing him and getting her rocks off too, since it would’ve been so long. Instead, the classy suit combined with her strawberry-blonde hair rapidly falling out of its knot gave Cassandra an air of depravity. Outright sexiness. She was a normally untouchable businesswoman who’d taken one look at his flight suit and needed a taste.

Her tongue darted out to lick his swollen head.

Ryan dropped his chin to his chest. God, that was good.

Hot and wet. Just the right level of pressure as she dragged her tongue flat along his shaft.

His urges won the battle. He dipped his hands down to push roughly into her hair, wrecking her classic perfection. Hairpins pinged across the linoleum floor. Reddish locks tumbled around her face just as she opened her lips.

Wet suction blasted his spine. Stripped away his last bit of sense.

She was a flight groupie.

Hot for it. Hot for *him.*

Slender fingers ringed the base of his shaft, stroking with her mouth. She sucked him deep, then tickled the underside of his cock with her clever tongue.

All the while she stared at him, eyes wide like some porn starlet.

Tiny shakes shivered his arms as he tried not to face-fuck her. She wasn't *actually* a pilot groupie, not some random chick he'd picked up at a bar. Maybe it had started that way, but somewhere along the way they'd moved on. In a good way, there was no denying. That meant he couldn't just wrap his hand around her neck and force her to take all of him.

Ryan ground his back teeth together as he resisted the orgasm swirling in his balls. Holding back the groan that started low in his chest was impossible.

Eyes glittering, Cassandra drew back far enough that her wet mouth hovered over his dick. Her lips glistened. She darted out her tongue to circle the ridge behind his head, then formed a deliberate O with her lips and sealed over him. Sucked deep again.

He forced himself to loosen his grip on the base of her skull, to pull his hips back. His cock slipped out of her mouth with a wet pop. Cassandra's soft sound of disappointment only cranked him higher. "Baby," he said, "you've got to back off."

She grinned and swiped the back of her hand across her chin. Moisture glistened on her lower lip. "Make me."

"How about if I just pick you up and throw you over my shoulder?"

She giggled, then leaned forward to suck him into her lips

again. Holy Christ, he'd never been with a chick who laughed while sucking him, and fuck if it wasn't amazing. Ryan couldn't even put words on why, but he was about to blow.

Tugging her off his dick required herculean effort. He ought to get a medal.

Her glistening lips turned down. "Why do you keep stopping me?"

"Because if I don't, I'm going to come in your pretty mouth."

"Maybe that's what I want." She grinned at him, all devilish temptress. "I've never blown a fighter pilot before."

Boom. That was all he needed. His head spun off into the ridiculous stories he'd been trying to hold back.

She claimed him again. *Her* territory. Sharp fingernails dug into his ass. The pressure built deep in his balls. He held on to the back of her neck, his grip way too tight. She didn't seem to mind. Her mouth remained firm and determined. So, the groupie wanted the taste of something fast and wild? He could give her that. Right fucking now. Sizzling tingles started at the base of his feet, in his boots, and rocked up through him in a white-hot rush.

She swallowed.

Ryan's vision tried to go gray, but he pushed it back with the last scraps of his willpower. He wasn't going to miss a second of the avid way she licked the last drip of his come. A satisfied smile curved her mouth.

Bowing his head, he clung to the contented wash of sensation that loosened his knees and swept away the last of his tension. Cassandra had done that. Just her. She'd ripped the bones out of his limbs, taken him down to the marrow.

He'd never say a damn word about the degenerate fantasies he'd been spinning.

Not ever.

Chapter Sixteen

Cass accepted Ryan's hand up, her knees achy. The linoleum wasn't exactly comfy, but she hadn't given that a thought as she sucked him off.

Wow, that she could even think such a delicious phrase threaded a wicked thrill into her skin—let alone that she'd actually done it.

Ryan's chest heaved as he gathered her close. He nuzzled her unbound hair. Although a raging lust zinged through her body, she accepted the consequences of her actions—he needed a minute.

"So," she said, kissing his neck. "Does that count as my bold thing?"

A deep chuckle vibrated out of his chest and into hers. "I'd hate to seem like a jerk for complaining, but that wasn't what I had in mind."

"Either way, I got it covered."

He pulled back to study her face. The sunlight through his living room bay window lit his irises, making them shine with more green. Some of the shell-shocked bliss faded, as if words made sense again. "What did you do?"

"Oh, no you don't, Major. I want my turn. Now be a good boy and help me come."

"Right away, baby."

She would've thought him too exhausted after that decadent blow job, but he was still a man—a man stacked with layers of lean, strong muscle. He hefted her off the floor and hauled her over his shoulder, just as he'd threatened. Cass squealed, suddenly looking down his back. She looped her arms around his middle, overcome by a bubble of hysteria. Joy and lust mingled in her blood as he walked her to his bedroom.

Ryan pressed a kiss along her bared waist, gripping as much of her butt and upper thighs as he could palm. "Don't move, woman. You don't want me to drop you."

She was still giggling, but she managed to say, "You won't drop me."

"No?"

"Too manly man. My own personal Neanderthal."

"You teasing me, Miss Whitman?" He gave her a quick slap on the ass.

It wasn't a particularly hard smack, especially through her wool dress skirt. Cass only registered a slight sting, but they both froze.

Almost awkwardly, which was a surprise considering how easily he'd handled her, Ryan set her on the floor beside his huge king-sized bed—a bed big enough for a guy his size. He ran a hand though his short hair. "Sorry," he said gruffly.

"Hey." She caught his forearm and kissed his knuckles. "It's okay. I didn't mind. In fact, it can be kind of...exciting."

"Can be? You have experience with that?"

"I'm shy, Ryan, but I'm not a saint." She shrugged. "Things happen in the heat of the moment. Believe me, I'll tell you if you go too far."

"After the fact. It shouldn't be your responsibility to keep me in line."

Cass inhaled, calming her ravenous body. She tipped her head but his thoughts were impossible to read. Sometimes he was too closed off, which really didn't match his hard-charging hometown-boy persona. She tried to console herself that they hadn't even met a week before. Not many people gave up their secrets that quickly, even if that was sometimes her impulse. After she got past the initial frigid hesitation of making a one-on-one connection, she couldn't see the point in holding back. By then the hard part—taking the daring first step—was over.

"Look," she said, her tone conciliatory. "There are times when I just get *really* excited. Almost...numb? A slap can be nice. It cuts through the buzz. Takes it up a notch—like a hard tickle or nibble." A raging blush flamed across her cheeks as she spoke, crawling its way down her throat. She wanted him to understand. She didn't want him feeling guilty, nor did she want him assuming she got off on being tortured. They were new. Communication was tough but vital. "Does that make sense? Ryan?"

He slumped onto the bed. "Sorry I overreacted. I, ah...I'm not usually one for losing control like that. Any of that."

Well, didn't that light her fire all over again?

Cass loved the feel of her slinky smile. "Are you saying I make you lose control, Major? Because I like the sound of that. Very much."

He pretended to consider it for a minute. At least his humor had returned, shaping his mouth into that delectable male grin. "Seems to be, yeah."

"See? Such a lovely caveman."

"Next time I'll drag you by your hair."

She unbuttoned her blazer and shrugged it off her shoulders. "Now there's no need to make fun."

Her skirt came next, shimmying off her hips. Ryan's eyes widened when he caught sight of the flesh-colored stockings and garter set. She stripped the silk camisole shell to reveal a matching beige lace bra. The color wasn't the best on her, she knew, but the last thing she'd wanted was for her underwear to do the talking at the gallery. She wanted to save that sort of communication for Ryan.

"Now, where were we? You were going to make me come? Because that six and a half minutes seems about four months ago."

"After you," he said, standing. He gestured to the bed, which was covered by a lovely forest-green down comforter.

Cass lay down. She stretched fully, from the tips of her outstretched fingers to her pointed toes. The waiting tension hadn't disappeared, making conversation possible. His bedroom was typically masculine, with white walls and the clean, strong lines of an oak dresser and nightstand. She couldn't find anything by way of photographs or personal knickknacks. The simple refuge revealed nothing more about him than she already knew.

Her perusal ended when Ryan crossed to the windows and

shut the dark green drapes, closing out the sun. It was still the middle of an ordinary Thursday. Cass was going to be his. She welcomed back a hot surge of pure lust.

The unzipped flight suit draped over his hips. A plain black T-shirt hugged every curve and ripple of his upper body—shoulders and pecs and the long line of his back. The drab and black made him look harder somehow. None of the softness that could be found in civilian clothes. Pure functionality. This was what a man wore when he went into battle.

The primal kick in Cass's bones came as a visceral shock. She hadn't thought herself the kind of girl to find that sort of machismo attractive, let alone so damn sexy. The undeniable violence of his profession ran right past ideas of feminism and enlightened thought, bypassing pretty theory to settle as a hot, wet rush between her legs.

She shifted her thighs. "When do you need to be back to the base?"

Ryan stepped out of the flight suit then peeled away his T-shirt. Even now, mere minutes on from his orgasm, his penis was an undeniable presence—or maybe she was simply fascinated as her gaze returned again to the bulge in his briefs. Lucky, lucky girl.

"Maybe three if I push it." He offered an almost bashful smile. "Sometimes it's good to be in charge."

"Sometimes? Sounds like heaven to me."

He knelt at the foot of the bed and worked his way up, slowly, until he sprawled between her spread thighs. No being coy—not in that pose. "Now, tell me more about this bold thing you did."

"I thought we were waiting until after?"

"Nah. I want details. I'll reward you accordingly."

"Meanie. I went down on you just like that," she said with a snap of her fingers.

Ryan caught the lace top of one stocking between his teeth, grinning up at her. Then he let it snap back against her thigh. "Not my fault you're easy."

She whacked him on the shoulder, laughing. "Here I thought you were a gentleman."

"Not quite." He stroked a thumb along the crease of her pussy. The wet fabric of her underwear molded to her folds. "Now spill. What did you do?"

Cass closed her eyes. Maybe that way she could concentrate as he unfastened her body from her thinking mind. The connection was tenuous enough already. "I talked to my boss at the gallery. Laid out my case. Said that I'd been there for nearly two years, working my cute ass off."

"So cute," he said, licking along the seam of her panties. His tongue teased underneath the elastic.

Her skin shimmered beneath his patient attention. This encounter had so little in common with the lunchtime quickie she'd initiated. Nothing about them was ordinary. They were...potent. Creative. Exciting. All of that helped loosen her inhibitions—as it did every time. She let her thighs relax then tugged down the lace of her bra. After wetting her fingers, she smoothed her nipples. Tweaked them. Teasing herself like Ryan did.

He hadn't missed a single bit of it. A glance down to where he propped on his forearms revealed dark eyes and an intent expression. Cass warmed with a blush that was a small part embarrassment and a huge part passion.

"You seem to have lost the flow of your story," he said.

"Someone's distracting me."

"This is nothing. Not yet." He unhooked her garters and pulled down her underwear, all with deliberate care. "I'll stop if you don't continue."

"Fine, fine." Cass forced out a shaky sigh. "I asked him for permission to head up the next summer exhibit. The woman who'd been in charge of it had her baby six weeks early. No one was prepared for her to need time off, and obviously she's super distracted. I'd assisted her on previous shows, so I know her contacts and her methods. Thought I'd be able to fill in and have a shot at proving myself."

Ryan's hands and his tongue had become languid. He pulled up to look at her fully. "And?"

The happiness she'd kept in her chest all morning came shining out. She couldn't help but smile like a goof, no matter that he'd stripped off her panties. "He said yes. The exhibit opens in July, and I'm in charge."

"Damn." He edged up to lie next to her on the pillows. "That's... Cassandra, that's great. Really." With a tenderness that belied their dirty deeds but that marked their relationship as something special, he smoothed the hair from her cheek. "I'm really proud of you."

"Don't be yet," she said with a laugh. "I have a heck of a lot of work to do. I've never done all of it on my own."

"Does that mean you don't think you can do it?"

She looked at him, at the firm confidence he had in her. Why should he? He barely knew her, in truth. Maybe it was some side effect of his own attitude toward life. He just assumed everyone else would do as well as he expected of himself. She liked the support, but she didn't know if it was warranted. Time would tell if her bold step meant a future in her dream career or a permanent relegation to the world of steakhouses and Grand Canyon tours.

No. No more doubting.

She loved her work at the gallery. Contemplating the long hours and endless tasks actually felt like a reward, not a burden. She'd kill this show or die trying.

"I can do it," she said. "That doesn't mean I'm not nervous."

"Understandable. I'm still proud, though."

Cass laughed and touched his upper arm, not surprised to find her fingertips trembling as she did. "Who knew? My caveman fighter pilot is a softie."

He growled, grinning, and rolled on top of her. "Hardly."

The faint smell of sweat and some spicy deodorant was an unexpected aphrodisiac. With Ryan's solid weight pressed on top of her, she was back in mind of strong muscles and the fierce, controlled sting of his temper when he'd dressed down those pilots. She liked his understanding and encouragement—appreciated them. She downright *craved* how soft and feminine and sexy he made her feel.

"Uh-oh," she said as he worked his mouth down toward her breasts. "I'm in trouble, aren't I?"

"Oh, yes. You are."

“With no one to save me.”

“No one at all.” He flicked his tongue against one exposed nipple, sending a hot shiver down to her belly. His hips settled against hers. The stirring of his renewed erection made her breathless. That she could do that to him made her head spin, all pride and greedy eagerness.

“I think I should be scared, Major.” She rubbed the bristling softness of hair at the back of his head. “I'm not in the least.”

“Oh, but you should be. Now where are those condoms?”

Chapter Seventeen

By the next evening, Ryan was curious as hell. He'd called Cassandra late the night before, and even after more than an hour on the phone, she hadn't given up the goods. She'd only reiterated her request that he should wear a nice suit and meet her at The Deuce Lounge at CityCenter.

At least she'd picked a classy place, all leather and wood with high-level gaming tables at one end. Weird gold-tone chandeliers reminded him of spiky Tribbles, but they went strangely well with the modern, honeycombed ceiling. The place looked like what a really hip version of Spock would dig for his time off.

He turned back toward the bar he'd been leaning against, tired of keeping his eyes on three different doorways and one wide curtained area—trying to spot Cassandra. The bartender was giving him a nasty look, probably because Ryan took up valuable space and had only ordered a Coke. Since he had no idea what Cassandra had planned, he wanted to be sharp.

He tugged at the knot of his tie. He wasn't used to wearing the damn things, not having much occasion for formal attire other than his uniform. Never had in all his life.

A ridiculous attack of nerves clenched his stomach. He wasn't above admitting that he liked control. Every bit of his life was ordered. On track. Yet here he was, waiting on Cassandra's whim. Obeying blindly.

For fuck's sake, the woman could lead him off a cliff by his hard-on and he'd willingly go. Then thank her for the privilege.

"Excuse me, is this seat taken?"

"I'm sorry, but yes—" The words tangled in his mouth as he turned. It was Cassandra...but not.

She wore a slinky burgundy dress cut halfway down to her

navel. The inside curves of her breasts were bare and just begging to be touched. Something about her makeup was different, her eyes dark and smoldering. Her lips glistened with a deep red color. She'd even done something to her hair so that it tumbled around her shoulders in loose waves like a '40s starlet.

He leaned one arm on the bar, the better to angle toward her. "No, go right ahead."

In a feat of sexy wiggling, she managed to slide up onto the seat. She leaned forward to signal the bartender, giving Ryan a prime view of the back of the dress—or the lack of it. The low-cut front had nothing on the slash that plummeted almost all the way to her ass. The tender divots at the base of her spine caught shadows.

"I'm Cassandra. What's your name?"

"Ryan."

"Are you visiting Vegas?" Her voice was smoky, every syllable sleek.

So that was her game. A stranger pickup. Christ, that was hot. If he didn't know better, he'd have thought she plucked the idea straight from the darkest corners of his brain.

He should tell her to stop. That they didn't need this to enjoy a classy evening on the town—the sort of evening he'd always pictured delighting in a confident, elegant woman. But the launch sequence had already fired. He could no more ask her to put aside the games than he could keep from wanting them. Wanting *more.*

"Yep. In on business."

She stroked down the lapel of his suit jacket. "That explains why I haven't met you before."

"If I'd ever met a lady like you, I'm sure it would have been memorable."

"Oh, I'm definitely memorable." Even though she leaned close and stretched up, she didn't quite speak in his ear. The bar was busy and filled with the chatter of customers, but anyone could hear her. "For five thousand, I'll give you a night that'll still get you hard when you're old and gray."

Ryan yanked back on reflex, his muscles freezing. She

looked back at him with heat in her eyes, her face a perfect mask of sultry control. His gaze tripped over her from head to toe. She couldn't possibly be serious.

Her façade cracked. A tiny hint of a smile curved her red-painted mouth.

He clenched the edge of the bar with a sudden rush. This wasn't just a stranger pickup. He was a john and this gorgeous hooker would be his for the night. His mind fogged over the possibilities.

"That price seems steep."

She scratched a dark red nail over his tie. "I promise I'm worth it."

"Why don't you let me pay for your drink and I'll give you my answer in a minute."

Cassandra sipped her martini. When she popped the olive into her mouth, she made a deliberate O with her lips. "If you think it'll take you that long to decide."

Two dark-suited security guards popped up out of nowhere. One tapped Cassandra on the shoulder. "Miss, you'll have to leave."

"Excuse me?" she asked, her eyebrows arched in a regal tilt.

"Such activities are not allowed on casino grounds."

Ryan snapped to attention. Holy shit hell. Busted. Cold embarrassment turned his spine into a pike.

Totally dropping character, Cassandra giggled. "No, you see, it's not what you think."

The taller guard shook his head. "We're asking you to leave, ma'am. You can go willingly or we can get the police involved."

"Okay, okay." She glanced over her shoulder at Ryan. The sparkle in her eyes invited him to join in on the joke.

He wanted to, but it would be much easier once he hustled them out of there. Taking Cassandra by the elbow, he shuffled them outside to the sidewalk. Hot spring air tickled at the back of his collar.

"I can't believe we got busted. *I* got busted." Cassandra was full-out laughing, looking back toward the guards who'd followed them all the way out. "They actually thought I was a call girl."

Ryan shook his head. Now that they were back among anonymous crowds, he could relax. No one had asked for his name. There'd been no threat to his real life. The adrenaline left over from that scare only heightened his arousal.

He caught her by the wrist and tugged her near. "Well you do look...unbelievably expensive."

"Is that right?" She sobered and pushed her lower lip out in a pout. "There's a reason for that. I *am* expensive, remember?"

"I don't think I could forget five grand." His fingers dipped into the back of her dress and grazed over the top curve of her ass. "So how does this work? I've never hired an escort before."

"You just leave everything to me, big boy," she purred, accentuating the compliment by giving his cock a quick pet.

She led him to a rank of limos but didn't let him hear what she told the driver. Although Ryan was the john, she was still running the show.

Slipping into the seat of the black-and-chrome limo, he didn't want to admit how much that bothered him. She'd obviously put a lot of thought into the night. The least he could do was at least *try* to enjoy the ride.

Watching Cass slide into the limo was a treat in itself. The dress gaped ever so slightly to reveal a glimpse of one nipple. The uniformed driver shut the door behind her smartly.

"Since I'm paying, shouldn't I pick the destination?"

She shook her head and crossed her legs. The slit in her skirt parted along the long length of her pale thigh. The woman was as hot as a jet engine. "Not this time. Later, if you like."

"How long is it going to take to get there?" His words felt like they were chipped out one by one.

"About twenty minutes. More or less."

Ryan stretched his arms across the back of the seat and unfurled his legs to their full length. Intimidating, maybe, but he was fine with that. More than fine. Fuck sitting back and enjoying the ride. He couldn't let it go. If she wanted to be a call girl, she was going to listen to her john.

"Good," he said, admiring every sleek inch of her. "Get over here. If you're worth it, you'll make me come before we get there."

Wide blue eyes flashed but almost immediately drooped heavily with lust. "You're the boss, mister."

She scrambled over the seat until she straddled him. The ankle-length skirt split over her legs and barely covered her pussy. He scooped hands under it to grip her thighs.

The game would dictate no foreplay for hookers. No kissing. She'd do her job and get a dude off. Underneath it all, she was still Cassandra. He wanted to make it good for her.

When Ryan went for her mouth, she shied back. "Not a chance, mister. We're just here for fucking."

Goddamn. He hadn't thought he could get any harder. Was there anything she wouldn't consider? Was there a limit to what she might accept of his perversion?

No. Don't think about it tonight.

"Just fucking? I can do that." He ran his touch up the inside of her thighs until his thumbs met at her hot, slick center. "No panties?"

She linked her fingers around the back of his neck. "They get in the way of business."

"Holy hell." He was absolutely raring to go. He delved between her lips to dabble in her wet pussy. "I want you to ride me, sugar."

The look she flashed from under her lashes was everything smutty and sexy. An absolute minx. "I've done a lot worse for five grand."

She attacked his belt like a woman on a mission, opening his fly and dragging his cock out into the air. The rubber slipped on with fast, efficient moves. She rocked up on her knees. Her clenched fist positioned him at her entrance, lingering there for a second.

Then he was engulfed in her tight, wet sheath. His hands clamped around her hips until a tempting voice whispered in his ear.

"Oh," she gasped in his ear. "You've got the biggest cock of any of my customers. So huge inside me."

Her words went straight to his head, swirling deep into his

brain. Customer. John. She was the hooker who'd only meant to do a job, but she was getting more than she'd expected. He'd give her so much more—an orgasm so shattering that she'd never remember the encounter as an exchange of money for flesh. She'd remember it as the best of her life.

He shoved her skirt until it rucked around her waist. His hips surged up, driving into her. A fast, dirty fuck. Grabbing that tight ass, he grazed his fingertips down her soft cleft, down past the tight pucker of her anus. The spot where they joined was dripping wet. Her lips clung to him on every short thrust.

"God, right there." She scraped his scalp. "Fuck me hard. Use me."

His balls smacked the curve of her ass, over and over. He ought to have more finesse but there was nothing. Just blind red lust. The tight clench of her cunt over his throbbing cock. The grind of their hips.

Ryan wrenched a hand into her hair, pulling so that her face bent up toward the ceiling of the limo. Her throat was a glowing white column. He set his mouth there, overcome by the need to mark her. Claim her—this wicked whore. He grazed his teeth over her skin and bit roughly when that wasn't enough.

She shuddered and he felt it all the way down to his cock. He plunged in and out of her. Urgent. Ruthless.

Bracing her hands flat against the roof of the limo, she kept chanting the whole time. Begging for his dick. Asking him to fuck her harder. This was more than a game and less at the same time. It was access to some broken part of himself that reveled in his depravity.

His orgasm grabbed him out of nowhere, tingling through his balls and slamming out in a hot surge. Ryan buried his face between her tits. "Fuck Christ, yes," he growled against her skin.

Thrusting one last time, he pressed his fingers over her clit. Cassandra's pussy cinched down on him as she bowed her back. She tunneled her fingers into his hair, panting, gasping, until her body went rigid.

Only then did Ryan feel his heartbeat thumping at triple time. His breathing, choppy and super-speedy, washed across her chest and back at him. He was a fucking mess.

Cassandra didn't seem to mind. Her arms wrapped around his head then petted down his back. Holy hell, he was still totally dressed in his suit.

A lazy hum rolled up her throat. "If you always fuck like that, mister, I have no idea why you're paying for it."

A surprising laugh shook his shoulders. "Maybe because you promised me you were worth it."

"And?" She curved a hand under his jaw and pulled his face up. Her kiss was feather soft, but only until she traced across the seam of his lips with her tongue. Her makeup remained flawless. "Was I?"

"Every fucking penny."

Chapter Eighteen

They sat primly side by side in the limo. Cass had brushed her hair, making it sleek and sultry again. Her dress was wrinkled and probably had wet spots on the back, but she couldn't help that. The hickeys and bite marks on her cleavage were also beyond hiding.

At least she'd kept Ryan from kissing her—partly out of call-girl cool and partly because she'd had the makeup professionally applied. "Give me slutty elegance," she'd told the girl in the beauty shop. Presto! Convincing enough to get kicked out of a casino.

She wanted to hold his hand, but that wouldn't be in character. She'd thought that what she and Ryan shared was fairly anonymous—the dressing room, the lunchtime quickie. Aways there was laughter and teasing, especially during the euphoria that followed. This was the first time she'd decided to keep playing the game, even afterward. Holding on to the cool businesslike reserve of a hooker was more difficult than she'd imagined.

So in an odd way, the charged silence inside the limo was reassuring. They weren't just screwing. Always, even from the beginning, there had been more.

The limo pulled to a stop. "Here we are," she said in her faux-starlet voice.

Ryan had managed to put himself back in order too. "You know, this is the longest I've had to wait on anything in years."

"Because you're a man who gets what he wants."

His eyes gleamed. "Tonight I do."

The limo driver opened the door, offering his hand to help Cass out. His lips quirked as he caught sight of her chest. She only handed over an extra forty dollars and smiled.

Ryan followed, his eyes on the darkened marquee as he buttoned his suit coat. She'd always loved that particular male ritual. So few aspects of a man's appearance seemed deliberate. Guys were generally of the shit, shower and shave persuasion. A suit made them pay attention to their looks.

It also displayed Ryan's nerves. He'd just had a fab quickie but he was still on edge.

He was getting trickier to figure out each time they met.

Cass pushed aside reality, willfully diving back into their game. She hooked her arm through his. "C'mon, you monster. I have plans for us."

"We're going to the movies?"

"Classic cinema."

"Why do I still think this is going to be unseemly?"

"Because you're a clever boy."

They entered through the heavy double doors. The décor was straight out of 1950s Rat Pack cool—modern for its time, but so quaint and amusing now. Renovated neon lit the lobby in crazy hues, dancing over dark brown shag carpeting. White paper Chinese lanterns swung each time new theatergoers walked in. However, no amount of pretty accents or mod, angular pieces of furniture could disguise the dusty smell of an old building that had seen better days.

The festive atmosphere more than made up for the theater's slightly decrepit state. All types of people had gathered inside, from openly gay Village People guys to hipsters and college students. Even another few men wore suits, which she hoped would help Ryan ease back from feeling conspicuous.

"Two tickets, please," she said to the young woman in the booth.

Ryan, his mouth close enough to send shivers down her nape, snorted, "Classic cinema, my butt. *Behind the Green Door*?"

"Have you seen it?"

"No."

"Is it older than both of us?"

"Yes."

"Then shut up, mister. Or do I have to take a lot of backtalk with my five grand?" The ticket girl only lifted an eyebrow. Cass blew her a kiss before steering Ryan past the milling people. "Come on. I want to get a good seat."

With her arm linked through his, she could feel the tension gathering in his muscles. God, he was built. She was nearly to the point of getting used to it, that every touch would reveal steely flesh—just like how she was nearly accustomed to him being hung like a horse. That wouldn't do at all. She curled her fingertips into his biceps, enjoying his soft inhalation.

"I thought you said you wanted good seats," Ryan said as she settled onto a worn velvet cushion.

She looked left and right along the back-most row. "I did. Right here."

"Cassandra."

"Hm?"

He sat tensely beside her. Whatever game they'd been playing was impossible to find in his expression. "I'm an officer."

A tiny shiver worked up her bare back at the idea of being left alone in this adventure. She'd been bold. She'd taken a huge chance by dressing up like a tart and dragging her lover of one week to a viewing of vintage porn. What if she'd got it all wrong? She didn't know if it would be possible to recover from being pointed out as a fool.

Too freaked by that possibility, she pushed ahead. It was either that or call the whole thing off. She wasn't quite ready to give up on feeling so confident and utterly sexy.

"Look, mister, you paid for a memorable time and I'm going to give you one." She leaned close, her hand sliding up the inside of his taut thigh. "You're not going to do anything worth getting worked up about."

Cass nearly laughed at the disappointment in his voice as he said, "Really?"

"Promise." The theater had steadily filled with people, but they remained alone in the back row. The lights dimmed. "Now close that delicious mouth of yours and watch the movie." She flicked a look down to his crotch. "Maybe you'll learn something, mister."

"Take notes?"

"Sure. It's not every day that a john can learn what gets off a hooker."

"Gets off...?"

His words trailed away as the movie screen flickered green. Some of the theatergoers cheered as the title came up. They sounded drunk. Good. If anyone were to attract attention, it would not be them. She was just a fancy piece of ass on the arm of a six-foot-plus stud wearing a perfectly tailored suit. *Nothing to see here, officers.*

Snickers and giggles from the audience were the rule of the day. Cass couldn't help but smile, and neither did Ryan seem able to remain serious.

"God, it's just so *seventies,*" he whispered, his smile bewildered.

"See? Classic."

But he was right. It was so lame, in fact, that she found herself thankful for their quick fuck in the limo. She couldn't imagine squandering such potent arousal on this cinematic cheese. A shame, because Cass had liked the concept: a girl gets kidnapped before being forced to have sex onstage—multiple times—for a theater full of costumed observers. Bad lighting, bad acting and unspeakably bad mustaches made it nearly unbearable. She and Ryan would wind up screwing to alleviate the boredom.

Worst case, they'd grab a couple bottles of wine from the liquor store across the street and head back to her place. Ryan hadn't been by yet. They could make up some new fantasy.

Cass was ready to suggest that they leave when the kidnappers hauled Marilyn Chambers's character in through the rear entrance of a seedy theater. She was really very pretty—all pouty and vulnerable. Her breasts were nice too. Exactly the right size and, *quelle* shocking, *natural.* Her hands were bound. That simple image did quick work on Cass's flagging interest.

By the time five women had stripped Chambers, displayed for a small crowd of masked observers to see, Ryan had grown quiet. He shifted in his seat. The women kissed and sucked at one another, silencing most of the theater. Both the film's costumed audience and the real-life one in that 1950s theater were enraptured. Imagining everyone else getting turned on too was a surprising bonus.

The movie wasn't any more explicit than a modern porno. In fact it was relatively subdued—some oral and missionary. But the public venue, the unexpected pleasure of finding it erotic, and the tense restlessness of Ryan right beside her…

Cass sank into her arousal, happy she could fulfill the role she'd wanted to.

She dragged her hand along the inside of her own thigh. The silky fabric parted. She slid her fingers along her clit, circling, rubbing, her back arching slightly as her breathing picked up. The weird lighting and funky jazz soundtrack didn't matter now. Watching the leading lady get fucked by a well-hung black guy was more than doing the trick.

Ryan glanced at her, giving her some serious side eye. His lips parted. Oh, she liked that. He looked that way after he came too, all disorientated and wrecked. She relished that this silly idea of hers had caught him off guard too. His eyes dropped to her lap.

The rate of fucking on-screen picked up the pace. Groans and breathless sighs were the only soundtrack now. Girls continued to work at Chambers's tits, sucking and fondling. Cass reached up with her left hand and rubbed her bare nipple. She tweaked it. Pinched it. She remembered how roughly Ryan had bit her breast, there in the limo, and was rewarded by another surge of wet need.

Ryan's hand rested on her near thigh. His fingers pulsed in a steady clench. So tense. Cass spread her legs. The fabric barely covered her pussy. She dipped the tip of her finger inside. So slick. She went for two fingers, pushing deeper, holding still. She stayed quiet. Ryan seemed hell-bent on keeping this relatively discreet, so she'd come in silence if she had to.

Maybe what his brain wanted and what his dick demanded were two different things. He turned in his seat, blatantly watching her now. Cass played it up for him. She opened her mouth, head pressed against the top of the seat back. The noises from the film followed her when she closed her eyes. Wet slapping. Grunts. A quick smack.

She was so lost to the moment that when Ryan took a nipple into his mouth, she almost cried out. That hot surprise jerked her arousal up ten notches.

"Don't close your eyes," he said against her breast. "You're missing out."

He circled his tongue so smoothly, so deliberately, teasing her as she was teasing him. The thrust and smack of bodies ramming together grew faster and faster. Cass clutched the back of his head to force him closer to her breast.

The very unobtrusive sound of his fly zipper being undone made her gasp softly. *Oh, yes. Bring that big boy out to play.*

Ryan continued to work her breasts. He angled his body away from the center aisle, using those gloriously broad shoulders to shield them from the casual glance. The folds of his suit coat helped conceal what he was doing with his engorged cock. He stroked. He pumped. He didn't make a sound.

God, the film's on-screen audience had degenerated into a mindless orgy. Naked aroused bodies were everywhere. Only, Cass wasn't as interested right then. She was too busy watching the show she and Ryan performed for one another. The sight of his head bowed between her tits was delicious. In the near-darkness, she only caught flashes of flesh as he jerked off. All the while the erotic sounds of a full-on seventies sex party filled her ears.

Cass bit her upper lip until she tasted blood. Her fingers worked. She arched against Ryan's mouth. He pushed her hand out of the way and slipped his fingers inside. Compared to the fat girth of his cock, even his three fingers weren't as large, but he certainly knew how to use them. He fidgeted with the angle, finding the sure spot. She bucked off the seat.

Like in the dressing room, he clamped his free hand over her mouth. Against her ear he whispered, "If you make a sound, we'll get caught. We can't get caught, Cassandra. You're a hooker. Do you know what guards do to hookers in jail?"

She closed her eyes, bathing in his deep, hushed rumble.

"I'd make you hold on to your cell bars, your arms stretched up. Christ, your tits would look great. Your stomach. I'd make you stand there naked while I beat off for a while."

So close now. His fingers jammed inside her, his thumb pressing on her clit. The hand he held over her mouth smelled of his arousal.

"Then I'd fuck you, my dirty whore. Right there against the bars, your gorgeous legs wrapped around me."

For how much she'd been waiting for it, her orgasm took her by surprise. Her mind glazed over. All she could do was ride the fierce wave and keep from grunting with the pleasure.

Ryan had withdrawn his fingers, returning to his own body. He needed no time at all. A couple tight jerks and he gave up his release. Hot wetness spurted against her bared thighs. She grinned up toward the ceiling, as limp as a rag.

Only a few seconds passed before reality jumped back between them. Ryan did up his fly. Cass arranged her dress. Even though the movie was still hard at work in all its vintage-porn glory, they fled the theater, laughing like kids.

Chapter Nineteen

They had to take a taxi back to where the F-150 was parked since limos didn't normally cruise past theaters showing classic porn. It wasn't long before they arrived at Cassandra's apartment. Ryan stood behind her with his flight bag slung over one shoulder while she tried to put the key in the lock. He probably wasn't helping, what with one hand splayed over her stomach, his thumb brushing the edge of her dress where it plunged down below her cleavage.

She persisted past the trembling in her hands and threw open the door.

"This is it," she said with a wave of her arm. "It's pretty small, but it works for me. At least I'm out of my parents' house."

He dropped his bag at the end of the couch before taking a look around. So this was Cassandra's place.

To the left was a small kitchen with ceramic floors and a bistro-style table in the corner. Farther on was the living area, with an open door providing a glimpse of a bedroom.

Nothing had a specific theme, nor did any of it match. The couch was upholstered in blue and set at an angle from an oversized chair done in cream with orange pillows. Framed prints shared wall space with paintings on canvas and what he figured was an African mask. Somehow it all worked together, making the place comforting. Nothing fussy. Just as sunny and inviting as the woman who lived there.

He spotted a collection of snapshots perched on a side table. One of them was a round-cheeked girl with a huge gap in her smile. The girl's bright red hair shot almost straight up from her ponytail like duck fluff. "Is this you?"

A pink blush rushed up her face. "Yes. I'd just lost my top teeth. I was pretty stoked that the tooth fairy gave me two bucks."

Another picture was a teenage Cassandra wearing a white tank top, tiny shorts and clutching a gold trophy. "You ran track?"

"All four years of high school. I went to State my senior year."

He held up the silver-framed photos so that he could look at the three versions at once—from the children to the one most certainly grown up, still wearing the guise of a call girl. All certainly had their charms, but he was ready for the real Cassandra to come back.

"I think I'm going to get cleaned up," she said as if she was thinking the same thing. She pushed her hair back over her shoulder and shot him a naughty look from under her lashes. "Somebody seems to have gotten me messed up."

He couldn't help but chuckle. Yeah, he'd done that. He'd come all over her leg in the back row of a seedy theater. He had no idea how he would've covered that with his chain of command had they been caught...

They hadn't been. They'd escaped free and clear. Now he had to convince his raging imagination that it was still a one-time-only thing. That task was becoming nearly impossible.

She sauntered past him, hips swinging in that dangerous excuse for a dress. "I'm going to run a bath. You're welcome to join me."

As if he'd pass up that opportunity.

He followed her into the cramped bathroom like a puppy on a string. The garden tub wedged into the corner was a welcome sight. As much as he'd like holding a wet, naked Cassandra in his arms, squeezing himself into a regular tub might have been too much.

"Nice," he said.

"Isn't it though? It was one of the biggest appeals about this place. After a long day on my feet, there's nothing better than a soak."

It was fairly obvious she made it a regular practice. The thick rim sported squat candles and a few brightly colored pots and baskets of girly things. Ryan emerged from his suit before he ran the water. He passed on adding anything else—not that he'd know what he was doing anyway.

He froze with his hand under the spigot, hot water sluicing over his skin, when she casually dropped the slender straps of her dress and let it pool to the floor. He still wasn't used to the beautiful lines of her body, half hoping he never became that complacent. The day he didn't appreciate her perky breasts and their pink nipples would be the day he belonged in hell.

Watching her wash off the makeup was strangely intimate in the tiny room. If they lived together—or if they were married, even—it might be something he saw every day. Something he'd eventually take for granted. He and Ashleigh had never lived together, with her stuffed in a tiny dorm on campus while he rented a room in a dilapidated house shared by four other guys. So watching Cassandra bend over the sink to splash water over her face, one foot rising behind her for balance, was sort of...nice. Far more intimate than he'd ever stopped to consider.

She scrubbed a hand towel over her face. "Phew. I just don't get how some women wear that much makeup every day."

Sitting on the edge of the tub, he grabbed her hip and tugged her near, until she stood between his knees. "It's probably because they need it. You don't."

"You are an unbelievable sweet talker, Major Haverty."

"Am not, Miss Whitman. I'm speaking the truth."

She didn't answer with anything other than, "Come on. In we go."

He got in first, then let her nestle across his lap. Her ass snuggled flat against his groin. Only the fact that he'd already come twice kept his cock from rising to attention. Her sleek body was even softer when wet. The ends of her hair floated in the water and turned a deeper red.

With a hearty sigh, she leaned back against his chest. "I don't think johns normally pay hookers to take baths with them."

He cringed slightly at the return of that fiction. Cassandra was a good woman. Quiet. Normal. He was surrounded by the proof of it. Which probably meant she was humoring him. Ashleigh had humored him until she...couldn't anymore. He had no intention of pushing Cassandra that far.

"Then maybe it's best if we don't pretend," he said softly. "We're better the way we are."

She craned backwards to look at him. A flash of hurt sparked in her eyes. Ryan stole a fast kiss, eager to make it up to her.

The whole night had been fun—too much fun. He'd tried all his life to be a different guy, one who didn't get off on such elaborate play. Cassandra, with her cheery personality and rocking body, ought to be enough. Instead he'd gotten caught up in the fantasy of making a call girl scream. He hadn't even learned his lesson when they were hustled along by security.

In the theater, he'd been sure he could behave. But when she'd started playing with herself... How could he resist? He'd been able to scent her musky arousal. When her eyes drifted shut as if she didn't even need him there—exactly like a prostitute finally getting a chance at her own pleasure—raging determination had surged up. He'd help the hooker get off whether she needed him, not because she was his for the night. Bought and paid for. *His.* He'd tasted her breasts and sunk his fingers in her wet pussy without another thought to their surroundings.

Cassandra deserved more than that. She could be more to him. With him. He needed to appreciate her for what she was. Not what disturbed fantasies he wanted to mold her into.

So that was it. The end of their games. He'd give it all up for a chance of embarking on something special together.

There in the tub, he carefully steered the conversation away from their night. He'd much rather hear her voice rise and fall with excitement as she told him about diving into preparations for the gala. It was enough to be able to listen to her talk. Her voice soothed him.

No matter the softness of the moment, he couldn't keep his hands still. Strokes down her arms turned into caresses across the tops of her breasts. When he dipped to circle her nipples, he was rewarded with her quiet gasp. She bowed up into his touch and her ass pressed back against his groin. He didn't seem capable of being around her without getting hard.

He snuck his fingers down her body to circle the shallow dip of her navel. Then lower to her curls. Her lips bloomed under his touch. Inside she was even slicker than the water quietly lapping against them both. He flicked over her clit with two fingers.

A few minutes later he reached out of the tub and snatched a condom from his suit pants. Entering her this time was almost like coming home—comforting after the craziness they'd indulged.

He pushed slowly inside, his arm around her waist. She draped her head back on his chest. The only sounds through the small room were their matched breathing and the quiet slaps of the water against the tub walls.

Since they were both spent, they barely rocked together. Ryan enjoyed the slow build and teasing clench of her pussy. Even the end was slow. Cassandra moaned low and gentle. Ryan's orgasm eased over him in a langorous wave.

Once the water cooled, they retreated to her bedroom. The bed was only queen sized, which did his big body no favors, but they huddled under the covers together. When he pulled her against his side with an arm around her waist, they managed to find enough room.

She traced idle patterns over his chest. "God, I'm going to be exhausted at my parents' house tomorrow. Ugh, and then the restaurant."

"Is that a complaint?"

"About my shift? Maybe." Burying her face in his shoulder, she giggled. "About being exhausted? No chance."

"Do you see your parents often? When you're not doing tours for them, I mean."

"Oh, yeah. More than I want to, probably." She traced a single fingertip down the line of his abs. "How about you? I don't even know where you're from. Do you see your family often?"

He closed his eyes and held back a sigh. The bare facts were bound to come out, but he still didn't like discussing them. "I was born and raised in Charlotte County, Virginia. I never knew my dad. My mom died."

Cassandra's head popped up. Soft lips had parted. "I'm so sorry, Ryan."

Shrugging against the pillows, he closed his eyes. No better way to ignore the pity on her face. "It was almost three years ago. She was a mess there at the end. A full-blown drunk."

"I really am sorry. I can't imagine what that must have been like."

He petted over her hair, which was lying damp and unbound around her shoulders. "Tell me about your parents."

She hesitated, as if debating whether to accept his diversion. With a tiny nod she said, "They've been married almost thirty years. Met in college. All they've ever wanted is what they have. A business they love and all their family nearby. They don't really get why I love art, but they try to be supportive." Her jaw cracked on a quiet yawn. "Letting me go to France was a really big deal. I do mean *let*, by the way. I practically had to pry Mom's hand off mine at the airport."

Ryan had no idea what that would feel like. Amazing, maybe? His mom had rolled her eyes when he'd finally told her that he intended to become a fighter pilot, then took another drag off her Newport before she sarcastically told him good luck.

If he ever had kids, he'd be damned sure they knew he loved them.

The weirdest thing happened as he drifted off to sleep with his arms full of warm and contented female. His mind filled with visions of a girl with red hair wearing a miniature bomber jacket and running over a lawn with a toy F-16 in her hand. The picture almost jerked him up out of his sleepy daze. He'd wanted a family for a long time. An idle wish, however, was different than imagining specifics.

Rather than deny himself, he let it lead him off into dreams.

Chapter Twenty

Mid-May in Vegas was an odd sort of limbo. Spring break was well over, but the summer tourist surge hadn't jumped on them yet. No matter, Cass was swamped. She'd led three tours to the Canyon over the previous two weekends. Her dad's arthritis was seriously limiting his ability to make consistent commitments. Emily, her sister, was laid up with an infected ingrown toenail of all things, which meant Vision Tours had scrambled to fill its rosters.

Ryan had become a bright spot in her routine. He worked on base steadily during the week, participating in a new Red Flag against some group of Marine pilots. She still smiled at his unimpressed assessment of their fliers. They met on the weekends, but their sex games had dropped off to nothingness. She liked to think it was because of how hellaciously tired they were by Friday night.

At least she hoped that was the reason. Not once had he mentioned the specifics of their first two weekends. The roles they'd undertaken. She was beginning to wonder if she'd imagined how much he enjoyed the roleplaying. Or was he holding back on purpose? If she weren't so ridiculously satisfied every time he finished with her, she might have resolved to investigate.

As it was, Cass's bank account still smarted from their initial few dates, and she knew Ryan's must too—although he'd never admitted it. So quiet dinners in, lots of lovemaking and lots of lazy late mornings had been their weekend agenda. That was better than good. It was fantastic.

Then there was the gallery.

At eight in the morning, well before it opened to the public at eleven, she pushed in through the employee entrance. Cool air conditioning stroked her cheeks. The scent of the place was always changing, depending on the exhibit. Sometimes the atmosphere was permeated with old smells, old ideas—canvas and linseed oil paints that had once been mixed by hand. At other times it was clinical and sharp, when the cleaning lady's lemon-scented chemicals overpowered everything.

That was especially true as they transitioned out the last of their recent student acrylics exhibit in preparation for the Bellocq photographs.

Cass tugged on her lightweight cardigan, knowing from experience that the gallery would cover her in goose bumps. "Good morning, Mr. Talbert," she called to her boss. As always, he sat in his tiny wedge of office off the coat room.

He waved. After a few more taps on his keyboard, he joined her. Handing over a stack of gilt-edged envelopes, he said, "The latest RSVPs."

"Thanks. I hope to have the caterer pinned down on her estimate by the end of the week. Hopefully we'll have a better idea of attendance by then. Sara said I should give them a polite shove to see if their numbers come down, if only by five percent."

"Good. Oh, and Mr. Hungerford is actually coming."

"The owner? Wow."

Mr. Talbert pushed his wire-rimmed bifocals up on his nose. A slightly embarrassed smile made his face seem even rounder. "Apparently he's a huge admirer of Bellocq's work."

"The man took pictures of naked women," Cass said with a giggle. "I'm not too surprised."

"Will you be bringing anyone with you? Or too intent on working that night?"

Cass picked at a cuticle with her thumbnail. She hadn't asked Ryan if he would be her plus one and didn't want to presume. They weren't that far along. "I have someone in mind, but I need to ask him. I'll know before I talk to the caterer."

The next six hours passed in happy productivity. She was on the phone for half of it, arranging press for the opening, gently reminding loyal patrons to RSVP, and coordinating the incoming photography shipments. The rest of the time was spent working with the gallery's head decorator to discuss how the prints should be displayed. Spacing, lighting, theme, chronology—all were meticulously considered, sometimes passionately debated.

The give and take of ideas filled her with pride every time she realized that her opinion and training mattered.

She was being paid the equivalent of cheap cat food, but the hours were so invigorating. This was what she loved. Every bit of it. Her mom had once told her that a job was a drag, but a career made you bounce out of bed in the morning. That was Cass all over the place.

Which made five o'clock all the more difficult to face.

She drove home, napped, ate a meal midway between lunch and dinner, and got ready for another six hours at Blakely's. Another six hours of Tommy, Cynthia and now, best of all, the return of Tommy's mother, Julia. The pinch-faced woman had been on holiday in Italy for two months, somewhere on the Riviera. They'd only barely tolerated each other while Cass and Tommy dated, but now Julia smelled blood in the water. There was no longer any reason to be polite.

She had returned on Sunday. It was Tuesday night. If both of them made it to Friday without skinning one another, Cass would French kiss a lemur.

She struggled into her Blakely's uniform, too cranky to even bother with her stockings. Screw them. The customers were always polite, the money was always fabulous—but damn she was tired.

On her way out of the apartment, she grabbed the letters from her mailbox. Water bill. Credit-card bill. *Congratulations, Miss Whitman, it's twins!* With a grumble she shoved them into her purse and hurried out to her car.

Four hours later, her feet ached. Her head pounded. Tips were slow, in part because the kitchen had run out of Blakely's famous French onion soup. Apparently this minor disappointment was excuse enough for stiffing the waitstaff. To top it all off, a particularly bitchy woman from LA had lodged a complaint against Cass.

She was on break when she learned. Gilly slipped into the employee's eating area, which was like a six-foot-square closet where they huddled away from the bustle of the kitchen.

"Hey," Gilly said. "That diva at table seven? She cornered the Witch and gave her a dressing down. Something about the salad?"

Cass shoved away the last of a piece of cheesecake. Her stomach had gone sour. "There was a long hair in the salad." She gestured to her own head where she'd secured her hair in a tight bun. "Mine? I don't think so. The woman blamed me personally. I got her a new one, but that didn't put an end to her complaints. The steak was overcooked, the bread pudding was cold. Eighty-five trips back to the kitchen, swear to God."

Gilly grinned. "Quite the rant. Feel better?"

"Not really. Not if Julia's going to blame me for what happened."

"You know she will. That's why I thought you might need a heads-up."

Cass licked her fork. "Thanks," she said soberly. "Better get out of here before you're caught giving aid to a condemned prisoner."

"I'll take my chances." Gilly fidgeted with her pen, even now, four months since quitting smoking. "Hey, remind me. When is that gallery opening of yours?"

"Second Saturday in July. Can you come?"

"Should be able to. My mom isn't flying in for her annual torture of a visit until later that month."

"Cool." Cass stood and stretched. Her back ached as if the dessert chef had flamed her with his mini blowtorch. "I'd love to have you there. My family's planning to come too, which makes me extra nervous, but it'll be good to have fans in the stands."

"Do we get to cheer when you make a particularly astute observation?"

"I'd rather you didn't."

"Don't worry," Gilly said with a wave. "I'll be too busy people-watching all the fancy-dress patrons ogling the nudie pics and eyeing your fighter pilot."

She tried to keep her response down to a casual shrug. The fact was she didn't know if they'd reached the point where making long-term, nonsexual plans was on the table. The previous few weeks had done a great deal toward upping her confidence, but she wasn't at a place to start bossing around a hot, fantastic guy. Part of her still blinked at the unbelievable stroke of luck that had permitted her to reside, even temporarily, in too-good-to-be-true land.

"I haven't asked him yet," she muttered.

"Idiot."

"What?"

"I said, I'm heading back out to the floor."

"Right."

Stopping off in the locker room, Cass reapplied her lipstick and checked her hair. Her fingers brushed the Bellagio chip she always carried in her purse. Strength warmed her on the inside, along with the knowledge that she couldn't keep doing this forever.

She was ready to return to the floor when Julia Blakely met her in the kitchen, barring the way. The woman's posture was like that of a snake about to strike. Arms crossed. Back slightly arched. Chin tucked against her wiggly throat skin. The new facelift looked great, in all honesty, and she took really good care of her body. Those assets only accentuated the few places where aging had taken its toll.

"My office," she said. Then she snapped her son's name. Tommy appeared from the rear of the kitchen, as if summoned by magic. Gilly called her the Witch for a reason. "You too."

The kitchen staff watched them go, not making any attempt to hide their curiosity. Even the head chef, who would've given Gordon Ramsay a run for his foul-mouthed money, looked up from where he prepared another set of dishes. Working in the steakhouse meant always having a live audience, no matter the kerfuffle.

"This is your fault," Tommy hissed as they followed Julia back through the building.

"Oh, really mature, Tommy. What are we, six years old?"

"You should've done more."

"More? I did all I could to please that wingbat. Some people don't want to be happy. They want to be pissed off and take it out on others. They're miserable. End of story."

"What, is that supposed to mean something, huh? Is that a jab at me?"

"Defensive much? Come off it."

"No, I won't," he said, his eyes practically pulling into his head as he got riled up. "You called me miserable when I told you about Cynthia."

Cass pressed a hand against her lower back as she walked. It was either that or curl it into a fist and give it a go. "Sure I did. I called you a miserable son of a bitch."

"Totally uncalled for. I was trying to apologize."

"Sorry. I missed that. My ears stopped working when you said you'd been boinking my Barbie doll coworker."

"Don't bring Cynthia into this."

"You brought her into this when you turned monogamy into an option."

"Maybe we would've done better had I know you prefer quickies with random strangers."

"You asshole."

Tommy waved his hands, brushing her off. His signet ring winked in the light. He was so damn proud of having graduated from the Cornell MBA program, but he still bowed to his mother's wishes regarding every detail.

A long time ago, they had bonded over being perpetually trapped by their parents' businesses, their successes, their wishes. That's where the affair had started. Cass had loved having someone who understood how stifled she was. Everything had been...decent. Stable. A teensy bit dull. But what the hell—she hadn't known any better. She hadn't caught a glimpse of how it could be.

Stepping into Julia's office was like crossing a medieval prison yard toward an awaiting guillotine. It didn't need to be that way. Just like her relationship with Tommy, she'd since come to understand how important it was to adore, *really* adore, how she spent her time. Time at the gallery. Time with Ryan. She wasn't going to compromise anymore.

"Miss Whitman," Julia said, her address staunchly formal ever since learning of the breakup. "I have received a very serious complai—"

"Save it," Cass said.

"Excuse me?"

"I said, save it. Please. My head hurts. My back is killing me. And I want to shove a high heel into your son's eye socket."

"How dare—?" Tommy began, but his mother beat him out when it came to being heard. Pure bitchy hostility trumped bluster.

"You have some nerve talking to me that way. You know full well that we must take any complaint seriously. The customer is always right."

"The customer was a psychotic drama queen who felt like kicking a lackey. She must not be able to afford one full-time, so she rented me for the hour." Cass untied her white apron. "What happened to loyalty, huh? I've worked here for nearly two years."

Julia steepled her fingers. "We both know why."

It was Cass's turn for a harsh, "*Excuse me*?"

"My son took a liking to you."

"Mother—"

"Oh, now you both can just can that shit." Cass squelched the attack of nerves that came with cursing. She was too upset to care. After balling up her apron, she flopped it onto Julia's desk. A few papers took a satisfying swan dive toward the floor. "I'm done. Really, really done. Tommy, I hope you and Cynthia and your skinny short dick are very happy together."

She was out of Blakely's and back in her car before another minute passed. Free. She was free. Screw the bills and the future. No one deserved what she'd put up with for so long. Her hands shook like an unbalanced washing machine. She could barely get the key in the ignition. None of it mattered.

Ten minutes later, her heart still pounding, she found herself traveling not toward her apartment, but toward Ryan's place. A red light gave her time to debate. The adrenaline was wearing off, as was her momentary flush of bold attitude.

Never had she...shown up. Unannounced.

She whipped out her cell phone. "Hey," she said breathlessly when he picked up. "Can I come over?"

"Uh, sure. You okay?"

He sounded sleepy, sexy, his voice a little slurred. Screw being timid. She wanted that voice in her ear all night, just like she wanted his hands, his mouth, his dick. Every bit of him.

She giggled at the power of her greedy and quite frankly *rude* thoughts. That didn't sound like her at all, which was part of the fun.

"I'm just fine, baby. If ever there was a night for celebrating, this is it."

Chapter Twenty-One

As soon as he hung up the phone, Ryan scooped a pair of jeans off the carpet and dragged them on. He didn't even bother doing up the top button or grabbing a shirt.

Because he then spent the next fifteen minutes shoving laundry under the bed and dishes in the dishwasher.

He normally wasn't a slob. Not at all. He'd grown up with enough of that crap. Having to wade through piles of filthy clothes to find something to wear had left him with a healthy appreciation for order, as did years in the Air Force, but the last week at work had been hell. Thirteen-hour days didn't leave him much time to clean.

Instead he'd gotten in the habit of calling Cassandra, if she didn't have a shift at Blakely's. She'd chatter about which prints had been selected to display at the gallery—something about choosing between Bellocq's originals or some other guy's version. While throwing a microwaved meal down his throat, Ryan was never sure he understood what she said about the nuances. Light and shadows. Along those lines. Then he'd spend way too long saying good night before passing out, usually while watching the evening news.

Exactly as he had tonight, until the phone had woken him.

He thumbed the remote to turn off the TV right as his doorbell chimed. Scrubbing the top of his head in a useless attempt to neaten his hair, he opened the door.

Cassandra stood at the threshold. A huge smile pinched her cheeks up and made her eyes sparkle. She tossed her hands wide. "Congratulate me."

"Congratulations," he said automatically. "What for?"

She launched herself into his arms, a lighthearted laugh spinning around them. "I quit the restaurant."

"That's definitely worth a congratulations."

Her smile only widened. "I know." Hooking her hands over his shoulders, she leaned back. "Dang, you look good."

Heat set up residence in his cheeks, but there was no way he'd admit to blushing. "Um. Thanks. I think?"

"You really have no idea, do you? All those lovely angles and muscles." She sighed dramatically, then traced the bottom of his oblique as it veed down to disappear into the gaping waistband of his jeans. "I totally came to the right place to collect my reward."

"Is that right?" He kicked the door shut, then hefted her into his embrace. His hands curved under her thighs as she latched around his waist. The kiss he claimed was flavored with her enthusiasm. "What makes you think you get rewards from me?"

"Hmm. Maybe the fact that you've got me halfway to your bedroom already."

He deliberately spread his fingers over her ass. She still wore the charcoal-gray skirt of her uniform. The way she'd leapt into his arms had twisted the material around her hips. She only wore plain pantyhose that evening—just as she'd done for weeks. Shoving aside a flicker of disappointment, he scoured his evening beard growth along her neck until she shivered.

"Nope," he said, shaking his head as he deposited her in the middle of his bed. "This is me being entirely selfish."

She leaned back on her elbows, grinning up at him the whole while. With a wiggle of her toes, she dropped her high heels to the floor. "I don't believe you. Not in the least."

"Believe it." He snagged a condom from his dresser drawer before he crawled over her. He had to taste that smile again.

With her fingers gliding up her blouse, she slipped button after button free. The bra she wore was only a shade darker cream than her skin. Incendiary lust mixed with the excitement in her eyes.

"I tell you what," she purred. "How about we each get what we want?"

He laughed and carefully lowered to press her into the mattress. His forearms bracketed her head. "Works for me."

He probably should have rewarded her, just as she'd insisted. Start by spending plenty of time licking her all over, with extra attention paid to her lovely, luscious pussy, but she didn't give him a chance. Her clothes were stripped off in the midst of hot, wet kisses and giggles—every one of those from her. Ryan might have groaned a few times, especially when her hands delved under his jeans to wrap his cock in a firm grip. Cassandra pushed his jeans down over his ass, grabbing and gripping as she went, then wiggled them all the way off his legs.

He slipped the condom on, groaning again as he sank into her. Perfect. Tight. So wet that he'd like to stay connected to her forever.

She nuzzled her face against his chest, fingers tunneling through his chest hair. "Mmm. Right there. I love the way you feel inside me. The way you fill me up. Just blissful, baby."

Those soft words went straight to his head, dove down his spine and made his hips move. Easy and gentle, he pushed into her again and again. She took every inch of him—arms wrapped around his ribs, legs curled around his calves.

Ryan was the one fucking her, but he was also the one who felt surrounded. In the best possible way.

Their climaxes rolled out with slow power. Cassandra's head tilted back as she gasped. Her slick pussy contracting over his cock was all he needed for pleasure to stream down his back, through his limbs—a long, hot, melting orgasm. Just right, exactly as she'd said. Just what he'd needed. What he'd always hoped would be enough to keep him satisfied.

Afterward they curled together on the bed, still on top of the comforter. She'd tossed the scraps of her uniform into the corner with a smug smile before nestling into his arms. He hadn't even turned off the lights, which meant he was treated to every inch of perfect skin as he petted her with soothing strokes.

"Okay," he said, smoothing her hair back from her head. "Tell me what happened."

Her grin reawakened as she told him the story. Lithe hands fluttered as she talked, and she proved to be an entertaining storyteller. As she repeated the owner's lines, her voice even pitched squeakier. She managed to sound like a pissy older woman. Her eyes narrowed on Tommy Boy's words, but not with crankiness. With a genuine flare for acting. No wonder she'd been so good at playing a French maid and a high-class hooker.

The beautiful, heartfelt orgasm they'd just shared gave way to needier memories. So many roles she could assume. So many games they could play.

He wanted to growl at himself. More than that, he wanted to grab a cleaver and cut out the part of his brain that couldn't be one hundred percent satisfied with the present. With that *perfect* moment, where Cassandra lay naked and sated in his bed, her smile as fresh as spring sunshine.

Didn't matter. He was halfway to hard again, positively high on deviant possibilities—all of which would mean turning Cassandra into someone else. That was an even more nauseating idea than knowing she'd lose patience with his immature desires one day—the day she called it quits.

"I didn't even give notice," she finally finished, sounding gleeful. "Just stomped right out of there. The only thing in my locker was my spare skirt and button-down. Maybe a pair of flip-flops. I didn't even care."

"Good for you," he managed to say. Stalling for time, he shifted her in his arms so that she lay sprawled over his front. His back pressed into the bed, with her softness melded against him. "Doesn't sound like they deserved you for even a second more."

She kissed him, fast but somehow innocent. Her mouth tasted like a win. "You're good for me, Ryan Haverty."

"Me?"

She stacked her hands over his chest, chin on top. "Yep. You."

Shit, he didn't deserve the worshipful way she looked at him. That smile would fall away right quick if she knew what he'd been thinking, if she realized how ungrateful he was.

"Bull," he said. "This was all you."

"Well, I am kind of awesome, aren't I?"

Ryan gave her ass a sneaky squeeze, which produced the

fortunate response of making her body wiggle. He dug his fingers lightly into her sides, just above her hipbones where she was ticklish. A naked Cassandra wiggling against him was something he'd do his damnedest to have more of at any opportunity. He'd shove whole parts of his busted, disgusting libido into a box and lock it away forever.

"Not just kind of, baby."

"Okay." She laughed. "Totally awesome. I rock."

"You do."

Her smile turned wistful. "I should have walked out of there ages ago. I mean, I can make the bills if I go mega full-time at the gallery. It'll just be a bit tight."

Although Ryan had managed to bite back most of his words, one question niggled past good sense. "Why were you ever with that jackass?"

"He wasn't always that bad."

She pushed up. He thought for one blissful second that she was just going to sit straddling him. He'd be willing to listen to her recite details about every single one of her exes if she sat in that position. Unfortunately she burrowed under his blanket. Her hair pooled on the white pillowcase.

Ryan climbed under the comforter too. There was no reason to stay away from her gorgeous body when he had permission to touch it. "I guess I'm going to have to take your word on that. Because all I've seen is prime jerk attitude."

"Will you turn out the lights?"

He tilted his head. There was a lot they still didn't know about each other, which meant he wasn't sure how to take that request. "Is that your way of telling me to shut up?"

She laughed. "No. But I think this might be easier to explain if you're not watching me. You're intense sometimes."

"Me?" he teased even as he did as she asked and flicked off the bedroom lights. "Intense?"

"Every now and then." In the dim light creeping through a crack between the dark drapes, he saw her lift a hand and squeeze her fingers together. "A wee bit. It can be intimidating."

"Sorry. I don't mean to be."

"Don't apologize. The energizing part of it outweighs the intimidating."

A truncated hum worked its way up his throat when he had no idea what else to say. He'd learned the hard way to go after what he wanted. The details were just that—details. Things to dodge or leap over on his way to a goal. He couldn't really help how everyone else took it, but... Well, shit, there was no way to think this without sounding like an idiot, but he wanted Cassandra to *like* him.

"Tell me about Tommy," he finally said.

She pressed her face into his biceps in the dark. "I'm being honest. He wasn't that bad at first. Wasn't at all bad, actually. He came across as sincere. He listened to me rant about my family whenever I wanted, and I only had to listen to him about his mom in return. Plus he seemed...comforting, I guess? Safe. Normal."

He could definitely understand the appeal of normal. It seemed like Cassandra didn't understand that she was *his* normal. His comfort. How long had he hungered for just that sort of refuge?

Uncomfortable with the dark turn of his thoughts, he fought to bring them back to the teasing they both enjoyed. Anything but being trapped in his own head.

"His eyes are about the size of the tip of my pinkie."

Her fingertips dug into his ribs. "They are not."

"Are too." He tickled her back until she giggled and writhed. "Itty-bitty piggy eyes."

Giggling still, she smiled against his chest. "Okay, maybe. Only when he's pissed. Until I proved to be unreasonable when he misplaced his skinny rod in Cynthia, he didn't have any reason to be pissed at me. We had a lot in common."

He couldn't help the snort. "Like what?"

"Feeling stuck in one place. Afraid to move on." Her fingers trailed down his chest almost absently. "Like I said, you're good for me. One small, bold move is making waves."

Be damned if that wasn't both a surprising weight and a feel good at the same time. "Are you going to stay the night?"

"I probably shouldn't. I bet you have to get up ridiculously early."

He shrugged, then stroked a hand over her hair. "Tomorrow's not too bad. Only six."

"Six a.m. isn't bad? You're insane." Yawning, she hitched a leg over his. Her toes dug softly into his calf. "See? I should go."

He buried his smile against the crown of her head, their bodies surrounded in darkness. "Yet you're not moving."

"You're not kicking me out, either."

"No. I'm not kicking you out."

Chapter Twenty-Two

Ryan called two nights later.

Cass had just finished painting her toenails following a powerwash of a shower. Her brain ached from hours of scanning catalogs, photographs, estimates, and her endless to-do list, but she never tired of the responsibility. The chirp of her cell phone made her nick the slightly spongy paint on her big toe, but seeing *Major Haverty* on her caller ID silenced her grumbles.

"You're up late, aren't you?" she said, leaning back against the pillows.

"Night sortie. I get to sleep in tomorrow."

"You won't be able to, you know."

He chuckled. "I'll give it a try. I have excellent sprawling skills."

She poured a second glass of merlot from the half bottle on her bedside table. Between the wine, the shower and Ryan's low rumble in her ear, Cass sank into a delicious lassitude. "While we working stiffs trudge into work? Doesn't seem fair."

"Ha. Don't try and play that with me. You were probably all bright and chipper this morning, cute as hell."

"Bounding into the gallery while birds tied ribbons in my hair."

Except for the *Cinderella* animals, they weren't far off in painting a picture of her enthusiasm. Maybe because working at Blakely's or for her parents had always been so frustrating, she was actually surprised. She kept expecting the other shoe to drop. One day she'd find the gallery an odious grind.

It hadn't happened and she doubted it would. This was, quite literally, what she loved doing—what she had trained for. What she was *really* good at.

Time spent at Hungerford flew by. She never accomplished quite as much as she planned, but knowing she got to do it all over again the next day made her grin like a silly kid. She'd tried to thank Ryan a couple more times, knowing he had been the kick-start to her current happiness. He always waved it off as if what he'd done was no big deal.

He was a great guy. Fantastic, even. On that small point, however, he was wrong.

"What're you doing?" he asked.

"Painting my toes. Watching *Tremors.*"

"What channel?"

"TBS."

Cass found herself relaxing as their conversation stayed pleasingly...normal. Silly stuff and ordinary stuff. Neither of them mentioned their early forays into bold, brazen sex—hadn't at all since those first two weekends. She tried not to let that bother her. Ryan was hot, adorable, polite and built like a star athlete. Nothing he did for her, or to her, fell short of fabulous.

He seemed happy enough. He hadn't brought home another kinky outfit for her to wear. She wouldn't have minded if he did, and in fact the roleplaying had been sort of...liberating. He just didn't seem to desire it like she'd first assumed. Maybe his interest had been a whim—as much a whim as her decision to have sex in a dressing room.

So they floated along in conversation, two people rapidly becoming a full-fledged couple. They played Six Degrees of Kevin Bacon until Ryan admitted that he used his laptop and the Internet to cheat. How else could he get from *A Few Good Men* to Charlie Chaplin in only three steps?

Most of all, Cass loved hearing about his work. *Such* a turn-on. He and the other pilots in the Aggressor Squadron had flown two hops against a contingent of Canadian hotshots—one this afternoon, and one when the sun had finally set. She couldn't imagine the training, concentration and nerve he must have. He'd always come across as an intense guy, of course, but Ryan was a relatively cool customer compared to what his job required.

"I want to see your plane sometime," she said, turning off

the lamp on the nightstand. The only flickering light came from her old television as a subterranean worm tried to eat Michael Gross and Reba McEntire. Her toes were fully dry, so she shed her robe and slipped her legs under the covers.

"I would've shown you last time, but you preferred checking out my apartment."

"Mmm. I particularly liked the entryway. Great view from where I was."

"Are you hiding in the dark?"

Cass froze in the middle of taking a sip of wine. "How did you guess that?"

Lordy, his laugh was sexy. She set the glass aside and settled even deeper into the pillows propped along the headboard. A curl of heat nestled in her belly.

"Because of who you are," he said. "You wouldn't say something that bold with the lights on."

A protest immediately came to mind. After all, she'd been a long way past bold when they played their games. *Are you man enough to fuck me right here?* She'd whispered that in his ear just before they got busy in the sex shop. Then French maid, the call girl, blowing him on his lunch break.

Not exactly timid.

Cass sat up in bed. She'd picked the naughty goth costume. She'd initiated the call girl pick-up evening. She'd even gotten off to the idea of him in his flight suit. What if she'd been so completely misguided as to pin all that on Ryan? And why? Because he'd stared a few extra heartbeats at her stockings. That wasn't conclusive proof. Maybe he'd chosen the French maid's costume to be safe, going along with what she'd already established as fair game. On the spur of the moment, a naughty outfit must've seemed safer than handcuffs or a paddle. Instead of having a laugh, she'd turned it into full-fledged roleplaying by adopting that ridiculous accent. He could've been being polite, not wanting to tell his one-night stand to cut it out.

The idea that she'd been projecting her desires on to him the whole time came as an unsettling possibility. He hadn't brought it up again because he wasn't into it. He hadn't gushed about their hooker evening because, frankly, he was probably happy to have escaped it without being arrested.

Kinky, fun sex with a new girlfriend—perhaps that's all those initial encounters had been for him.

She was the one huddled in the dark. She'd bet an entire year's wages that Ryan didn't need a security blanket to speak his mind. The boldness she'd assumed of herself with regard to their sex life had always been wrapped up inside a persona.

What was she if she didn't have that? What was her relationship with Ryan?

Safe. Normal. Even chatting on the phone about a B-grade horror flick was special.

She'd spent six months with Tommy, bargaining with herself about the same issue. She'd thought *normal* was good enough. She'd thought working at Blakely's and putting off her dreams had been good enough too. The last thing she wanted was to start thinking of her time with Ryan as sinking to those levels of...ordinary.

They were capable of so much more.

"Cass?"

Blinking, she rubbed the rush of goose bumps from her arms. "I'm here. Just refreshing my drink."

She didn't like lying to him and was horrible at deception in person. Only the cell phone's lackluster connection made the attempt even worth trying. Her brain was crowded as she sorted and resorted six weeks' worth of intimacy.

Then she shut it down. She needed time to make sense of what she felt, what she wanted.

As a stalling tactic, she ran headlong into the big question of the evening—the one she'd been putting off. After a deep breath she said, "My parents are having a barbeque in a couple weeks."

The question in her voice was unavoidable. She was still made of *at least* fifty percent scared little girl. Even a miniscule clue about his reaction would give her the nerve to ask outright.

"Oh, yeah?"

Well, there were way worse replies.

She burrowed her nose, eyes, forehead into the nearest pillow. In her mind she pictured how fantastic he'd looked the other night after she quit Blakely's. The sleep-mussed hair. The bare feet and the open fly of his jeans. She wanted that. For a good long time. That meant making them more permanent, by tiny steps. He would be *so* worth it.

So in she jumped. Again.

"Do you think you might want to go? I mean, I know meeting my parents is a big thing. I'd understand if you don't want to."

"I'll go."

"You will?" Her head popped up as if powered by jack-in-the-box springs. The fat, chugging beat of her heart became thin and fast. *Racing.* Giddiness sped around her body, animating each cell. "That'd be great. The last guy I brought around to their place was Tommy."

"And we both know you've upgraded."

"Ha! Watch the ego, Mister Fighter Pilot."

He laughed. "That's *Major* Fighter Pilot."

"I'm warning you, though. They can be overwhelming. Lots of big personalities. They're good people, though."

"I'm not surprised. They raised you, after all."

"Dang, you're suave."

"So you've said. Or gasped and screamed, more like."

Ooh, but he was lowdown. Because gasping and screaming was exactly what she had in mind. He was miles away, which didn't settle right on her heart.

The movie ended almost in tandem with the return of her restless arousal. It was probably time to sign off and go to sleep. She hugged the phone to her ear, not wanting to end their connection.

She had it bad.

Cass slipped her hand beneath the comforter, touching herself. She was wet already, primed and ready to go. The whole conversation had been one long foreplay session—not because they talked dirty, although the occasional innuendo was unavoidable. It was his voice, his humor, his quiet intelligence.

Rarely had she felt so special.

She flipped off the TV. Sure enough, he was right—the question on her tongue became so much easier to speak. "What are you wearing?"

Ryan's low chuckle was a caress in the darkness, petting along her nerve endings. Languid heat spread across her skin like warm water. "Isn't the guy supposed to ask that?"

"Go ahead, then."

"What are you wearing?"

"A pink T-shirt."

She heard his heavy swallow even over the phone. "That's it?"

"Oh, and my pigtails. I was thinking of you."

He moaned softly.

Well, that was interesting. Maybe the either/or option she'd considered earlier didn't apply. If they *both* enjoyed the roleplaying...

Luckily, this was an experiment she could easily conduct. Just like before, the worst case would be if he didn't go for it. She had to try. She didn't want to bury her head in pillows and cloak her fears in darkness. Not with Ryan.

Bold. Daring. She could do that. All she needed to do was consider the potential payoff. They didn't need to sacrifice amazing on the altar of *safe*. Her fighter pilot deserved better, and so did the woman who wanted to be his.

So all that remained was whether she could sound like a sex goddess. She certainly felt like one when she was with Ryan.

This was it. Time to give it a try. There in the dark, she convinced herself that she had nothing to lose.

"You've reached Cassandra's midweek phone-sex hotline," she said, pitching her voice to a slightly husky English accent. "How can I help you?"

Silence.

For the first time since touching herself, she pulled her finger away from her clit. She heard his breathing. That was all. Her insides twisted in crazy, hideous contortions. Waiting.

Waiting for him to say *anything.* Even just "knock it off" would be better than nothing. At least then she'd know.

She let out a shivering breath. His name was on her tongue, to be followed by an apology—probably one steeped in giggling embarrassment.

Then came his whisper. "Don't stop."

A heavy, blazing thrill seemed to press her into the mattress. What she'd felt when he agreed to go to her parents' Memorial Day barbeque was nothing compared to this relief. It wasn't just her. She wasn't alone in thinking this was sexy as hell.

"Hello?" she said, accent in place. "Fellow, this is costing you $1.99 per minute. Either hang up or let's talk."

He cleared his throat. "I've never done this before."

"Then I'll make it easy on you," she said softly. "What are you wearing?"

"Boxer briefs."

"Take them off, please."

After a quick rustle, his breathing became ragged in her ear. She closed her eyes, picturing him lying in the dark, his hand stroking that thick miracle of a cock. Her fingers returned to the slick folds of her pussy. She let a sultry smile shine through in her voice.

"You have quite the prick, I'm sure. You're hard for me, yes, my darling?"

"Very."

"If I were there with you right this moment, I would watch you work. The tendons of your wrist as you stroked. The flare of your nostrils as you inhaled. The fast rise and fall of your magnificent chest. My pleasure would be in soaking up each detail, everything that says you're utterly mad for me." She didn't know about Ryan, but the frankly sexual talk was doing a serious number on her head. The slip-slide of her arousal had flared to a backdraft. "Are you there, my big boy?"

"Yes." He was breathless now, the word harsh.

"Oooh, good. Because I'm so very hot for you. I'm touching my pussy."

Another moan. That rumble brought her closer. So close now.

"Do you know," she said hoarsely, "what we English girls like best in the bedroom?"

"Tell me."

"Why, my good fellow, we simply *adore* a good...hard...spanking."

Ryan grunted the word "fuck" and sank into another groan, this one long and unmistakable. Letting go of all her tension, Cass dedicated herself to her own pleasure. Lordy it came fast. Every giddy, crazy, sexy thing they'd shared came crashing down—especially his last satisfied groan. *She'd* done that. A rush of power threaded through her desire, higher, until her orgasm left her gasping his name.

The bedroom shadows eased into focus. Oh, but she felt good. Rather than spoil the moment by trying to analyze what they'd done, she said, "Lovely, my darling boy. So lovely."

And hung up.

This was definitely an experiment she needed to try again. Cass eased toward sleep with her body sated and her mind awash in possibilities.

Chapter Twenty-Three

The Whitman home was a sprawling tract house in the tidy suburb of Henderson. Red Spanish tiles covered the roof. The walls were a brownish stucco, and dark green trim surrounded the doors and windows. The front yard had been carefully landscaped with pea gravel and arrangements of desert plants. There was even a white picket fence, though it was in miniature and surrounded a cactus garden nestled along the walls.

With Cassandra's hand snug within his, Ryan had a weirdly nostalgic feeling as he walked up the flagstone pathway to the front door. He'd always wanted a house like this one. Nothing huge. Just a neatness that said the owners cared about their home and family.

Meanwhile, he was about to walk in holding the hand of their daughter—with whom he'd had kinky phone sex. Not just phone sex, but a serious mind fuck when she'd slipped into a naughty English accent and worked him like a pro. *Again.* As if she had a direct line to exactly what wrenched him into knots—what he'd been trying to ignore for weeks.

"You ready?" she asked.

He shifted the huge bowl of fruit salad propped under one arm. Cassandra had prepared it, but he'd insisted on carrying it for her. "I fly planes and bomb the hell out of bad guys. Why wouldn't I be ready for your family?"

She patted his biceps. "It'll be okay. You don't have to be nervous."

"I'm not nervous," he said, but even he heard the tension threading through his voice.

Parents loved him. They always had. They'd loved him way back in high school, when anyone in their right mind would have kept their daughters way away from him and his trashy mother. Not many had looked past his role as the school's quarterback hero. He'd been able to charm them too by being forthright about his intentions. Since he had a plan—going to college and then flying—he hadn't been about to screw up anyone else's life.

This was different. Explaining why was beyond him, but it was.

Cassandra didn't knock, instead just throwing open the door and calling out, "We're here."

A middle-aged, slightly faded copy of Cassandra emerged from what must've been the kitchen, wiping her hands on a dishcloth. "Hey, darling."

The women hugged, then Cassandra stood with an arm looped around her mother's shoulders. "Mom, this is Major Ryan Haverty. Ryan, this is my mom, Betsy." Her eyes twinkled.

"Major Haverty, happy to meet you."

They shook hands. "Please, call me Ryan."

"Only if you promise to call me Betsy." Her bright smile was an exact mirror of Cassandra's. She was still slim too, probably from regularly leading hiking trips.

"I see where Cassandra gets her good looks."

"Oh, you are a smooth one, aren't you?" She laughed and shook her head as she led them down a hallway lined with pictures of Cassandra and another girl. "Did Cass tell you how happy we were that she dumped that scumbag and quit the restaurant? So far you seem like a definite improvement."

"Mom," Cassandra moaned. "There's no reason to get into any of that."

Betsy waved the dishcloth at her daughter. "There's no reason not to. When you got rid of Tommy, we all cheered. No harm in telling the truth."

When Ryan smothered a laugh, Cassandra slugged him in the shoulder. He brushed a kiss over her cheek in apology.

They emerged into a comfortable family room. A huge sectional couch in brown leather took up most of two walls. The third supported an enormous flat-screen TV. "Now this is the life." Ryan laughed.

"I thought you'd like it." Betsy's brow wrinkled in confusion. "Now, where did I put that man?"

"Dad's not a footstool, Mom." Cassandra rolled her eyes. "He *is* able to move under his own power."

"Pish, I know that. I just thought he'd be watching the coverage."

They followed Betsy through a set of French doors that opened onto a wide deck. "The coverage?" Ryan echoed.

He felt like he'd lost the thread of the conversation. Being part of a close family must be like that—already knowing what the other person was talking about. He had no frame of reference.

Cassandra laced her fingers through his. "The Indianapolis 500. Dad's a freak for anything that drives fast. If we stick around too long, we'll be sucked into watching the NASCAR race this evening too."

"If anyone around here understands the appeal of fast cars, I'd be willing to bet it's this guy." Mr. Whitman stood over a barbeque that was just heating up. He was a tall man, only a couple inches shorter than Ryan. "I'm Keith."

"Pleased to meet you."

They shook, then Keith shrugged at his wife. "It was a commercial break. Thought I'd get the barbeque up and running."

"What, so you can let it sit there until the race finishes? Go sit. Enjoy."

Keith waved her off, reaching for the bowl of fruit salad. His knuckles were pretty gnarled for a man his age. Ryan might have stared if Cassandra hadn't told him about her dad's arthritis, her voice laced with worry.

"Let me take that from you." Keith placed it on a table against the side of the house, which was covered with plates and platters of everything from pasta salad to a cheese plate. He aimed a tsking noise at Cassandra. "Not that you had to bring anything, little girl."

Ryan quirked an eyebrow. "Little girl?"

"I'm younger than Emily by two years," she said with a shrug. "I'll always be the little one. Nothing I can say changes his mind."

Next Ryan was introduced to Cassandra's sister, Emily,

and her family. Her husband Robert was hippy-dip granola with his goatee and longish hair, but he seemed like a nice guy. Their daughter was about seven and looked an awful lot like the picture of Cassandra with her teeth missing, except that young Claire's hair and eyes were brown.

She looked up at him with a teddy bear under one arm. "You fly planes?"

Ryan hadn't ever had much interaction with kids. He glanced around for some help, but Cassandra had abandoned him. She stood at the food table with her mom and sister, chatting away. "I do."

"Does that mean you're in the Army?"

He shoved his hands in his pockets. "Um, no. I'm in the Air Force. The Army only has helicopters."

"My grandpa was in the Army. A long time ago. I like the Army best. See?" She held up the bear, which was white and sparkly but inexplicably dressed in a tiny pink T-shirt and camo pants. "Susie's an Army bear. She's from Build-A-Bear. She fights bad guys."

"Well, dang." He pulled from his pocket the toy he'd bought on impulse during his lunch hour on Thursday. He'd been in the BX, picking up a Red Bull and a Slim Jim in order to get back to his maintenance logs, when he spotted it. When he'd realized it was even painted in Aggressor gray like his jet, he plunked it down onto the register. "I think Susie's too big to fly this."

Claire's big brown eyes went huge. "No, I think she could. She'd fit." She nodded earnestly. The thick bangs cut across her forehead wiggled with the move. "She would."

"Then I think maybe she should have it."

After snatching it away, Claire threw a "Thank you" over her shoulder as she ran to show her mom.

The women leaned down in tandem. Though Emily had light brown hair like Keith, the three shared a significant strain of resemblance. More than that—they even moved in similar ways. As one, they looked up from Claire to smile at him.

Ryan rubbed a hand across the back of his neck. Being the focus of so much attention was uncomfortable. He had to admit that seeing them all grin was kind of fun. Instantaneous acceptance.

Just...weird.

The next couple hours were much more enjoyable than he'd expected. After the Indy pre-race interviews wrapped up, Keith grilled steaks and hot dogs, politely but firmly refusing Ryan's offer of help. They ate while gathered around a glass-topped patio table under a green umbrella. By the time they all devoured seconds—and thirds for Emily—barely a dent had been made in the piles of food.

Keith pushed his chair back and patted his belly. "I tell you what, this is why a man's got to own his own business. To be with his family on the best day of the year."

Cassandra curled her hand around Ryan's knee. "Dad, what about Christmas?"

"Christmas is good too."

"Honey," Betsy said, "we're so proud of your event. We're all going to be there."

Ryan glanced at Cassandra out of the corner of his eye. She still hadn't invited him. He'd assumed at first it wasn't a family-and-friends sort of thing.

She squeezed his thigh, perhaps sensing his discomfort. "Later," she whispered. In a louder voice she said, "Mom, it's an exhibit."

"Yes, that." She beamed. "Will it be those flower pictures? Like Monet? I like those."

"Um, not...exactly."

At the other end of the table, Emily and her husband were whispering. Ryan caught a quick, "Not now," from Emily, but her husband stood anyway.

Robert held up his bottle of Bud. "Everyone, we've got a bit of an announcement." Emily blushed and ducked her chin.

Claire jumped up and down in her seat. "I'm going to be a big sister."

"Oh, honey!" Betsy squealed and clapped her hands. "Is it true?"

Emily grinned. "In December."

The entire family broke into happy chatter. Betsy and Cassandra leapt up and swallowed Emily in hugs. Keith and Robert exchanged several rounds of backslapping. Even Ryan got dragged into the excitement, hugged by both Betsy and Claire, who spent most of her time dancing around the table chanting, "Big sister! Big sister!"

By the time the noise died down, they'd shifted back into the glorious living room. Everyone staked out positions on the couch, apparently in it for the duration. Cassandra slipped off her sandals and eased against Ryan's chest. He wrapped an arm around her shoulders, trailing his fingers up and down her bare arm. The whole scene was just so damn homey.

He found himself drawn into the NASCAR race on the huge television. Planes were his big adrenaline rush, so he hadn't thought stock cars would hold any appeal. Keith had been right—the speed was, as always, intoxicating. Drivers only zoomed around in circles for hundreds of miles, but with the surround sound it was almost like being there.

After the fiftieth lap, Cassandra left to get a drink from the kitchen but took forever to come back. Ryan went looking for her.

She was in the kitchen all right, but her mom had caught her in a whispered conversation. He hung back.

"Cass, we're going to need you more this summer. Probably the fall too."

She shook her head. "I don't think I can."

Betsy's eyes widened. "Your sister can't do tours in the heat when she's pregnant."

"I know, Mom, but I'm working more than full-time at the gallery. That means working weekends. They don't pay me enough to be picky and make my own work schedules."

"If you're worried about the money, your dad and I will help. We can put you on at full-time. Give you the best routes so you get good tips."

"I don't know, Mom..." Her voice trailed off in a way Ryan hadn't heard before. Hesitant. Even scared.

He didn't like it. At all.

He stepped fully over the threshold. "Cassandra, can you

come explain what's going on? Your dad keeps cheering for wrecks. That's not something we generally do on base." He held out a hand.

The laugh she dredged up sounded strained. She slipped her small hand into his. "That sounds like him."

They never made it back to the living room. In the hallway she pulled him to a stop with a playful tug. "Hey, are you ready to get out of here?"

He curled his hands around her shoulders, then trailed up to brush his thumb along her jaw. "You sure?"

Other than catching her mom gently strong-arming Cassandra, he'd been having a pretty good time. He and his friends created makeshift families at their various duty stations—to have somewhere to go for holidays, if nothing else—but that wasn't the same as being smack in the middle of a real one.

She looped her index fingers through his belt. "Yeah, I'm positive. I've had enough for one day."

Ryan kissed her softly. Although he'd sworn he was going to keep things strictly PG while in her parents' house, his body didn't want to listen. He needed to pull back. "Then of course we can go. Anywhere you want."

Chapter Twenty-Four

Cass really liked riding in the passenger seat of Ryan's giant Ford. The truck made her feel tall and solid, so unlike her low, cramped Honda. The early evening air was still warm, but not oppressive. They'd left off the A/C and opened the windows. Wind tossed her hair back from her face as she stretched and snuggled into the leather bucket seat. She didn't even know where they were going, having simply asked Ryan to drive.

Emily pregnant. Tours all summer and fall. That wasn't how she'd wanted the rest of this year to be—this year when she might actually get unstuck. Her stomach knotted around all that rich barbeque. Not good.

She wasn't surprised when they arrived at Nellis. After flashing his ID at a security guard, he drove her back beyond the hangar where she'd seen him chewing out those pilots. Rows of jet planes lined up like overgrown toys or movie props. He parked, then reached in the backseat for his leather flight jacket and credentials. They didn't say a word. He only smiled before coming around to open her door.

Wow, but he looked absolutely amazing. His neatly pressed forest button-down brought out the green in his eyes. Wranglers hugged his thick thighs, flaring to drape over polished brown cowboy boots. After helping Cass down, he shrugged into his flight jacket and adjusted the collar. She swallowed tightly as he ran a hand through his hair, which was dark with shadows. Against the backdrop of those planes, he was a man in his prime and in the place he belonged.

Crazy to think she might belong with him.

She looped her arms around his neck and kissed him. No warning. No explanation. She needed to.

However, she ended the embrace before she was ready. Ryan's easy grace had stiffened. He was in his element.

Apparently that meant he had a certain professional distance.

"This way," he said, taking her hand.

He walked her down the line of planes before stopping in front of one in particular. *Maj. Ryan Haverty* was stenciled just below the seam sealing the cockpit.

She smiled, reaching out to touch the machine. "You have your own plane."

"You sound surprised."

"I don't know. I thought maybe you shared them." She mock glared at him. "Don't laugh! What I know about the military could fit in a shot glass."

"Okay. Air Combat Command 101. We have our own planes. That's Tin Tin's," he said pointing, "and that one is for the Princess herself. They're all the same F-16s, but none of them flies exactly the same. The smallest variations can make a big difference in the air."

She eyed his friends' fighters. "Who's the better pilot?"

"I'm not a major for nothing."

"I'm serious."

"Leah," he said, sobering. "By far. She's...gifted. Jon's a genius. He never makes technical mistakes, but he still has something to prove."

Cass liked these frank assessments. They revealed so much about not only Jon and Leah, but about Ryan's capacities as a leader. "What about you?"

His sober expression turned almost sad, although she couldn't say why. "I just work harder than anyone."

"*Just?* That's huge."

He shrugged. "That's what I bring to the table."

Apparently changing the subject, he moved on to some of the technical aspects of the plane. Cass had to hide her grin. He likely wore the same glazed-over feeling when she talked art, but his enthusiasm was catching. Cannons and hardpoints, g-force and dogfights. The unfamiliar terms blended together.

"Sorry," he said, chuckling. "I know I can go on. I just love this damned thing." As if realizing what he'd revealed, he cleared his throat. "I'd let you see inside, but the ladders are back in the hangar."

"Some other time," she said, dazed enough by what he'd already shown her. The idea that he sat in that cockpit every day, as routinely as she drove her dinky Civic, and flew a thousand miles an hour was overwhelming. His day job.

He was just so...*cool.* There wasn't another word for it, although a few choice adjectives came to mind. Impressive. Potent. Sexy.

They jumped back into his truck and drove to the outskirts of the base. He kept a blanket in the back of the cab. They lay on the lowered tailgate, her head pillowed by his chest. The desert evening closed in around them, illuminated by the lights from the base and the runway.

"This is my favorite spot," he said.

It was a simple, almost throwaway sentence, but Cass took it for what it was: an invitation into his head. Maybe even into his heart. No matter what they'd shared so far, those invitations had been few and far between.

"A good thinking spot." Voice neutral. No gushing girly stuff. She was proud of herself.

He made an affirmative grunt, petting her waist. "Your family's great. I had a good time."

"I'm glad."

"That's big news, about your sister."

"They've been trying for a long time. They never intended Claire to be an only child. I'd almost given up thinking about it. Just resigned, you know?"

"It'll make your parents' business trickier, though."

"I'm sure they won't mind." Cass sighed. "We all help out. That's family."

He angled up on his elbow, looking down at her face. "I heard you and your mom in the kitchen. About you taking more tours."

Her skin went cold. "Oh."

"Is it what you want?"

"You know it's not. What choice do I have?"

"Tell them no. They can hire other tour guides, I'm sure."

Cass pushed to a sitting position. She shivered. Without a word, Ryan slipped out of his flight jacket and wrapped it around her shoulders. The leather still held his scent, his heat. "You don't understand how things have been lately, with the economy. Vegas is all...shriveled. My folks keep cutting costs, but there just aren't as many tourists." She choked back a surprising sob. "They need me."

Ryan leaned forward, cupping her cheek. "*You* have needs too. Their job was to raise you up to be your own person. Your own interests. *Your* future."

"I don't know about that," she said with a wobbling smile. "Sometimes I think they'd rather I was more like Emily. She's always loved the business. If they could build a big Kennedy-style compound and have us all live together, they would."

He cocked a sexy grin. "I'm not down with that."

"Me neither, goosey. But maybe you can see why it's been so difficult for me. I'd love to just go for it—do what I want, when I want."

"Yeah, but now I've been in the mancave, overcome by a food coma. That would blunt anyone's ambitions."

"Even yours?"

"Hell, I wanted to stay and finish the race."

His humor, as always, eased her back from the cliff of her nerves. She took a deep breath and asked what she'd been putting off. "Would you like to come to the exhibit opening?"

"I'd love to. I'd begun to wonder if you were going to ask me."

"I wasn't sure if it would be your kind of thing. Sort of tame." She pressed her cheek against his chest.

"Baby, anywhere you're at is my sort of thing."

Cass giggled. She went to tickle him on that special spot above his ribs, but the flight jacket made a crinkling noise she hadn't expected.

Feeling inside the warm leather, she found a stiff place in the lining. "What's this?"

"Blood chit."

"A what?"

"It's a message in a bunch of languages. That way if I'm ever shot down, the locals will know to return me to the nearest US outpost."

She zipped right on past the idea of him being shot down. That was forbidden territory. "Does that work?"

"Who knows. It goes back to WWII when it was in French and Russian. Now it's Pashto, Persian, Arabic."

"You were in combat."

"Four tours in Afghanistan and three in Iraq." Mentioned so blithely, he summed up his whole wartime experience in a few words. Cass could only make the attempt to wrap her head around that gut-wrenching information. He squinted toward the desert stars. "Seems like a helluva long way from here."

The whining roar of an aircraft engine fired to life.

"Oh, nice," Ryan said. "A C-130. I hadn't expected anything to take off tonight."

"Are we okay here?"

He nuzzled behind her ear. "No, baby, I've put you in terrible danger."

As the engine noise grew steadily louder, Cass couldn't help her sense of anticipation. They were right under the flight path. The huge transport was, relatively, a small speck in the distance, but soon it'd be flying right over their heads.

"You want earplugs? I think I've got some in my glove box."

"Will I need them?"

Ryan broke open a wide smile. "Either that or cover your ears."

Minutes passed. She felt jumpy and jittery, like a kid waiting for Santa Claus. Finally the C-130 began its long journey down the runway. They were still seated on the truck's tailgate, but Cass felt the vibrations shaking into her butt and crossed legs. A heavy bass rumble messed with the rhythm of her heart. She held Ryan's hand until the sound became too powerful. With her palms pressed against her ears, she watched in mute wonder as the transport's front wheel lifted from the ground.

It didn't seem possible. It was too big.

The gigantic engines overcame gravity. The rear wheels lifted. Like a huge bloated metal bird, the C-130 thrust through the air, growling directly overhead. Cass couldn't breathe. Her whole body shook. A hot wash of air that stunk of gasoline followed in its wake.

Then it was gone.

She tentatively lowered her hands, her pulse frantic. "Wow," she whispered.

"Wow's right." He looked nearly as satisfied as after he'd just climaxed. Cass realized her competition wouldn't ever be limited to other women. Planes and danger and flying Mach two...or Cass Whitman. Intimidating. How in the world was she ever going to live up?

"What's it like, flying?"

He turned those gorgeous hazel eyes on her, still wistful. "Amazing. Breathtaking."

"How did you know it would be that way? What got you started?"

Rubbing the back of his neck, he seemed to almost hunch in on himself. The posture wasn't defensive, not in the classic sense, but Cass immediately felt the distance.

"You remember that coach I mentioned? Dan?"

"Yeah."

"He took me and a couple guys from the team up in his Cessna. It was only a small four-seater, but damn." He shook his head. "Changed my life."

"How old were you?"

"Sixteen. I was already pretty lucky not to be in juvie, but that gave me the extra push to get my act together."

"Juvie?"

He flinched, then exhaled heavily. "I got caught with pot when I was fourteen, at some party in our trailer park. The cops showed up. I was completely busted, probably because I was too high."

Cass couldn't take it in fast enough. Pot. Being high. Trailer park. She'd just seen Ryan with his fighter jet—in his element. Images of his childhood were a million miles away, like someone else entirely. Maybe that was true. He certainly wasn't that kid anymore.

"They hauled me down to the station, probably just to scare some sense into me. I could've called my mom." He shrugged. "It was a Friday night. She wouldn't have been home. So I called Dan. I was on the JV squad, only a freshman. He showed up anyway. The cops let me off without charges, but soon enough I wanted to be safe behind bars."

"Dan rip you a new one?"

"At first. It was his disappointment that got to me most. I'd never..." His voice trailed off. Cass took his hand, quietly begging him to continue. "I'd never had anyone give a damn before."

The lump in her throat was thick and hot.

He adjusted his shoulders against that old burden. "So yeah, after that it was just getting away from what I'd been. Made varsity as a sophomore. My grades were still pretty bad. Got into a crappy community college. Found out the military doesn't care where your degree comes from. By the time I arrived at OTC and then flight school, I'd really hit my stride."

She touched his face, the slight evening stubble scoring her palm. "And he lived happily ever after."

"Sure."

His cell phone rang and he was quick to answer. Cass could've smashed the thing with a sledgehammer. She wanted more. More of who he was, but the moment was lost.

"Yeah, sounds good," he said. "We'll be there in a bit." After hanging up, he jumped down from the tailgate—not that it was much of a jump for such a tall guy. "Jon and Leah are at a club. Sounds like fun."

Not only was the moment lost, he had it in lockdown. He'd never made plans for both of them without asking her first. Cass tried to hide visible signs of her frustration.

"You dance?"

"Me? Oh, hell no." Ryan laughed, donning his All-American armor. "Although Princess is a serious diva when she drinks, and Tin Tin's always good for a few laughs."

Apparently that was what he needed right now.

As she hauled herself into the passenger seat, Cass decided to let go of the heavy, unexpected emotions brought on by their day. Soon enough Memorial Day weekend would be over, and she'd need to decide what to do about her family.

Chapter Twenty-Five

They were halfway across Vegas when Cassandra's wiggling and twisting in the passenger seat caught Ryan's attention. "What are you doing?"

"I wasn't really dressed for a club." She slanted an unreadable glance at him before bending her head to her knees and giving her hair a shake. "Since no one asked me, I'm getting ready."

He tightened his fingers around the steering wheel. Her voice only carried the slightest hint of reproach and she'd been smiling—but he felt a pinch of chagrin anyway. No denying that he'd signed them both up to meet his friends.

He'd wanted out of there. Flat-out truth.

Having ditched those embarrassing years a long time ago, he didn't like revisiting them, no matter that Cassandra deserved some honesty. She'd taken a risk inviting him to meet her family, letting him see why she sometimes felt trapped. Quid pro quo and that shit. That hadn't made the facts any easier to spit out.

He'd escaped. End of story. He didn't want to have to drag up the crap all over again.

When she sat back up, her shimmering hair was tousled into a mess reminiscent of when they'd awaken wrapped up together on weekend mornings—or not long after they'd gone to bed, the strands tangled as they got busy. She stripped the demure short-sleeved sweater she'd been wearing, leaving only a clingy, strappy top that showed off her breasts.

"How the hell did you do that?"

Cassandra grinned at him as she reached behind her back. "Girl magic. Wait 'til you see the rest."

Be damned if the next twist of her shoulders didn't have

her bra falling into her hand in a lacy pile. The perky mounds of her breasts pushed against a top that now seemed skimpier. So far her nipples were bare pokes, but he hoped that wouldn't last long. Ryan's mouth watered.

After digging in her purse for a minute, she dabbed something on her lips and eyes that made her even hotter. More sultry. From suburban princess to club girl in two minutes flat.

That ability to turn herself into another person entirely...

He shifted in his seat and tried to use logic, rather than letting his dick do the thinking. She still wore the same jeans as at her parents' house, but they looked entirely different with an inch of her bare skin showing above the waistband. Her mouth was more lush than normal, glistening with a gloss that reminded him of their epic lunch break, the one where she'd wrapped her mouth around his cock until he exploded. Her breasts bounced slightly as the Ford chugged over a speed bump in the club parking lot.

More than that, even her demeanor had changed. She wasn't the cute younger daughter who'd spent the morning assembling a fruit salad. The slinky curve of her waist reminded him of how she looked while riding him to a ravishing finish. The eighteen inches between her knees—was that intentional? As if she were inviting him to imagine the possibilities. She used her clothes to adjust her outlook on an intimidating world, like a chameleon changing the color of its skin.

She angled one arm across the open window and smirked at him. "See? Girl magic."

"I'd complain about false advertising, but you're way hot normally."

She giggled. "I'd kiss you for that one, but I'd get lip gloss all over you."

"It's probably not my color."

The club was housed in a sprawling industrial complex on the edge of town, which meant that Leah must've picked it. Jon preferred the lux, big-money places nearer the Strip that sported one or two idle paparazzi hanging around outside. Tin Tin might never make the papers, but apparently his family was hooked into some invisible uppity-up information network. They spit nails whenever they learned of Jon out boozing it up. However, the venue on that night's agenda wasn't the type—more like where the locals went to get their fuck-the-tourists on after work. Ryan stripped down to his white undershirt so he wouldn't stand out too much.

He kept an arm slung low on Cassandra's waist as they wove through the club's different levels. There was no way to miss how her hips started working the second a heavy bass line wrapped around them.

He might even be willing to dance with this woman. Such a sap.

They found Jon sitting at a table on the highest level, of course, where the music was muted and the atmosphere as refined as the place got. He'd staked out a corner table where he could see everything. A bleach blonde in a sparkly top cut down almost to her black leather pants leaned over the table. Jon dismissed her as soon as Ryan and Cassandra walked in. She flounced away with a pout on her collagen-injected lips.

Ryan held out a chair for Cassandra, then sat next to her. "I hope we didn't interrupt anything."

Jon's eyes narrowed. "What do you mean?"

"The chickie," Cassandra explained for them both. "She looked pretty interested in you."

The shrug that folded his shoulders said he didn't care in the least. "No challenge."

Ryan couldn't help but laugh, letting go of the last of the tension he'd been holding. Jon could be such an egotistical jackass. Only his unstinting loyalty to his friends made up for his arrogance. "Where's Princess?"

"Shaking her ass down on the hip-hop level, I think." He waved for the waitress, who came bounding over, although she'd been serving another table.

"What would you like?" she asked Jon with a smile.

By the time the drinks arrived, Leah had reappeared. Sweat dampened her forehead and stuck dark strands of hair to her cheeks. She draped herself in a chair beside Jon and smiled at Cassandra. "Glad you lovebirds could make it. I was beginning to think you were keeping Fang strapped to a bed."

Cassandra's eyes sparkled, even in the dim light of the club. "Now that's not a bad thought…"

Ryan groaned. He stretched his arm across the back of her chair, trailing touches over her soft shoulder. "Geez, don't give her any ideas."

"Hush, you." Cassandra folded her arms on the table and leaned in. "Feel free to give me all the ideas you want."

"Help me out here, Tin Tin," Ryan said.

Jon only crossed his arms over his chest. "No way. Don't you know this is a one-in-a-million chance?" He waved between the two women. "They look like they're setting up for girl talk. Girl *sex* talk. We may never have this opportunity to peer into the murky depths again."

Keeping his smile in place became a bit more difficult when his insides twisted. If Cassandra gave him the least hint, Jon would pick apart their dynamic in seconds. The shudder Ryan gave wasn't the least bit forced, but he played it up anyway. "Like I really want to know about Princess's murky depths."

Cassandra walked her fingers up his thigh. "You don't have to play. I know you two dated, remember?"

Laughing, Leah picked up her margarita. "Yeah, but there was no depth-exploring. Trust me on that one. We were all sorts of shallow. Probably why it ended so damn quickly."

Ryan watched Cassandra out the corners of his eyes. He wasn't sure if he hoped she caught the implication—that yeah, they had been getting down and dirty, but he'd let slip more with her than with any other woman. The realization of just how much she'd edged under his skin was both appealing and chilling. Not frightening, because he still had his balls. More like unsettling. Nerve-racking. He was living at DEFCON 1, always locked and cocked.

He managed to shift the conversation but couldn't keep control of it for long. Leah had just waved for another round of drinks when she leaned across the table and crooked her finger at Cassandra. "I bet Fang hasn't even told you what hot shit he is, right?"

Confusion wrinkled Cassandra's brow. "What do you mean?"

"You're dating a freakin' war hero," Leah said on a grin. Her voice had started to slur the tiniest bit.

Ryan rubbed a hand across the back of his head. "Don't be ridiculous. We've all been over there. Done what we had to. That's all."

Most of the time, he didn't mind the shit-talking—trading stories when the drinks got too deep. No way did he miss the way Cassandra's eyes darkened. She'd lost her tip-tilted smile.

As oblivious as always, Leah went on. "My favorite is the way Fang got his first Distinguished Flying Cross. I was there for that one."

Jon aimed a smile at Cassandra. "Your boy rocked it out."

"Outside Fallujah," Leah said. "Remember?"

"Course." Ryan wrapped a hand around his beer bottle, but there was no cooling his palms. He had the sudden, ridiculous wish that the music in their corner of the club would crank up. Make more talking impossible.

"It was a thing of beauty," Leah said with a shake of her head.

"Do tell." Jon's sly smile said he knew exactly what this was doing to Ryan.

"We were flying low already because it was getting dark and there were too many friendlies on the ground. Fang here spotted a convoy and pushed even lower. Took out half the thing all by himself—with his 20-millimeter cannon." She even provided sound effects. "Though they were trying to strafe him with anti-aircraft guns. Just *fab* flying."

Ryan risked another glance to where Cassandra took it in with wide eyes. Her mouth fell open as her gaze darted between Tin Tin and Princess.

Across all the times he wondered what it would be like to have someone waiting at home for him, he'd never considered the actuality. That person would be worried, scared shitless sometimes, when he was just doing his job and protecting the rest of his flight. As far as he could tell, his mom hadn't had a clue. He'd done the good-son thing every time, telling her when he was going over. She'd always seemed surprised when he called to say he was home, like she'd forgotten where he went.

There it was, almost four years after the incident Leah described, and Cassandra responded as if to fast-breaking news. Her breathing had gone shallow while her fingers clenched his knee.

Ryan wrapped his hand over hers and pried it free, finger by finger. After lacing his hand through hers, he drew it up to his mouth and feathered a kiss over her white knuckles. “That was awhile ago.”

Her eyebrows rose, her smile looking forced. The corners of her eyes were pinched. “Oh really, Major? You wanna tell me you wouldn’t go back?”

“If I was told to,” he said with a forced shrug.

“Right. You’re an instructor.”

“For now,” Leah added blithely.

He could’ve killed the woman. Buried her body in the desert and let the javelinas have her. Instead he kicked her in the shins.

“What the hell was that for?”

Jon smirked. “Have another drink, Princess, and you won’t care.”

Pushing away from the table, Ryan tugged Cassandra up. “Want to go dance?”

Her smile became more natural, just enough that his chest loosened in response. “I thought you didn’t dance.”

He wrapped an arm around her waist. Having her snuggled against his hip both wired him up and calmed him down. He traced idle patterns over the silky-smooth skin above her waist, enjoying how her muscles jumped under his touch. “I don’t. However, making a strategic retreat when appropriate? I do that.”

She stretched up on her toes and pressed a kiss to his jaw. “I’ll take what I can get. Come on. We’ll see you guys in a bit.”

Jon saluted them with his glass of scotch while Leah signaled the waitress. Again.

Ryan let Cassandra lead the way, holding tight to her hand so he didn’t lose her in the sweaty press of bodies. She wove through the crowds to the retro room, where ’80s pop spilled out the door on a wave of synthesized notes.

Robert Palmer's "Addicted to Love" was in full swing when Cass wrapped her arms around his shoulders and started a cruel, grinding shimmy. Ryan couldn't help but laugh even as he palmed her hips and did his best to keep up without looking like a spastic chicken.

Addicted to Cassandra, was more like it.

Chapter Twenty-Six

Abandoning the tension of the previous few minutes, Cass lost herself in one song after another. It wasn't difficult, considering the perfect match of music and dance partner.

The DJ spun what sounded like Cass's very own "If I Were a Stripper" playlist. Classic '80s sexiness, but always with an element of cheeky humor. Years spent traveling with her family into the desert, and hanging around their home office where Mom always played music, meant she could either learn to love it or go bonkers. She'd chosen, quite predictably, to go along.

As she dug her hips into the throbbing beat of Aerosmith's "Rag Doll", her thoughts flew far from those childhood days. She gave herself to the moment. The air in the club was heavy with the humidity, wet with the collected sweat and respiration of so many dancers. Particolored lights flicked up and over and around a hundred bobbing heads. The ceiling in that particular room was low, giving Cass the impression of dancing in a broad, square cave. They were primitive people reveling in the dark.

"Raspberry Beret" by Prince faded into "I'm Goin' Down" by Bruce Springsteen, which made Ryan smile.

"You like this?" Cass shouted, right up close to his ear.

"Gotta love The Boss."

"Oh, yeah. You're a keeper."

She swiped a slick piece of hair off her forehead, then dipped in time to the next bass-drum kick. Sometimes she caught a flash of skin or a couple leaning into one another's space, but mostly she kept her eyes on Ryan. Her dear Major Haverty had absolutely no grace for dancing. Apparently he saved his rhythm for sex where his lean hips never failed to find the right pulse.

She appreciated his willingness to humor her and wow, did

he look fantastic. He'd stripped the respectable button-down, leaving only a plain white T-shirt. To say that a dose of sweaty dancing did the boy's body good was an understatement. The white cotton plastered to his chest and hugged his shoulders—her own candy ready to be unwrapped.

She liked how he gave her space to move, not hanging on her and trying to cop clumsy feels. A slightly bemused humor tipped his lips into a half-smile. Never had she been with a guy who made her feel that everything she did was special. That laser-beam intensity of his could be intimidating as hell, but it was also a potent drug.

She looped her forearms around his neck and pulled up close. A quick lick along his throat left a sexy, salty taste on her tongue. Ryan seemed to take that as she'd intended: an invitation. He grabbed her ass with both hands, reintroducing their hips. Nearly six weeks together meant she was becoming more familiar with his body's responses. He wasn't hard, not yet, but his hands had taken on that edgy, filthy tension that said he was in the mood to get busy.

Cass was running on adrenaline but wasn't quite ready to give up the night. A hefty dose of emotion waited for them outside the club, and she didn't feel strong enough to face it.

"Let's get a drink?" she asked when the song ended.

Ryan nodded and, damp hands laced together, led her back to the corner table where the noise was so much less. Leah was nowhere to be found, but a rather curvaceous brunette sat next to Jon. They made for an odd couple—his lean, buzz-cut precision and her rounded flesh. He seemed far more interested in her than the stereotypical bleach blonde from earlier in the evening.

"Hey," he said. "This is…?"

"Julie," the woman supplied.

After those casual introductions, Ryan left to grab a Red Bull for himself and a beer for Cass.

She and Julie chatted for a bit, but soon the conversation lagged. Glancing around, she looked for Ryan in the crowd by the bar. His tall frame was easy to find, and a nearby black light turned his T-shirt into a neon beacon.

"*Une femme aux courbes très généreuses*," Jon said, almost to himself.

She turned to find his gaze on Julie's bare shoulder. *Such lovely curves?* Cass laughed.

He lifted one arched eyebrow, pausing in the motion of taking a sip of scotch. She couldn't remember his having ordered another, just nursing that one round. "*Parlez-vous français?*"

"*Oui. Il y a un an que je l'ai etudié à Montparnasse.*"

"Oh, don't you two start," Ryan said. He set Cass's Corona on the table and settled in, his arm around her shoulder.

"Where did you learn?" Cass asked.

Jon shrugged. "Prep school."

"Your accent is great. That means you kept with it."

"Watch it, baby," Ryan said with a rumbling chuckle. "You catch Dimples here being sincere and it'll blow his cover."

Leah appeared like some sort of amped-up version of herself. Her ponytail was a thing of the past. Long dark hair, all a tousled mess, made her look like she were already suffering from the regrets of a morning after. Three shots of tequila were neatly balanced in one palm. In the other hand she carried drippy lime slices and a salt shaker.

"Time to get this party started," she said, her voice fuzzy. "Here, Tin Tin."

"I drove, Your Highness. No thanks."

"Fine." She slammed two shots herself, one after the other. Julie took the third. "Fang, you remember that time we found Alley Cat's stash in his footlocker?"

The story built on itself, returning inevitably to the trio's history together. A half hour passed without Cass being able to contribute a word. Worse, her stomach knotted over each new detail of the danger they'd faced together.

Finally she leaned close to Ryan and said, "I'll be back. Ladies' room."

She slipped away before he could reply.

Soon she stood leaning against a stall's graffiti-smeared wall. A mash of words and images filled her brain. Jon's provocative smirk. Leah's fabulous rack, which was inevitably followed by a reminder that she'd slept with Ryan. The worst, however, was the smooth slither of dread that coated Cass's skin. Every round of war stories choked off the blood to her heart.

Literal war stories.

Finding Ryan sexy and potent had been much less complicated when reality stayed clear of her fantasies. Even seeing his fighter jet hadn't brought it home, not like the eager way Leah and Jon bragged up Ryan's daring. He was ambitious in life, having pulled himself out of a slummy childhood by willpower. Heck, she was still trying to process that new information as it was.

Knowing he was equally determined in combat soured her stomach. His profession made her family's trips into the Canyon seem no more dangerous than heading to the 7-Eleven for a Slurpee.

Shoving off the wall, she washed her hands and splashed water on the back of her neck. She couldn't hide in the bathroom. She needed to head back out there and smile, even if the pilots' histories and nicknames and bewildering Air Force terms made her feel as competent as a rock. Rarely had she been more of an outsider. Even knowing, logically, that Ryan would be equally lost among a group of her colleagues from the gallery—or even with her family—didn't help. None of them were in the habit of flying faster than the speed of sound, risking death every time they clocked in.

What if I can't handle it?

She'd only just risked standing up to the owner of a family steakhouse. No one but a fool would think she'd reached a point far enough along on the mouse-to-superhero spectrum to endure getting seriously involved with a fighter pilot. Putting on a few accents was embarrassingly naive by comparison.

The door to the ladies' room swung open. Leah staggered in, with Jon right on her heels. He nodded once to Cass, his expression stripped of flippancy as he followed his colleague into the handicapped stall. For a moment she wondered if Ryan had actually got them wrong. Maybe they'd snuck away for a quickie in the bathroom. The sound of Leah retching put the kibosh on that idea.

Not knowing the dynamics of this particular drama, Cass stood rooted next to the pair of grungy sinks. Jon's voice pulled her free of indecision when he called, "Cass, could you bring us some towels?"

She grabbed the freestanding roll of brown paper towels off the backsplash. Inside the handicapped stall, Jon squatted while using the cinderblock wall for balance. He was remarkably calm despite the situation, managing to keep his mod-style dress slacks clean. A watch that looked super expensive gleamed on his wrist as he held Leah's hair back from her face. The woman had no apparent concern for the state of her khaki cargoes. She knelt before the toilet in the classic kowtow of a barfing drunk.

Cass ripped off a length of paper towel and handed it over. "You seem rather…practiced at this," she said softly.

Rolling his eyes upward, Jon had ditched his playboy cool. Lines of tension marred either side of his mouth, which turned down in a grimace. "You could say that."

"I can hear you both." Leah's voice echoed inside the toilet bowl.

"You can hear us," Jon said, "but you won't remember a thing."

"Fuck off, Tin Tin."

"I can leave you to mop your own face, if you want."

Leah groped blindly behind her until he wedged the paper towel in her hand. His expression of weary patience shifted Cass's assessment. Maybe he wasn't nearly so bulletproof as he projected. She remembered what he'd said about his call sign, back when she first met him at the 64th's hangar. Rin Tin Tin. *For my unerring loyalty.*

She ripped off another hunk of toweling and handed it over. "You weren't lying, were you? About your call sign."

He shrugged. "I never lie."

Before she could dissect that tiny statement, the door to the ladies' room banged open again. "Jon? You in here? I can't find—"

Cass turned to find Ryan, whose tense expression eased as soon as he caught sight of her.

"There you are," he said with obvious relief. He crossed the bathroom with a few long strides and gathered her close. "I was looking for you."

"Sorry." Standing on tiptoes, she wedged her face into the crook of his neck. "Didn't realize I'd been in here so long."

"You okay?"

"Yeah, fine. Just needed a minute."

His frown returned, just slightly, and he held her gaze. When Cass offered nothing more, he angled his head toward the pair of toilet groupies. "How is she?"

Leah sat up and wiped her nose with a towel. "*She* is right here."

"Same ol', same ol'," Jon said tightly. "You two get out of here. I got this."

"Nah, it's my turn. Besides, what about that girl Julie?"

"You can owe me. I drove Her Highness here, so I'll get her home."

Ryan hesitated, then nodded. "Thanks, man. I'll see you both Tuesday. That means you too, Princess."

"Bright and early, Major Fang," she said just before doubling over again.

Cass followed Ryan through the crowd to the muffled quiet of his giant Ford. She hadn't had very much to drink, but her mouth felt fuzzy and her head even worse. They'd stretched from one extreme to the other, from her parents' cozy, homey living room to a dingy bathroom stall—with a C-130 taking off somewhere in the middle.

"Is she always like that?" she asked.

"Yeah."

"Is she dangerous?"

He frowned. "Like, as a pilot? No way. She'll be the second one in the hangar Tuesday morning."

That made her smile. "After you?"

"Yeah, after me," he said with a soft chuckle. "She just... I think she gets bored."

"Life at normal speed?"

"Something like that." A shrug lifted those wide shoulders. "I wasn't joking when I said she and I didn't work. Her craziness was a serious part of it. She holds on too tight, then spins off when it's time to let loose."

He keyed the ignition and drove. Cass tried to keep her eyes open, but the heaviness of the long day dragged down her lids. A gentle nudge on her shoulder roused her from near-sleep. She blinked to find them sitting in her driveway.

"You want to come in?" Feeling sandblasted and turned inside out, she swallowed. They had yet to spend the night together without having sex, which made her wonder how he'd take her next request. "You're welcome to stay, but I don't feel up for much."

"Crash out together?"

"Would you mind?"

He leaned across the central console and kissed her forehead. "I'm in this for you, baby. All of you."

They were inside her house, curved in bed like a crescent moon, before either spoke again. "Maybe I pushed too hard dragging us to the club," Ryan whispered against her temple.

A rush of warmth urged her to dig deeper. She wanted to grab hold of his rare moment of contemplation and, despite her fatigue, ask him to keep talking. Just as he had there by the runway. For that privilege, she would've forced her weary body to take a rain check on sleep. The boldness she'd discovered with Ryan, however, was no magic potion to cure years of caution.

This was good. Curled into his body, surrounded by the strong assurance of his arms and the quiet comfort of his breathing...

Better than good.

"Nah, let's take it as a positive sign," she said. "That we...we have something here. We both wanted the other to spend time with our families." She touched his face. "Because they are your family, aren't they?"

He offered a tight nod. It wasn't as if she'd cracked him open entirely, but that small concession felt like a victory. Ryan

Haverty was a good man, only shy in ways no one would assume of an ambitious fighter pilot. In time he'd open up. She put her faith in that and closed her eyes.

Chapter Twenty-Seven

Ryan was never more in control than when he wrapped the throttle in his left hand and the side stick controller in his right. Information hammered at him from all angles and directions. The radio buzzing in his helmet. The heads-up display directly in front of him. Multifunction displays over each knee. He'd needed a ridiculous amount of practice and studying to learn how to process it all, but damn if it hadn't been worth it.

Everything was worth feeling like he rode on top of a rocket, the entire world unfurling before him.

He'd worked for that very sensation. The impressiveness of it. He was bigger and badder than the rest of the world—and tiny at the same time. Almost insignificant among the cogs that kept even the simplest operation on track.

Princess flew to his right, among the canyons, dipping low along the topography. Her grace in the air meant that uneven terrain was the best place for her. The innate skill she displayed was almost enough to make him forget that one of his best pilots spent her nights praying to the porcelain goddess. Leah's display at the club had been almost two weeks ago, but she'd apparently reenacted it again on Wednesday night.

"Target acquired," came Tin Tin's voice over the radio, mired among the hums and clicks.

Ryan tapped his display and reviewed the radar over his right knee. "I want Kisser to take this one," he reminded them. The pilot was still relatively new to the squad. They all would benefit by better understanding how he flew.

"Roger," Tin Tin replied. When in the air, his smartass tone was entirely absent—all business and calm calculation.

The squad swooped low in formation then swung around to the south. Everyone in place. Everyone with a mission. Kisser took the mocked-up flight path with as much efficiency as he'd yet demonstrated.

Spinning relentlessly through the checkpoints and hard lines in his head, Ryan watched his men and women for any weaknesses. Despite the intensive nature of that training session, no one even bobbled. They were more than ready for the next Red Flag. They'd take out the NATO forces like automatons.

Through their cohesion, they'd help save lives.

His satisfaction in that thought was only matched by knowing he had somewhere to be that night. Someone waiting on him.

Since quitting the steakhouse, Cassandra had worked almost nonstop at the gallery. She was grinding herself to the bone, intent on excellence for her first gala. On the phone the night before, she'd confessed that most days she forgot to eat lunch. Ryan tried to convince himself that the out-of-control sparkle in her eyes meant she was doing the right thing—working hella fuckin' hard for what she wanted. He knew what that was like.

He was still going to make sure she ate a decent meal when she got to his place that night. Stuff her with the orange chicken she loved. Chinese food might not be the healthiest junk ever, but at least it would funnel some calories down her throat.

How fucking crazy was that? There'd be no late-night paperwork cram for him. Not tonight. Not when he knew he'd disappoint Cassandra by bailing.

He'd also disappoint the rest of his squadron if he didn't get his head back on track. He pushed away thoughts of his girl, then ran through the data one more time.

"Let's bring it around, ladies and gentlemen," he said after queuing his radio. "One more run. This time's for the gold. I expect the best, people. Trajectories on line."

A chorus of "roger" and "affirmative" streamed in and dove right to his guts. Good people, every one of them.

His team was the best of the best.

Ryan carried the container of orange chicken back into his bedroom. "Hey, did you want any more of this?"

Cassandra sat on his bed, reclining against the pillows. *All* of the pillows. She'd even stolen both of his. His laptop was perched across her knees.

"What?" She blinked at him as she tried to focus.

He wiggled the box. "More chicken."

"Nah, I'm fine."

"There's one last spring roll too."

She rolled her eyes then smiled. "I swear, I'm fine. You might have to shove me out of here with a forklift."

"Whatever," he said, lacing his voice with amusement. "You're tiny."

"And you're a sweet talker. Both of which we've said before." She laced her fingers through her hair, pulling it into a ponytail. The rubber band from around her wrist snapped everything into place, uncovering creamy shoulders left bare by a thick-strapped tank top.

She'd shown up in her classy day clothes. A sundress printed with a geometric pattern that flirted around her knees had been topped by the black cardigan she always wore at the gallery. In a big way, Ryan had enjoyed uncovering her sleek body from under that professional layer. That she transformed from polished to panting because of him did crazy things to his guts.

Leave it to him to finally find a fantastic woman with classic taste and a picture-perfect background...and all he longed to do was muss her up. Turn her into a sweaty, gasping sex kitten. The only thing better would be if she talked dirty again, but that had ended with their game playing. Plain ol' Cassandra didn't cuss, no matter how rough they fucked.

Shit, that shouldn't be a disappointment. Not at all.

In the hour since ordering Chinese, she'd changed into the tank top and a tiny pair of yellow jogging shorts. She'd taken to packing an overnight bag whenever she stopped by.

Now that he *did* like. A lot. If he had to choose, he'd rather have Cassandra waking in his arms than whispering foul, breathless words in his ear.

But he was a selfish idiot—one who didn't learn very well from past mistakes. Because he sure as hell didn't want to choose.

"Goddamn it," he muttered, shoving the leftovers in the fridge.

Determined to be good, he scooped up the sheaf of rent-by-mail movies on his entertainment center. He checked them out as he walked in the bedroom. "I've got two action flicks, one of which is martial arts heavy, and *Monty Python and the Holy Grail.*"

She grinned at him. "That one, please. It's always funny, no matter how many times I've seen it."

He booted up the DVD player and dropped the disc in. "I wouldn't know. Haven't seen it."

"What?" Her mouth dropped open. Letting her knees fall, she pushed the laptop away. "How have you lived without ever watching it?"

After flopping on the bed, he folded his arms behind his head. "I don't know. Just haven't."

Cass planted a hand on his far side and leaned over him. Her eyes narrowed. "There's something about the way you said that... Tell me the rest of the story."

His grunt and shrug didn't put her off. He sighed. "We didn't have a VCR or anything. Or cable. Mom... Half the time we were lucky she paid the bills enough to keep a roof over our head. I didn't take over the bills until I was about seventeen. When I found enough money for a few luxuries, I wanted to watch war movies more than funny things."

Her lips moved almost as if she were repeating what he'd said. "You didn't take over... Ryan Haverty, how long did you do her finances?"

He sat up fast enough that she jerked back to her side of the bed. The soda he'd left on the nightstand was watered down, but he gulped it down like ice-cold water after a long run. "It wasn't a big deal. I just set up her Social Security check for direct deposit, then put her rent and stuff on auto pay."

Snorting a bit, Cass drew his computer back onto her lap. "You are the biggest softie ever. Of all people, you should get why I'm tied to my family."

"No, I get it." Shoulders stiff, he used the remote to click on the TV. "We gonna watch this?"

"Yeah, just hang on a second. Let me finish this up."

"What are you doing over there, anyway?"

Probably messing with her email—no good distraction from the sudden discomfort nudging at him. Most of the time he didn't even think about his mom, much less talk about her. How was it possible to still be so tense? Only a few hours before, he'd buried a raging hard-on between Cassandra's pale thighs until his body collapsed and his mind went blank.

It wasn't his family, or his lack thereof. It was knowing how much he'd been holding himself in check. In the weeks since that round of phone sex, he'd bit his tongue more than once to keep from begging her to bring back that naughty British accent. His yearning for more was becoming difficult to ignore.

Jesus, he'd couldn't name a more selfish prick.

The movie would need to be damn entertaining to clear out his head.

Cass slanted him a quick glance. Her lips curled up into what he had identified as her wicked smile. "I'm not doing anything," she answered, drawing out the last word.

He pushed up on his elbows, trying to peek around her. She only tilted the screen away.

"Seriously, woman." He curled a hand around her calf and tugged her closer. She didn't give up her grip on the laptop. This was rapidly becoming a much better distraction than some Englishmen making stupid puns. "It's my computer after all."

She giggled, then blew a lock of hair out of her face. "Okay, okay. I was just doing some shopping."

"That's it?" He ignored a slight pang of disappointment. "Why're you being all weird over that?"

"Oh, no reason," she said in a singsong voice.

She tilted the computer so that he could see the display.

God. She wasn't just shopping. She was *shopping.*

The screen was filled with row after row of pretty girls wearing raunchy-as-hell costumes.

Ryan's mouth went dry. Immediately. Even licking his lips didn't help. His throat clicked when he tried to swallow past the sudden constriction.

"Why are you looking at those?" His tone was strangled.

"Because I like them?" She bent over the top of the screen. Adjusting the cursor to hover over one of the pictures was awkward from her angle, but she managed. A picture of a blonde in a skintight white dress blew up to take over half the screen. Ryan's mind shifted to imagine Cassandra in that outfit, her strawberry-blonde hair pinned in a neat bun. "What do you think? Naughty nurse? You could be the doctor who gave me my injection."

"That might be the worst joke I've ever heard you make."

His brain and his body were operating on two separate levels, both of them practically out of body. Conscious thought ticked along, trying to make the connections. How much had she figured out? Did she know the depths he sank to, the ways he imagined her? Or was this a silly tease?

He didn't want to be humored, and he didn't want to turn Cassandra into someone there only to get his rocks off.

That was his brain. His body, however, was rocking and rolling, totally ready to go.

He still sprawled across the bed, leaning on one elbow toward her. He clamped down on her calf. Probably too tightly. He forced his fingers to loosen. If Cass bothered to look, a serious short-tent had popped out from under the silky material of his basketball shorts.

"You have a point," she said, and clicked away from the naughty nurse outfit. "Probably not the right choice."

Like he had any way to respond to that. If he said he didn't give a shit what puns she made so long as she wore that, he'd totally give away how hard it hit him. How hard it *made* him.

"There's a Vegas showgirl costume too," she added. "Although that seems silly. We could go down to the Strip and see one in person."

Not the same thing as having Cassandra wrapped in the tiny metallic outfit. Touchable. Within his grasp. A girl who chose to drag *him* back to her dressing room despite her hundreds of admirers.

"Ooh, look." She bounced on the mattress. "Bad schoolgirl. That one would look good on me."

She moused over to the girl on the bottom row, then opened the page. The tiny white shirt knotted between the model's *very* ample breasts was almost obscene wrapped over so much flesh. On Cassandra, though... Fuck, it'd be perfect. She'd look up at him with a smile that invited him to live out all sorts of filthy scenarios.

"That's good," he managed to rasp.

"You think so?" She nibbled on her bottom lip. "Would you be the mean professor? Who had to punish me for cheating in class?"

His hand lashed out to slap down the computer screen before he could even think. He latched on to Cassandra's thighs and yanked her flat.

She giggled, winding her fingers around the base of his neck. "I'm not sure how I should take that. Either you love it, or you think it's the best idea *ever.*"

Burying his face in the crook of her neck made the words easier to say. "All of the above."

Her hips shifted beneath him, then she squeezed her knees along his sides. "So I should order it?"

He snuck his fingers under the hem of her shorts. Deliberately, he traced a fingertip through her curls, discovering her lips were already wet. His mouth open over the curve of her shoulder, he licked. She tasted so fucking good. Always did.

His voice was still hoarse, but there didn't seem to be anything he could do about that. There would be no going back now. No more hiding what he needed.

"Yeah. Order it. *Later.*"

Chapter Twenty-Eight

When she was seventeen, Cass had led a tour that got trapped in the Canyon during a freakish, fast-moving thunderstorm. She'd kept the tourists calm despite her wild-horses heartbeat. They'd been able to find a rocky outcropping. Together the dozen anxious travelers had huddled together as Mother Nature offered a mind-bending show of strength. The air crackled with so much electricity that the hair had stood straight off her arm.

She felt like that now.

Ryan's eyes glowed with blazing passion, so dark that they appeared nearly black. The set of his jaw said his control was already a very thin, very tenuous thing.

Cass had found her answer. Whoa baby, was it a doozy.

She had liked their few roleplaying sessions. *Really* liked it, if she was honest. The ability to become someone else, if only for a while, freed her from so many expectations. She could curse and be as bad as she wanted, all with a trusted partner. What wasn't to love for a woman whose scale weighed more heavily toward cowardice than bravery?

Ryan, however... Ryan was that thunderstorm over the Canyon. Something powerful and sparking and absolutely electric.

Thoughts as to why he kept his kink under wraps, hidden even from her, flew away as he stripped her. Didn't merely undress her. He *stripped* her. Cass almost wanted to hide her body—that's how methodically and relentlessly he moved.

A potent rush of adrenaline held her still. She couldn't begin to keep up with him, not the way he leaped miles ahead of her in terms of arousal. Part of the fun was knowing she'd finally found his trigger. Like when she'd tempted him to join in that fun phone-sex session, she felt powerful. He already did so much to make her wobbly and breathless. Now she could return the favor.

Cool air washed over her bare stomach. She wasn't bare for long. Ryan laid his strong, broad torso over hers, their chests crushed together as he kissed her. Crudely. With so much force. His tongue plunged in, swiping past her teeth. He caught her moan, then dove deeper. She grabbed the back of his head, surprised when her instinct was to drag him even closer. The violence he swirled around them was intoxicating.

The boy wanted to play rough. Good. Because she wanted to be the sort of girl who could take it. All of it. No fear. Just a gluttonous, headlong rush toward her release. She shivered against a flash flood of pure sexual energy.

Suddenly Cass wanted to be on top. She wanted to see that furious arousal on his face, looking down on his lovely body as she rode her flyboy. With no small amount of strength, she shoved his chest. He didn't budge. Just thrust his fingers into her pussy. She groaned, hips lifting toward his graceless touch, and she shoved again. With all her strength. The fact she couldn't move him—not when he didn't want to be moved—propelled her up another notch.

"Do you want me to stop?" he rasped against her mouth. The words sounded like a threat, not a question. As if he'd take her anyway.

That she could push a good man that far. Dear God, what power.

She whimpered, again bucking against the rough drive of his fingers. Sweat dotted her skin—along her inner thighs, the insides of her elbows, the undersides of her breasts.

"I want," she gasped.

"What?"

"On top." She thrashed her head against the pillow, fingers clawing into his shoulders. "I want to be on top."

Ryan grabbed her ass with both hands and rolled. Clinging to taut muscles, she went with him. They misjudged the width of the mattress. Cass tipped over the edge. She threw out her foot to catch her balance. Her sole touched the floor but her weakened knees turned traitor, collapsing beneath her weight.

She sagged to the hardwood with a gasp of laughter.

"Shit," he said from where he sprawled on the comforter. "You okay?"

"Yeah. Now get your fine ass down here."

He scrambled off the bed and snagged a condom from the top of the dresser. Kneeling stomach to stomach, Cass ripped the T-shirt off over his head. He turned and propped his upper body beneath a bank of windows, as she dragged his basketball shorts down, down off his long legs.

"You're right." He was panting, even after the small break in their intensity. "You on top."

"Why?"

Hazel eyes were all darkness and passion. He sat almost straight against the wall, the backs of his knees pressed flat to the floor. "You set the pace. I don't trust myself."

Cass tipped her chin toward the ceiling as another gorgeous shiver worked up her spine. After a deep breath to calm her trembling, she rolled the condom over his epic hard-on. Masculine hands that were almost cruel—stiff with tension—guided her hips as she straddled him.

Oh...as he filled her.

A long moan rumbled in her chest. His arms crisscrossed up her spine. She arched back, then pressed her breasts together. Offering herself to him. With his face right there, Ryan caught a nipple and sucked. Back and forth. He opened his mouth, devouring more of her flesh as she found her rhythm. Each push of his cock met the grind of her hips.

"I love riding you," she gasped against his ear. "You hear me, Ryan? I fucking *love* it."

"Hell, yeah. Ride me, baby. C'mon. Fuck me."

Cass slid her palms high overhead, grabbing the window's lower sill for leverage. She bit down where his neck met his body. On a grunt, he cinched his arms behind her back. Their torsos smashed together. The wall supporting his shoulders meant he had nowhere to go. Each of their thrusts met that implacable barrier. He jammed her down onto his every upward plunge.

No such thing as setting the pace. Not for either of them.

Their bodies were in charge.

A fierce orgasm built in her belly and in her thighs, colliding right where they joined. Cass threw her head back on a screech, which throttled down to a low moan. The contractions still pulsed and vibrated when Ryan stiffened. Tendons on the sides of his throat jumped. With one last upward jerk, he gasped.

His head thunked backward against the wall. Cass bowed forward. His body was the absolute best place to rest, strong and solid. Her rock.

Chests heaving, they sat like that until the air chilled her sweaty skin. Ryan's erection subsided within her—such an intimate feeling. She licked the raw place where she'd bit down. He was salty and almost feverishly warm. Cuddling up against him was comforting, especially when he stroked her hair, petting, smoothing the disheveled strands.

"You okay?"

Cass giggled. "Of course I am." Then she sighed, playing with a whorl of his chest hair. "That was just...*wow.*"

"Yeah."

"Oh, c'mon. Gimme a 'fuck, yeah' at least."

"Woman, you have a filthy mouth."

"You bring it out in me."

His eyes rolled closed, looking completely sandblasted. He'd worn that same expression after the best of their games. Never, ever would she complain about the times when they made love. Earlier that evening on the couch had been wonderful, but there was a huge difference between wonderful and shattering.

As she and Ryan wordlessly disengaged and readied for bed, Cass couldn't shake the idea that she'd stumbled onto a treasure trove of knowledge. She'd been right, even there at the start when his gaze had caught on her stockings. The roleplaying got him off like nothing else, which complemented her needs and desires so perfectly that she almost shook with its rightness.

He still hadn't spoken. He hadn't shared in her ridiculously satisfied laughter. A quick push back through their early encounters revealed the same pattern. Extreme excitement and satisfaction followed by...silence. A silence that left her doubting they'd even shared the same experience. He closed off so completely that she'd nearly been convinced the turn-on was hers alone.

That sure as hell wasn't the case.

Brushing her teeth, she kept slanting him looks. He merely walked around his apartment, turning off the lights and checking the front lock, as if this mystery didn't exist between them. As if it wasn't growing with every minute that ticked by.

What was he thinking? Why had he hidden this from her?

She fought a shiver. How far, exactly, would they go when that naughty-schoolgirl costume arrived in the mail?

Gilly was running late for their afternoon coffee break at Starbucks, but Cass appreciated the opportunity to compose herself. She'd become a tangle of all things giddy. Her inner thighs were still sore from the night before, and the email on her phone stated that her costume had shipped. A nervous thrill made her bite her lower lip. She couldn't believe how excited she was. Still. All over again. They'd set their big date for the following Friday, which meant a whole week to anticipate.

Any niggle of doubt... Well, she could ignore that long enough to convince Ryan this was what they both wanted.

After setting a mocha on the table, Gilly plopped her purse on the floor next to her seat. She was dressed for work at the steakhouse, with her black hair threaded in a French braid.

"Now that is a bad-girl smile if I ever saw one," she said.

"Hey, you." Slipping her phone away, Cass knew it was true. She couldn't deny that Ryan made her feel delectably wicked. "Don't tease me. I can't help it."

"Good for you. Although I'm seriously jealous. Maybe I'll see if they have civilian tours of Nellis."

Ah, God. Always such a rush of adrenaline-fueled terror when she put the two together. Ryan plus fighter pilot. The combination that had once turned her on so fast now severed her air supply for entirely different reasons. She was falling for him. Big time. That meant accepting all of him, including the ridiculously dangerous job he'd worked toward since he was young—the job that had maybe even saved him from a wasted life.

She just needed time. Time and a few more of Ryan's reassurances.

"I'm not sure the pilots are there on display," she said. "They do work, you know. Speaking of, how's it been at Blakely's?"

Gilly took a sip of her drink and swiped whipped cream off her upper lip. "Oh, barrels and barrels of monkeys. I've actually been having a fun time."

"Oh?"

"Tommy and Julia have been psycho crazy ever since you left. I think it's because Cynthia expects everyone else to pick up her skinny-ass slack. She does the bare minimum, and then the Witch hits the fan. And it all starts over again!"

Cass blinked. "Wow."

Maybe on a different day she would've felt some sort of smug satisfaction. All she found was relief—relief that she'd escaped that toxic environment. Those people didn't influence her anymore, and they obviously had it a whole lot worse than she did. Her transformed life made her far too happy to wish them ill will.

"So yeah," Gilly said, grinning. "Fun times. At least no one seems to give a damn anymore if I'm ten minutes late."

"Ten. Yeah, right."

Gilly moved on to talk about her latest sculpture, which thankfully kept Cass's thoughts from straying back to Ryan. Their shared love of art was a hallmark of her friendship with the other woman, especially when waitressing had threatened to decompose their brains. With any luck, Cass would one day be in a position to show Gilly's work. The prospect of helping a talented artist find an audience was exciting.

"So, your turn," Gilly said. "The gallery first, then your hot fighter pilot."

Finishing her chai, Cass fought the rejuvenated bubble of excitement under her ribs. "Prep work for the gala is clicking along. I'm dog tired, but in a good way, you know?"

"Sure. I'm always that way in the middle of a big project."

"Mr. Hungerford, the owner, is looking over candidates to represent the gallery at an exhibition in Florence this August."

"You've got the qualifications for that, missy."

"I know. It's just...early? Like, I only just stepped up. Maybe if the gala goes well, I'll have a shot."

She hadn't told Ryan about the possibility yet, mostly because the odds seemed so long. Her intense hours and dedication weren't just for the upcoming gala, but for her future at the gallery. And hello, *Italy*. Wouldn't that be making a statement to the world?

"Now Ryan. Come on, give it up."

Cass shrugged. "What can I say? It's been fantastic. His friends are going to take some getting used to, but I like how much they all look after one another. Though now that I've seen his plane and heard them swap stories, I'm kinda freaked about how dangerous it all is. I mean, they're *warriors*. Bombs and crashes and deployments. It's all possible for Ryan." Her pulse had accelerated well out of proportion with that cozy cafe scene. "The most danger-prone guy I've ever dated patched roofs during his summer vacations."

"It's hot."

"Sure, but it's scary too."

"He's the shit, though, right? He's not some crazy cakes who does stupid crap to show off?"

"No," Cass said with a smile. That sounded about as far from Ryan as possible. She'd never worried about a wild streak—more like his determination. She could imagine him putting himself at risk for his friends, his fellow pilots, and that thought turned her bones to liquid.

Gilly looked at her watch. "Rats. I gotta go. You have just enough time to give me something good to think about tonight."

"I am not going to be your alone-time inspiration."

"Oh, come on." She grinned. "I promise that I won't say a word when I see him at the gala."

Cass almost flinched at that possibility. The strange thing

about having unraveled Ryan's big-time turn-on was how protective she felt of his secret. *Their* secret. She didn't want to have to justify why roleplaying worked for them. He'd be mortified, like that first time when the clerk at Anna's Boudoir knew what they'd done. She hoped that time and proof of her own eagerness would help him loosen up, but that meant discretion. She owed him that measure of trust.

So, a little something for her friend. Something vague.

"You know that scene from *Thelma & Louise*?"

"*The* scene? Brad and Geena on a table?"

"Yeah, there against the wall?" Grinning, Cass ignored the blush that flamed down her throat. "That was us last weekend. Ryan's version of a quiet Sunday brunch."

"I hate you. Officially. Just so you know."

Cass leaned in, as if ready to share another salacious secret. "Then he made breakfast."

"Ugh." Gilly rolled her eyes as she stood. "Come give me a hug so I don't have to plot how to blow up your house."

Laughing, Cass embraced her friend. "You asked!"

"I did, and I'm happy for you. Honest, Cass."

"Thanks," she said. "Have a good night at work."

"Suurrrre. I'll get right on that. See ya, hon." Gilly sauntered out of the coffee shop, her usual hip-swish in place.

Cass watched her go while wearing a stupid grin. Because she was happy for herself too. Forcing her anxieties to a low ebb, she grabbed her purse and portfolio. She had lots of work to do. The sooner she finished up, the sooner she could enjoy the rewards. All of them.

Chapter Twenty-Nine

Ryan normally assumed predawn phone calls on Saturday mornings were Leah. The ringtone wasn't his. Instead Cassandra sleepily fumbled across the nightstand.

"H'llo?" she muttered once she'd flipped open the phone.

Even though he was half-asleep, Ryan still caught the slightly frantic tone of voice that came over the line. Impossible to pick out the words. Rolling over put him in full-body contact with Cassandra, just the way he liked it. He curled an arm around her curvy waist and dragged her against his hips, burying his face in her hair.

That dirty-schoolgirl costume was slowly headed toward them. *Slowly.* As if by donkey cart. Ryan had checked the ground tracking number often since she'd forwarded him the email. Stupidly often. Every time, he had the idea that a pop-up window would appear and read, *Chill, dude, it hasn't moved far in ten minutes.* He couldn't shake the idea that the outfit was going to be trouble. He wanted to see Cassandra in it too damn bad.

It wasn't normal.

After a moment of listening, she rubbed a fist over her eyes. "Mom, I was up late last night. I don't know if I can do it." She trailed off, obviously listening to whatever her mother said. "I wasn't scheduled."

Going back to sleep was a losing battle. Ryan pressed a kiss against the nape of her neck. "What's wrong?" he whispered.

The voice pitched even higher. He could pick out every third word, but not enough to make sense of it.

Cassandra flapped a hand over her shoulder at him. "Yes, that was Ryan. Yes, we're being safe… No, Mom… Okay, okay.

Fine. Yes, I'll even be there on time."

Flopping onto her back, she heaved a huge sigh as she snapped her phone shut. "I probably don't have to tell you who that was."

"No, not really." He spread his hand wide over her stomach where her tank top had ridden up. "Do you have to go?"

She scrubbed her eyes again, then pushed to a sitting position. "Yeah. Dad woke up in a lot of pain, and Emily's morning sickness is kicking up. They need someone to cover the West Rim tour."

"You're going?"

"Yes," she said softly. "I'm sorry. I finally get a Saturday off from the gallery and let Mom totally guilt trip me into it. I'm going to have to talk to them soon."

Still lying on his side, Ryan curled a hand over her knee. He wiggled his fingers into the crease, tracing the tender skin. If he gave away what a sick shit he was once the costume arrived, their time together could be ticking down. That thought pinched his stomach into a gnarled wad.

"I could go with you," he said.

Her smile was definitely worth the offer. Still sleepy at the edges, but bright and shining. She swept sleep-tangled hair out of her eyes with the back of her hand. "Do you want to?"

He shoved off the bed and reached for a pair of shorts. "Why not? I haven't seen the West Rim yet, so might as well. Plus I'll still get to spend the day with you."

From behind, she launched at him. Her arms wrapped around his stomach. She curled her chin over his shoulder to lay a smacking kiss on his cheek. "You're the best boyfriend ever, baby."

Yeah, right.

"We'll see if you still say that after being trapped in a bus with me for hours."

It proved not nearly so bad as he'd thought. Out on the road, Cassandra popped up and gave chipper, well-rehearsed speeches to zombie-eyed tourists, but in between she was all his. As tour guide, she sat in the front seat—practically on display, which ditched any hope of privacy—but at least it meant extra legroom for him.

The last time he'd spent so many hours in a row on a tour bus, he'd been a senior in high school headed to away games. After an unfortunate incident before he joined the football team, no cheerleaders were allowed. Instead they followed behind in a van. If Cassandra had been a cheerleader, though... Ryan would've found a way to sneak her on the bus with him.

God, his imagination was in overdrive, as much as he hated it. She even acted just enough like a cheerleader as she explained peppy details about the Joshua Tree forest or whatever else they passed. She'd strapped her hair up in a high ponytail, and khaki shorts bared most of her sleek legs.

The hours they spent pressed together in the bus seat flew by. Before Ryan knew it, she ushered everyone onto a second bus as she provided options for the next four hours. They all arrived at a tiny welcome center.

Ryan swung his backpack over his shoulder, watching the tourists file into the squat building. Bright sunshine arrowed down at them as he and Cassandra stood in the middle of a dusty parking lot. "What just happened?"

"I've handed them off." She smiled, tugging on the straps of her own pack. "This side of the Canyon's run by the Hualapai tribe. We basically just get them here. I've got to be back here in exactly four hours, but other than that I'm good."

"Oh really now?"

She nodded. "Yep. Means the tips aren't as nice, which is probably part of why Mom had such a problem getting someone to fill in."

This was even better than he'd expected. He'd thought he would need to tag along behind the group and do his damnedest not to spin fantasies about getting lost in the wild with an innocent stranger with reddish-blonde hair.

Now he had her all to himself. The implicit temptation crunched down along his spine. "So what's the plan, Miss Whitman?"

"I figure we've got two options." She fished a pair of sunglasses out of her backpack and slipped them on. He'd never tell her, but the huge lenses made her look like a starlet shading her eyes from the flash of the paparazzi. "We can either hop a ride with a helicopter pilot I know and hike along the bottom of the Canyon. Or we can stick to the top. I figure either way we'll hike out for about an hour, then head back. Leave enough time for padding, just in case."

The sudden authoritative set to her shoulders was a bit of a surprise. He wasn't sure why since she'd been doing the job for years. Probably because she seemed to dislike it so much. Confidence looked fantastic on her. Always had.

"Let's stay up top." He didn't always do well in aircraft that weren't under his personal control. His feet would slam and his hands clench as if he actually held the throttle. "Better views that way."

"Good with me. You can go look out over the canyon if you want. It's right around there." She pointed past the visitor center. "I'm just going to check in and call Mom back at the office."

He did his best not to let the reminder of her mother get to him. So, he'd been doing raunchy things to the woman's daughter. For weeks. They were grownups. No big deal. Except Betsy and Keith would be disgusted to remember he'd ever been in their house if they knew what he imagined doing to their baby girl on Friday.

Because it wasn't just a bit of dress up. He wasn't going to simply ask her to give him a spin as he inspected the costume's fit. No, he wanted to be the professor. He wanted to punish his naughty student, to bend her to his authority.

Then he'd want to do it all over again.

His guts heaved another lurch as he walked toward the overlook.

Cassandra reappeared about fifteen minutes later, when his toes were practically over the drop. He put his camera away, just as he put away his nerves. She'd always enjoyed when he smiled, but that defense mechanism was getting damn rusty. "I can't believe there's no guardrails."

Her grin, however, was all natural. "Looks great though, right?"

That was for sure. The canyon stretched out at his feet. It

wasn't as deep or sharp as the more-famed South Rim, but it was still impressive.

She joined him with sure steps, as if they couldn't plummet miles and miles down along sharp rocks. Whether it was her years of familiarity, or her normal zest for life that made her fearless, he didn't know. He liked it. At the moment, when his doubts were so fierce, he appreciated that at least one of them was in control.

He reached out to curl an arm around her waist. "Standing here feels a little like flying."

"Really?"

"Mm-hmm." His gaze tracked along the streaks of earthen colors. Browns and reds and tans. The majesty of it. "Being on top of the world. Only thing missing is the speed sucking at your bones, trying to steal your breath."

"Still want to hike it?"

"Heck, yeah." He shifted his pack, then took a drag of water off his CamelBak. "You set for hydration?"

She rolled her eyes. "Not my first go at this, Major Haverty."

"Then lead the way."

For a full hour, she did. They walked along a well-beaten path until they got to a viewpoint that was unbelievably called Guano Point. That one made Ryan scratch his head. Even if, yeah, guano had once been practically farmed there, why not rename the damn place?

They only stayed long enough to snap a couple pictures before continuing farther on to where the trail narrowed. Cassandra proved to be a great guide. She pointed out historical notes, plant types and even identified a specific type of lizard that skittered across their path.

Ryan loved every minute. Even letting her break trail wasn't a big deal when he could watch her thighs flash from under the hem of her shorts. With her dark brown T-shirt and lightweight pack, he couldn't shake the image that she was an official park ranger—who had a thing for getting down with anonymous canyon visitors.

She drew to a halt right as he tried to ignore the possibilities inherent in such a remote location. He darted his gaze out across the canyon.

"Okay, so we've been out an hour. We can turn back..." Her voice trailed off.

"I sense an 'or' coming."

"I knew you were a smart boy. There's a tiny cut through this cliff. If we go down about thirty feet, there's something I can show you."

Said the ranger to the poor, innocent tourist from the Midwest.

He rubbed his hand across the back of his neck, coming away with a fine layer of sandy grit. Like it wasn't enough that the costume was, right then, somewhere outside of Indianapolis. There'd be plenty of time to fuck everything up later. Cassandra was in her element. She didn't deserve his incessant horn-dogging.

"Sure."

"Great," she said, grinning. "Come on."

The path took a fairly gradual slope, but soft shale and crumbling rocks meant that watching their footing became vital. She subtly pointed out where to step. Soon they spit out onto a small landing.

"Holy crap," he breathed.

The landing, carved out of the cliff, was about five feet by seven—big enough so he could stand there and not feel like one wrong cough would propel him over the edge. The ground fell away sharply beneath it and kept falling. Until the river winding through the bottom was nothing more than a tiny green thread. It was like they were practically floating *in* the giant crevasse.

"I know, right?" She pushed her sunglasses up on top of her head. "I do love this place. I just wish I didn't have to drag a bunch of strangers with me every time."

He wanted to kiss her. Right then and there. Over the past few days, however, he hadn't been able to find a way to even touch her without his head filling up. Clouding up. Drunk on Cassandra. Drunk on what he was going to risk. Soon. All the while hoarding every taste and look and sound while he still could.

So he shoved his fists in the pockets of his cargo shorts.

"Definitely worth the extra time."

She smiled. Christ, she looked so relaxed out here. Like she had all her shit together. Unlike certain people. "That's not all," she said.

With her hand curled around the inside of his elbow, she tugged him over to the wall. She smelled like sunshine blended with mesquite and creosote, all of it underlaid with her usual freshness and a dash of sunscreen. The brush of her shoulder against his arm sent a low-level shock wave across his skin.

"Look," she said.

A perfect, classic seashell was pressed into the rock—no, made *of* the rock. A fossil. Proof that where they stood had once been under water. That no matter what happened once the water disappeared, some things were marked deep. Permanent. Inescapable.

He touched the sun-warmed stone a few inches below the fossil. Gritty shale scrubbed against his palm. "Amazing."

"They're protected, you know. No one's allowed to take them or destroy them or anything." She laid her hand over his, fingers folding side by side. "So no matter where I've been, or what I've been doing...I can come back here. It's been the same forever." With a shrug and a smile, she said, "Some things are just that good."

He wanted that. More particularly, wanted it with Cassandra. Maybe... There had to be a way to hang on to all this. What was the point of such a perfect moment if he let it get away?

Chapter Thirty

Cass hadn't enjoyed a trip into the canyon so much in years. Maybe ever. Ryan worked magic on her mood. She loved showing him all the crooks and corners she'd learned across a whole decade. She would never enjoy it as much as the rest of her family, but somehow Ryan salvaged it.

Because she knew this would be her last tour.

Exhaustion pressed on her from all sides. She couldn't do what she wanted and still satisfy her parents' expectations. The life she'd started to build, finally, needed all her attention.

She took Ryan's hand and looked out over the gaping crevasse. He'd been in an odd humor all day. Maybe it was a sign that they were drawing closer, that he didn't feel the need to plaster on pretend smiles. The pretend ones were more disconcerting than none at all.

"Thank you for this," he said.

"No problem. Really. It's fun to see it through your eyes."

"I don't think you want to be in my head right now."

"No?"

After a shake of his head, his hair highlighted with streaks of gold, he sighed. "I'd have expected you to lead me somewhere for the purposes of jumping my bones. This is far classier."

"Educational too."

"Exactly. So you saved me from myself."

"That sounds incredibly tame of me."

He grunted. Face forward, he seemed to study where a band of bright sunshine streaked across layers of redwall limestone. Emily's husband could name each geologic nuance and its composition, but Cass was content with having retained much less. It was breathtaking, no matter the technical terms.

"I'm going to tell my parents this evening," she said. "I can't do this anymore."

Ryan peered down at her. "Are you sure?"

"I am. This..." Already she felt lighter for having said it aloud. That lightness gave her power. "I can't keep splitting myself into pieces. I know you don't like it when I give you credit for the last few months, but I wish you'd let me. Just a bit. If anything, you've helped me sort through what's important."

"Your family is important to you."

"Sure, but I don't need to live my parents' dreams. I have some of my own." She grinned, then let loose of his warm hold. "Here, take a picture of me. To commemorate this."

Turning carefully, she stood on the edge of the landing. She fluffed her ponytail and threw her shoulders back, ready for her closeup.

Ryan's face, however, had lost most of its color. "Get back from there, would ya?"

"What?"

He held out his hand, as if afraid a sudden movement would send her tumbling into the rocky abyss. "Come on."

"Don't be silly. I've done this for years. I'll hold still."

"Cass, I mean it."

"Just take the picture, damn it."

She almost apologized because she never cursed—not when they weren't playing. Maybe it got through to him. Ryan's mouth compressed. His frown revealed he was as upset with her as he'd ever been. He managed to snap the picture. Cass didn't dare ask to see the viewscreen.

"Don't *ever* do that again." His tight voice said this wasn't a request.

She tipped her head, trying to see into his brain. Lordy, he had a lot going on in there today. That didn't do a thing to dim her annoyance.

"I've been coming down here since I was in grade school. I don't take chances. This morning Mom asked me, a grown woman, if you and I use protection. Dad still asks if I've gotten my oil changed recently. They're laid-back about a lot of things, but my safety is a hypersensitive area. No way they would've let me lead a tour, *ever*, if they thought I couldn't handle myself. You could extend at least that much trust."

He appeared only somewhat chastened, which only pissed her off more. She got the feeling that if she protested, he'd haul her over his shoulder like he had at his apartment. Full-on caveman.

Feeling prickly, she turned away from the platform and headed back through the cliff-wall crevice. The shale still slipped like oily plastic beneath her boots. The flame of annoyance in her was ablaze now. Ryan followed closely. She wasn't sure what she'd do if he reached out to take her elbow. Southern gentleman aside, she didn't feel like being patronized.

They reached a solid spread of Muav limestone, its lackluster gray so uninspired when compared to stripes of orange and red. Cass took a healthy swipe from her canteen. The worry she'd been repressing for weeks fizzed in her chest.

"What?" he asked.

"You're a fighter pilot!"

He blinked. "Yeah?"

She smacked the lid back on the canteen and gave it a sharp twist. "So I'm supposed to just *accept* that you're in danger every day? Every day?"

"That's my job. You knew that. Cass, where is this coming from?"

"It's coming from the fact we're serious about each other now. Aren't we?"

His slight hesitation was too long. Too long to let her breathe. "Yes, we're getting serious."

She swallowed. Always so many threads to untangle with him. So she focused on one for now. "That means trust. I have to trust that you're good. The best. That you'll take every precaution to keep safe."

"Yes."

"Then give me some credit, okay?" Damn. She didn't like that her voice cracked. Her throat closed around the idea of Ryan wounded in the line of duty. Any nightmare scenario led to tears, so she focused on being angry. "This is my last tour.

I'm going to live in a gallery or a museum for the rest of my life. Paper cuts and paint fumes will be my on-the-job hazards. But you... God, Ryan, just look at what you're asking me to sign on for."

He rubbed a hand over his neck. The tight crimp of his lips hadn't eased. He watched her, as if trying to make a decision. Cass didn't know what she wanted or hoped. She only knew that their relationship had taken a turn.

To survive it, she craved more than a few reassurances.

She enjoyed the idea of giving herself to this man, handing her heart into his care. She spent a good many hours each day imagining just that. She needed to know he'd do his best to keep it safe.

Ryan shrugged free of his hesitation and crossed to stand before her. "I'm sorry," he said quietly. "I've been admiring all afternoon how well you handle yourself down here. Back there just took me by surprise."

She nodded stiffly. *More. Give me more.*

Hands loosely encircling her upper arms, he met her gaze squarely. She imagined he'd wear that same solemn expression when reciting his wedding vows. Joy that bordered on terror zipped down to her toes. She might be that far along, but she could never read him well enough to know if she lived alone in hope.

"I *am* good. The best. I take every precaution." Her words, echoed in his voice, began to ease her tension. "Cassandra, I'm not going to lie. What I do is dangerous, and there's the chance I'll be redeployed one day. But what I do is important." With a tenderness that left her breathless, he kissed her forehead. "I've been trusted with a responsibility that I never take lightly."

His double meaning was unmistakable. Or else Cass didn't want to peek into dark corners anymore. She circled her arms around his trim waist. He held on to her too, making her feel safe—like he always did. Strong. Whole. Vital. Maybe that's how she'd be able to stand it, by clinging to that feeling, and by believing that he wouldn't want to give it up any more than she did.

She tipped her face to find his throat, which was roughened

by a slight growth of stubble. Per Cass's request one bold evening, he no longer shaved on the weekends. The rough rub of those sharp hairs along her skin was too good to do without. Mouth open, she licked toward his ear.

"How much time left?" he asked against her cheek. He swooped in for a kiss that turned her blood to lava. Holy smokes, the man was a master.

Cass checked her watch. "You have seventeen minutes."

"Lemme make it worth your while."

"You got it, Major."

Cass sat on the edge of cushion. Her mom and dad occupied the giant sectional couch in the living room. The flatscreen still flickered, but *Saturday Night Live* was muted. Ryan had dropped her off after the tour. He'd offered to stay and lend his support. Although she wanted so badly to rely on him as her safety blanket, Cass had given him a kiss good night.

Her parents. Her stand to make. Knowing she had his backing would have to be enough.

So now she waited—waited for their reply.

Her mother exchanged a meaningful look with Dad. "You mean this, don't you, honey?"

"I do." She left it at that, afraid that too many words would see her hedging and making excuses.

Her father leaned forward and rested his forearms on his knees. Then he grinned. "I'd have been pissed off if you quit us before the restaurant."

"Keith, your language!"

"I mean it, honey. If she'd have chosen slinging steaks over us, I'd have protested." His humor faded as he looked at Cass. "I'm happy you spoke up. It's not your job to worry about us."

"Robert has good connections with the geology department at UNLV," her mother added. "We'll hire a student who needs part-time work."

"Worst case," Dad said with a laugh, "I play a mean game of

poker. You watch. I'll secure our retirement on one good hand."

Mom whacked him playfully on the arm. "You will not. Now, about this guy Ryan. What's going on with you two?"

"Mom." Cass rolled her eyes, but she was too elated to put up much of a fight.

"How was it having him on the tour? Did he have a nice time?"

As if she was going there. *Yeah, Mom, he yanked down my khaki shorts and fucked me against a cliff wall.* She hadn't found the nerve to look at her back yet. Probably a mess of scrapes. The deliciously sore muscles of her inner thighs were a much nicer reminder of those frantic, passionate minutes.

At least some of her anxiety had passed regarding his profession. If she wanted to be with Ryan—and God, did she ever—then it was a part of him that she would learn to accept. She almost smiled. What would he think if he realized she had more of a problem with his life as a fighter pilot than with their roleplaying?

Schooling her features, Cass tried to keep her voice even. "We're good, okay? Let's leave it at that for now."

Although she seemed ready to protest, her mother nodded once. "Decaf?"

"Beer?" her dad replied.

He grabbed the remote to catch the next SNL sketch. And that...was that. Cass leaned back against the couch cushions, smiling, still stunned. She was free—of the restaurant, of her family's business. She was even free from most of the unease she'd harbored about Ryan's job. Now she could sink or swim on her own, with the career she wanted as her incentive. The *life* she wanted.

More and more, that life included a certain gentleman fighter pilot.

Chapter Thirty-One

As Ryan stood before his bathroom mirror one last time, he couldn't escape his worry. He looked like a douche, wearing a sweater over a button-down shirt and a tie. With a shake of his head, he left the bathroom. Disgust dogged his heels.

The nauseating lengths a guy would go to in order to get his rocks off.

That wasn't really right either. He ran a hand over his head. It wasn't like he'd been dragged unwillingly into their newest game. He just hadn't expected so much anxiety chomping at him while he awaited her arrival. The turn-on, yeah, maybe. Maybe he could finally admit that his body was primed and ready. His mind hadn't yet caught up with the plan.

Since their epic beginnings, his relationship with Cassandra had been normal. Sane. Regular. Just like he'd always wanted.

Now he was pacing up and down the length of his apartment, wearing a bloody costume as well. The French maid thing didn't count. After all, he'd been wearing his dress uniform. That wasn't so much a costume as a regular change of clothes.

The whole sweater-over-a-button-down thing…

That was admitting to a whole new level of involvement. He wasn't just asking her to dress up because the sight of her turned him on. He wanted the whole performance, including his own participation.

Knowing that the schoolgirl outfit arrived at her apartment on Tuesday had been almost more than he could handle. He'd skipped out of seeing her through the week because he wouldn't have been able to keep from asking for it. Begging her to wear it. Early.

When the doorbell rang, he instantly knew why he'd put himself through this wringer. Cassandra was on the other side, with her awesome body wrapped in another tiny fantasy costume. Fuck, yeah. Every moment of freaking himself out would be worth it.

There was no turning back now. Backing out would stir up as many questions as going through with it. He could only hope he was man enough to salvage their relationship after turning her over his knee.

Christ. Just when he didn't think he could get any harder.

Except it wasn't Cassandra waiting when he tossed open the door. Jon and Leah tumbled past him like a couple of puppies.

"Hey there, Fang," Leah called. She headed immediately for his kitchen and shoved her head in the refrigerator. She wore a low-slung pair of hip-hugger jeans that dipped when she bent. Her tiny shirt ended two inches above her waistband. Ryan looked away.

"Yo, man." Jon flopped down on the couch lengthwise, his feet kicked up on the arm. The jeans he wore with a white-on-white striped dress shirt was pretty casual as far as he went.

Ryan leaned against the archway between kitchen and the great room. He crossed his arms over his chest, struggling to calm his erection and keep his voice below a shout. "By all means, make yourself at home, Dimples," he said dryly.

Jon grinned. He hated having his dimples pointed out, which meant that Ryan was in exactly the mood to do it. "We always do."

Leah reemerged with two beers in hand. "Next time I come over, I'm sticking a couple bottles of wine in your fridge. Cass would appreciate it."

"Cassandra doesn't drink much."

She handed one of the beers over to Jon, then flopped into Ryan's easy chair. "Fine, then I'd appreciate it. I don't like beer that much."

"Princess, no one's forcing you to drink mine."

Jon took a swig straight from the bottle. It looked odd since he usually preferred liquors with fancy names or bottles of wine that were older than all of them put together. "You got plans tonight, Fang?"

Ryan ran a finger under the ring of his collar. He had plans all right, but they involved Cassandra on her knees. Begging for his cock. Not the thing he discussed with his friends.

"Not really."

Leah bounced on her toes. "Cool. Then you can come out with us."

"Yeah, I heard about this new jazz club opening," Jon said, pushing to a sitting position. "It's got big money behind it. Going to be great."

Most nights, watching Jon and Leah annoy the tourists wasn't a bad way to spend his time. But not when he had prior commitments. An *epic* commitment, around which he'd based his whole week. He glanced at his watch. Cassandra would show up at any second. "I don't think so. I'm feeling kind of tired. Was just going to turn in."

Leah's eyebrows rose almost to her hairline. "Didn't I tell you the old man was going soft?" she said to Jon.

"He really is." Jon shook his head in mock sympathy. "Finds himself a spicy little girlfriend and the poor dude's just no fun anymore."

"Yeah, yeah." Ryan checked his watch again. His back went stiff. He was down to seconds. "I'm old. I'm boring. Maybe y'all should flee now, save yourselves."

"Not at all." Leah waved grandly with her beer bottle. "I think we should try to save *you*. Go get changed."

"Seriously." Jon eyed him from head to toe. "Why are you wearing that for sitting around the house, anyway?"

Fuck. Trust Jon to catch on to anything slightly weird. Ryan shoved his hands deep in his pockets. His mouth opened on an excuse, but he couldn't think of one in time.

The doorbell rang.

A cold sluice of something resembling fear trickled down his spine at the same time his dick perked up once more. The damned thing knew who'd rung that bell.

His guests both sat up straighter. Jon angled a look at Ryan, one eyebrow quirking upward. "Going to turn in, huh?"

As he trudged to the door, Ryan felt like he were wearing combat boots with soles made out of concrete. At the same time, his nerves sparked with prickly excitement.

How in the hell could he clear this up without his friends figuring out what was going on? No fucking way. Leah might be oblivious enough, with her mind set to getting her drink on. She wouldn't notice anything strange beyond his attempt to tell them he was just turning in for the night.

Pretty-faced Tin Tin, though. If anyone were going to twig, it'd be the original perv himself.

The doorbell rang again, the chimes annoyingly cheery.

Ryan opened the door.

Christ, she looked good. The outfit was mostly hidden under a lightweight knee-length jacket, but it didn't matter. Golden-red hair was pulled into braided pigtails and tied off with plaid ribbons. She hadn't worn much makeup, but something made her mouth pale pink and glossy.

She looked up at him with her chin pulled toward her chest. "I'm not late, am I, Professor Haverty?" Her bottom lip poked out.

Fuck. He was a dead man.

After a cutting motion across his throat, he hooked a thumb over his shoulder.

She craned up on her toes to look past him. "What? What's wrong?"

"Jon and Leah are here," he said, voice pitched low.

Her mouth dropped open for a second before she giggled. She tried to smother it with her fingers across her lips, but her shoulders still shook.

He wanted to find it funny. Christ, he really did. He'd have been able to see the humor involving anyone else, or if the story came up in some late-night bullshit session downrange.

Except it wasn't someone else. It was him. Being busted was imminent.

He pinched the bridge of his nose where a sudden, fierce pain had lodged.

Cassandra's blue eyes dimmed.

A serious stream of cuss words set up in his head. He was killing the excitement that had bubbled inside her only a moment ago, and he hated that. He couldn't seem to battle past the jet-engine roar in his ears.

"So you going to let me in?"

"Of course," he said woodenly. He stepped back and let her walk by. A fruity scent rose in her wake as he followed her into the living room.

"Hey, Cass," Leah called. She'd stretched her long legs out to rest on the black wood coffee table. "We're trying to convince Fang to come out with us. You're totally welcome to join in too."

Jon had frozen on the couch. His astute gaze darted between Ryan and Cassandra, moving over every detail—from pigtails to white bobby socks. Exactly as Ryan had expected.

A smirk curled Jon's mouth. He leaned back on the couch and stretched one arm along the back. His foot lifted to hitch over his knee. "No plans, Fang? Or maybe a late-night tutoring session?"

Ryan shot him a death look, but it didn't kill that plastic smirk. "Would you please shut the hell up?"

Leah's brow wrinkled. Her mouth turned down as she glanced between the men. "What am I missing?"

Cassandra laughed. "Can you keep missing it? These two have it covered."

Shrugging, Leah took another long drink. "Good with me. Last thing we need is a pissing match. If they don't get over it, you and I could always ditch 'em and go out on our own."

"I bet we could rip up the town." Cassandra flashed a smile at Ryan, obviously trying to get him to loosen up.

He sure as hell couldn't handle the idea of her out in public wearing the tiny costume hidden under her jacket. Every man for miles around would be drooling all over her. Hell, he was on the verge of it himself, even considering the raging embarrassment turning his neck hot as a branding iron.

He wrapped an arm around her waist and pulled her tight. "We're not going anywhere."

Jon stood and smoothed his shirt. "Come on, Princess. I think we're *persona non grata* right now."

She put her beer down on the coffee table and followed Jon to the door. "Give me a call sometime, Cass. I really think we should go out."

Cassandra agreed with a bright smile. Ryan managed to wave, but that was about it. He was numb. His feet were stuck to the carpet.

So screwed. He'd be hearing about this for years. He wrenched a hand down along his temple. He'd be seriously lucky if Jon didn't lobby to change his call sign to Professor.

Cassandra turned and leaned against the closed door. Her laugh was low and loose. "I can't believe we got caught. Again. Proof positive I was never meant to be a call girl. I'd be busted my first night. Again. We must have the worst luck ever."

His mouth opened and closed a few times. All he could manage was a quiet, "Shit."

"Oh, come on, baby. Don't be that way."

He wasn't above admitting that he stomped as he walked to the couch, surprised his back bent well enough to sit. It felt like a bayonet had been shoved up his spine, keeping him stiff and straight.

He couldn't explain. He didn't freaking *want* to explain. If they'd kept to normal shit, there wouldn't be anything to explain in the first place. Any man, even a class-A pervert like Jon, would admit that he'd found a helluva woman in Cassandra.

He had to go and demand more.

Her smile sultry, she came to stand in front of him. "I bet I know what'll make you feel better."

She untied her jacket, then dropped it off her shoulders.

Good God, she looked exactly as hot as he'd imagined. A tiny white shirt barely covered her breasts, tied practically at her cleavage. He could cover the pleated plaid skirt with the width of one hand. The entire, smooth expanse of her torso was bare. She angled one knee across the other leg and clasped her hands behind her ass—the perfectly petulant teenager.

"Please, Professor," she said in a slightly breathy voice. "Don't be mad at me."

Chapter Thirty-Two

It wasn't working.

Ryan was as stiff and as closed off as she'd ever seen him. Every movement radiated tension. He'd been really shaken up by his friends getting wind of his secret turn-on, Jon especially. Cass wanted to deck the smug butthead for poking at Ryan that way.

At the same time, she didn't see what the big deal was. So what? They enjoyed each other. It's not like they were having an illicit affair, where lives could be ruined if they got caught. Jon and Leah wouldn't run tattling to their CO about naughty Major Haverty's private pastime.

Cass crossed to the kitchen and grabbed a cold beer. She opened it, downing a swig to clear her head. The alcohol content couldn't have been much, but she wasn't used to it. A pleasant buzz nestled in her brain with the third hefty swallow. She took two more for good measure, just trying to decide what to do.

He still wanted it. That much she knew. For some reason he was resisting. He'd been avoiding her for days. All week he'd found excuse after excuse not to see her, always finishing on a rushed, "I'll see you Friday." She'd even prepared herself for the possibility that he might come up with a reason to cancel that evening.

She still couldn't figure out why. Was it her? Or was it something he had yet to explain?

Screw it. Half the bottle was gone. For months now he'd been telling her how great it was to do something daring. Well, this was her being daring—and she was prepared to call him on it if he didn't follow suit. She needed the truth, while Ryan needed a lesson in looking dark things in the face.

She adopted a different approach this time. No more breathy pleas. This called for good old-fashioned insolence.

Dropping onto the couch beside Ryan, she folded her arms beneath her chest and found a pout that matched her mood.

"What?" he asked.

"What? You're the one who wanted me here."

"Cassandra, it's not—"

"I mean, really, Professor. Detention's bad enough without you rubbing it in."

"Detention?"

"Yeah, and it's not fair. Those other girls were talking too. It's like you singled me out on purpose. What, am I supposed to be some example for the others?" She huffed out a breath that played with her bangs. "Like I said, not fair."

He shifted on the couch. "You don't have to do this, you know. You can go home. It might be better that way."

No way, buddy. You're not getting out of this so easily.

Cass turned on the couch, propping her head on her elbow. The position was sure to accentuate the low plunge of her knotted shirt and the white lace push-up bra beneath.

"You mean it? I can go?"

Wearing a frown, he said, "Sure. I'm not holding you here."

"Cool." She leaned over to the coffee table and grabbed her Hello Kitty purse. The Bonnie Bell lip gloss tasted of artificial strawberry as she reapplied it liberally.

"You going home?"

"Nah. To the mall."

"What's at the mall?"

"Yeah, right. Like I'd tell you. You'll only say how he's no good for me."

Ryan watched her lips with a ravenous need. Every muscle in his long, vital body was shaking, like a beast waiting to jump out of his skin. "Your boyfriend?"

"We're fuck buddies if that counts. He works at the tattoo kiosk."

"You can get tattoos at a kiosk?"

"Uh, yeah." She rolled her eyes as if he were the oldest person on the planet. "But, hey, I wouldn't expect a guy in his forties to know that."

"I'm twenty-nine."

"Whatever." She stood up. The miniscule hem of her plaid skirt would leave little to the imagination from his vantage. She gave him a cruel shimmy, smiling privately at his near-silent moan. "Later, Teach."

Cass actually reached the entryway where she'd hung her coat, the Hello Kitty purse dangling from her wrist. Her hand grazed the fabric. Then his low, hoarse voice found her.

"Not so fast, Miss Whitman."

Relief and a fast thrill zipped down to her toes, settling between her legs. She kept the insolent teenager front and center. With every ounce of attitude she could muster, Cass turned and cocked her hip. "What now?"

"Is he any good? Your, ah, fuck buddy?"

"Good enough, I suppose. He knows what to do with his tongue stud." She feigned a flash of panic. "Oh, shit, you're not going to tell my parents, are you?"

"Depends."

"On?"

"Come here."

Cass took her time crossing his living room, back to the couch. She gave Ryan a pointed look. He had relaxed into the cushions, just a bit. The sweater and tie made him seem almost like another person, as if Ryan Haverty had decided that Egyptian ruins were his passion rather than flying. Not exactly bookish, he was more like Harrison Ford when Indy suited up for time in the classroom—the academic every girl wanted to have a naughty streak.

His knees were spread. The thickening line of his erection trailed down the inside of his thigh, pressing against his slacks. Oh, yeah. She wanted that.

"I won't tell your parents."

"Oh, thank you, Professor. I don't know how to—"

"For a price."

She bit the tip of her forefinger. "It would be our secret? All of it?"

"Sure." A swallow bobbed his Adam's apple. "All of it."

"So that's the real reason, isn't it? You could've had four other girls in here. Instead...it's just me." She leaned over, her hands on the back of the couch, one on either side of his head. Any attempt he made at keeping his attention away from her cleavage was a losing battle. He gave in and looked. His luscious lips parted on a soft inhale. "Admit it, Professor. You wanted me here alone."

His lifted his eyes, revealing just how dark and needy he was. "And here you are."

"So...what do I have to do?" she asked in a whisper. "To keep you quiet?"

"Show me what's under your skirt."

"I don't have anything under my skirt."

He grabbed one of her braids. A jolt of pain swept across her scalp. Cass let out a surprised squeal and tried to wrench away. Ryan got a better grip on the tether, twisting until she couldn't move her head.

"I said," he rasped against her cheek, "show me."

"Yes, Professor."

He released the pressure and allowed her to stand. Cass stepped back, feet scarcely apart. The outsides of her thighs barely brushed the insides of his spread knees. She pinched two places along the skirt's hem, then raised the pleated plaid like a curtain. If porn movies had money shots, this was her own personal must-see moment.

She had to see his face. Because she'd meant it. She didn't have anything under her skirt, not even her bush.

Ryan gasped. They weren't touching at all, anywhere, but his body jerked. He rubbed a swift hand across his jaw, eyes fixed, gaze locked on her hairless pussy.

"Holy fuck," he moaned.

Cass smiled as innocently as she could, although on the inside she was pure raging sex. For twenty-four hours now she'd had time to get used it. The pain of her first wax had been pretty damn shocking, but afterward she'd gloried in how different she could feel. Panties had slid along smooth skin. Even the press of jeans between her legs had been more sensitive.

Every time, that brush of new sensation brought her back to delicious questions. What would it feel like when Ryan went down on her? What would it feel like when he fucked her?

She was gambling on *heavenly*, but wanted to know for sure.

Playfully, she dropped the hem of the skirt. "I've shown you mine, Professor. Now you show me yours."

"Undo my fly. Slowly."

Cass knelt between his legs. The trembling tension in his muscles was even stronger now, spiking her excitement. She slid her hands up along the insides of his thighs. Her thumbs cupped the underside of his balls through the soft fabric of his slacks. He sucked in a quick breath. Her every movement was slow, just like he'd ordered, until his fly hung open.

That gorgeous cock pointed due north, its head poking out from the waistband of his boxer briefs. Cass hooked her fingers under the elastic and tugged. The scent of his salty arousal made her lick her lips.

"Touch it," he said roughly.

Cass wanted nothing more, but she fell back on her role. "I don't know if I should."

"You've done it before, haven't you? That boy in the mall?"

"Yeah, but this is different."

He cupped the back of her neck. The pressure he applied there was not gentle. Cass resisted, their muscles fighting, but he was so much stronger. "I don't see how. A slut like you—what does it matter whose cock you suck?"

"He's not..."

"What?"

"He's not so big."

Ryan growled. He moved in for a fierce kiss. Their teeth banged together, their tongues tangling. He sucked her bottom lip, licking off her flavored lip gloss. One big hand slipped up her body. He cupped her breast, squeezing until she shivered.

"Now goddamn it, you snotty little bitch. Suck me off or I call your parents."

"Okay," she gasped. "Anything you say, Professor.

Just...don't tell, okay?"

He edged forward on the cushion, back straight, with the perfect vantage to watch her work. His expression was feverish. Cass rubbed her stinging lower lip where he'd bit. She pushed her braids back and lowered her head. The first touch of lip to cock pulled a heavy grunt from his chest. She pushed deeper, taking in that wide head. Already she tasted his salt, how ready he was to explode in her mouth.

She couldn't let that happen. If Ryan came now, he'd be right back where they started. It could take all night to get it through his thick skull that this was good sexy fun.

He stroked her face with his thumbs. "Beautiful," he whispered. "So fucking beautiful."

Cass cupped his balls, gently fondling as she sucked and swirled her tongue. His hips pulsed with jerky movements. His breathing picked up.

She slipped free, pulling back.

"I don't want you to stop," he said.

"But...I...I'm curious."

Ryan reached out and deftly untied the shirt where it was knotted at her cleavage. She was almost impressed that he could manage it with such unsteady hands. "About what, Miss Whitman?"

"I'm curious what you'd feel like." She rose up on her knees and licked along his jaw. Rough evening stubble scored her tongue. "Inside me. I've never been with a man so big before. Just punks with pencil dicks and no rhythm. It wouldn't be like that with you, would it? I want a real fuck by a real man."

With a tug, Ryan yanked her shirt down off her shoulders. Soon she was kneeling before him in the plaid skirt, the bobby socks and her white lace bra.

"If we do this, you'll have to listen to everything I say. You'll have to do everything I tell you to do." His voice was so different, so controlled, that her thighs loosened. Just wanting him. "Do you think you can do that?"

"Of course I can, sir."

He pinched her nipple through the fabric of her bra. "I mean it. If you disobey me, there will be consequences."

"If I *do* obey, Professor? You'll make it good for me?"

Gradually running his hand down her torso, he slid two fingers between the lips of her smooth pussy. He gave her clit a flick, then smiled a nasty, sexy smile.

"Yes, Miss Whitman. I'll make it *very* good."

Chapter Thirty-Three

Ryan was fucked in the head. Really, truly fucked.

And savoring every second.

Cassandra was on her knees between his legs, her beautiful tits mounded by the sheer lace bra. The tiny lick of a skirt barely covered her pussy.

Her *bare* pussy.

She'd lifted the skirt, and he'd thought his cock would rise up to meet her. Nothing but bare skin, gleaming with her juices. The only thought in his head had been *yes, please.* Cupping her hot, warm center in his hand had been awesome.

Even now she waited. Patiently. Her lower lip pouting out in petulance. She play-acted at defiance, but she was giving him everything. Her sexy self laid out on a platter.

It was so wrong and so right at the same time.

He circled over her clit one more time, then withdrew. He stuck his fingers in his mouth to lick her wetness. Sweet flavor rolled over his tongue.

"Oh, Professor," she said, eyes wide. "Are you a bad man?"

"You're about to find out, aren't you?"

Something angry and violent was running him down. Chasing him out of his head. No way could he think about anything from the outside world. Not right then. There was only him and her and their twisted game.

He stood abruptly. Fierce lust roared when she stayed kneeling, her face at cock level. "Go to my bedroom. Now. Bend over the end of my bed and wait for me."

"Wait?" Her words were still infused with petulance, which both grated at his spine and made his dick throb. "I thought you were going to make love to me."

He snatched her braid again. Pulled too tight. Tight enough

that a whisper of real pain flickered across her face. He wanted to back off at that moment—but then she licked her bottom lip. He watched her body roll up into the sting, soaking it in. Her smile was more than wicked. It reveled in the hot lust between them.

"I didn't tell you to give me any backtalk, did I?"

"No, Professor."

"Did I or did I not say you'd have to obey me? In everything?"

She curled her hands around the insides of her thighs. The plaid skirt brushed her wrists. "You did, sir."

As if prying off his fingers one at a time, he released her pigtail. Already he missed the rough silk of her hair wrapped around his fingers. He intentionally echoed every word. "Go to my bedroom. Now. Bend over the end of my bed and wait for me."

"Yes, Professor."

She hopped up immediately and almost ran toward the doorway to his bedroom. At the threshold, she paused and flipped up the back of her skirt. Then she continued on as if she'd never stopped.

Ryan needed a second. He pressed the heels of his palms to his eyes. It wasn't too late to quit this shit. Call a halt. But when he dragged his hands down his face, he smelled her arousal on his fingers.

He stripped his clothes before he could think twice, stalking toward the bedroom on legs he barely felt. His entire world centered in his cock.

Cassandra had obeyed to the letter. Her palms were flat on the mattress, her ass high. The skirt only covered the top curves of her perfect backside.

He stepped up behind her. "Miss Whitman, I'm tired of your impertinence."

She still kept it up, wiggling her ass at him. "I'm so sorry, Professor," she said, but in tones that taunted she didn't mean a bloody word of it.

"Did I tell you to stop on the way in here? Or to flash your smutty skirt at me?"

"No, sir."

He stroked up her back in one long pet, then fisted his hand around both pigtails. He pulled up mercilessly, until she had to stand and lean against his chest to avoid the pain. "You smelled like beer when I kissed you. How old are you, Miss Whitman?"

She pushed up on her toes, her ass sliding over his cock. "I'm nineteen, Professor."

He couldn't tell if the tremor in her voice was real. He wasn't exactly sure if he cared. He wanted to push her and keep pushing her, just to see how far she'd go. "That's not old enough to drink. Did I even give you permission to drink my beer?"

"No, Professor."

He shoved her down. She slapped her hands flat on the comforter. "Do you know what happens to naughty girls?"

Her entire body shuddered. "They're punished?"

"Yes." He drew the word into a hiss. Anticipation ate at him. His whole body was locked and loaded. He throbbed with wanting her.

"I deserve to be punished, Professor. Punish me. Spank me. Anything." She tossed her braids over one shoulder and looked at him. Lust sparked in her eyes, which had gone a darker blue than he'd ever seen. "Just please don't tell on me."

He cupped her ass, then under to her bare, wet lips. The touch he traced across skin was feather soft. With his other he worked at gathering up the wisp of her skirt and holding it out of the way. Baring her.

He yanked his hand back and smacked the flesh of her ass cheek.

She yelped once. Her hands fisted in the bed covers, but she pushed up on her toes. "Yes," she breathed. "*Yes.*"

His mind dimmed. Only Cassandra remained—and teaching her a lesson.

He'd started off relatively gently. A bare crack with his fingertips. He kept on, each smack harder and harder, until the reverberation ran all the way up to his shoulder. Until there was nothing but her ass, turning red under his tingling palm, and her body arching to meet every hit.

She kept up the stream of filthy talk. Calling him professor. Begging him. Telling him how wet she was. How much she wanted to be fucked by a real man.

Every word went straight to his head—pushed more and more shit away until there was just them. Just what they were making. Together.

His hand lifted in the air, he froze. “Miss Whitman, this is your last stroke,” he warned. “But if you can’t take it, I’ll be forced to start over.”

Cassandra pushed her face into the comforter. Her skin was flushed, her eyes glassy. “Yes, Professor. I’ll be good. Just please don’t stop.”

He used his left hand to pet over her back. Sweat had gathered in the dip at the base of her spine. “You’ve been a very good girl so far, but for this one I want something different.”

“Yes, sir.”

He bent low over her. The skin behind her ear was unbelievably soft as he brushed his lips there. “Don’t move,” he whispered. “Don’t say a word.”

He brought his hand down sharply over her wet pussy, fingertips aimed directly at her clit. Her body jerked. Her toes curled into the carpet in their bobby socks. Low and deep in her chest, a moan built, but she kept her lips sealed against it. He could let her get away with that much.

Ryan pushed two fingers into her sheathe, then dropped to his knees. He closed his mouth over her slick cunt. Licking along her wet length, he dipped his tongue between her lips. Juicy as a summer ripe orange. So goddamn smooth he thought he’d lose his mind. He fanned his hands wide over her tight ass, holding her apart. Taut muscles trembled under fever-hot skin.

He spread her folds with his thumbs. Her arousal soaked his fingers until he licked it away, her clit pulsing beneath his tongue as he circled. Around. Back the other way. Varying the rhythm so she couldn’t get complacent. So she’d be as mind-sprung as he felt. He curled his fingers inside her, stroking against the front of her sheathe—finding that small spot that made her thighs jerk and her hips thrust.

"Please, sir." She pushed her pussy against his face. "Please, can I come?"

He rocked back on his heels, stroked in and out. "Now. Come now, my dirty girl."

Her smooth lips clenched him and she screamed. Flat-out screamed, pressing her face into the bed, coming in violent pulses around his fingers.

That was it. Ryan lost all semblance of control. He grabbed a condom and rolled it on in a blink. He thrust into her with no finesse. No slow testing. His hands wrapped around her pelvis, under the tiny plaid skirt, fingertips brushing where her newly bare skin began. He slammed his hips against her red ass.

"Yes, sir," she gasped. "Fuck, right there. Fuck me. Own me. Use that prick in me."

Again and again. He pounded her. Unrelenting. Fierce. His cock ached. She bore down on him so strong he thought his brains would blow out through his dick.

Wet smacking noises filled the room. His harsh breathing. Her begging and panting.

Abruptly, he pushed her down and nearly threw her onto the bed. She landed with a bounce on hands and knees, but he didn't give her a second to flip over. He couldn't look at her. Not when it would mean looking at himself.

Ryan didn't even know himself at that moment. He only knew where his cock belonged. Inside this snotty little schoolgirl.

He slammed into her again.

With her braid in his hand, he pulled until she jerked up onto her knees. Her arms latched back around his neck. "Oh, God," she moaned. "Right there. You feel so good right there."

He slid one hand around her throat. Keeping his touch gentle was damn difficult when his limbs were shaking. He forced himself down to her breasts, cupping one soft mound. Squeezing, he kept driving into her from behind. He lined up her nipple between two fingers and pinched. She squealed. Her cunt clamped down as she came again. Juices poured over him.

His orgasm was a crashing jet, smashing into him with no control. He jerked once, twice. He was lost. A red haze covered him. Overwhelmed him. Tore him down to the foundation.

They stayed locked together in that position. The sweat started to cool over Ryan's body.

Cassandra melted first, her arms drooping from around his neck. She folded to the bed. Even as she slipped into a puddle, her mouth curved into a contented smile.

He collapsed next to her and smashed his face into a pillow. He couldn't look at her.

"Oh, my God," she breathed. Any trace of the petulant teenager was gone. There was only Cassandra. And Ryan. And his fantastic lack of control.

He rolled to his back. His chest still jerked with his rough breathing, his heartbeat rushing in his ears. As the blood left his dick, he started to get a few brain cells back.

Her shiver shook into his side. "That was fierce. *You* were fierce." She laughed. "Freaking fabulous."

Ryan pushed to sit, then swung his legs over the edge of the bed. One swift move took care of the condom.

He wanted to smile. To laugh. She liked that. Liked him when he was being charming. There wasn't an ounce of funny in him. He scrubbed his hands down over his face.

The bed shifted as she came to her knees behind him. A tentative touch stroked over his shoulders. "Ryan?"

"I just... Give me a minute." A fast push had him on his feet.

"Ryan." She grabbed his wrist. Pulled. He wouldn't let himself be moved. "Come talk to me about this."

He couldn't deal with this, not now. Not when he realized that he wasn't the man he'd tried to be.

The bathroom wasn't much of an escape, but at least it was something. "I need a shower."

Chapter Thirty-Four

Cass scrambled off the bed before her brain caught up with reflex. Not even bothering to tug off her miniscule skirt, she skittered between Ryan and his bathroom escape hatch. She braced her arms on either wall of the short hallway. He reared back as if touching her would burn.

"So, what, you think a shower will wash it all off?"

He tried to angle past her. "Quit playing, okay? No more insolent teenager."

"Oh, this isn't insolent teenager. This is full-grown, pissed-off woman."

"I'm tired. I don't want to get into this."

"Of course you're tired! We just had a monumental good time. If you think I'm letting you shut me down, now, after what we just did, you're insane."

Jaw clenched, Ryan clamped his hands around her upper arms, but he didn't try to move her. He just stood there, his eyes begging for something she couldn't give him—privacy.

"What?" she asked. "Can't do it, huh? Can't fight me unless there's a backstory and a hard-on involved?"

"You're making too much of this. I just want a shower."

"Bullshit." She shrugged from under his hands, poking a finger against his bare chest. "I call bullshit, Ryan. Now you sit your butt down and tell me what's been going on!"

"*Been* going on? What the hell?"

"Sure. You've been on the defensive about this almost since day one. I'm standing here dressed like a Nabokov fantasy, but you aren't man enough to tell me why it wigs you out—when only two seconds ago you couldn't get enough."

Movements stiff and clipped, he turned away and grabbed a fresh pair of boxers out of a drawer. Cass shucked what remained of the slutty schoolgirl getup. She snagged a soft white dress shirt from his closet. It wasn't as safe as talking to him in her own clothes, but at least she wouldn't feel quite so chilled. The contrast was huge between wearing that outfit when Ryan was on board...and when he was walled off by unnamed regrets.

He stood with his naked back to her, head bowed. His fists tightened over and over. When he finally turned, his face was twisted by some conflict she couldn't understand. To see him caught in such a moment pulled her close. She crossed to him, touched his shoulder. His tiny flinch made her drop her hand.

"Do you have any idea how much that turns me on? What we just did?"

Cass tried to find some humor—any glimpse of her Ryan. "I have an idea, yeah."

But Ryan wasn't home. He looked...hollow. Broken down.

"I've been like this for years. Just couldn't admit it. I'd look at *Playboy* or something but wouldn't get much out of it. Yeah, they might be hot. Might even be saucy or pretty. Then... Shit, I'd see an ad in a magazine of a cute woman dressed like a nurse or a goddamn librarian, and I'd get hard so fast I couldn't breathe."

"So? Ryan, I'm not getting it. What is the big deal?"

"What's the big deal?" His voice was an explosion in his small bedroom. "What do you mean, what's the big deal? It's sick, Cassandra. What we just did is *sick*."

This was full-blown Major Haverty talking, like when he'd laid into those pilots. After an initial reflex to retreat, Cass stood her ground—one small part frightened, one huge part furious.

"Oh, sure," she sneered, "you can say that now after you've just come. I didn't see you trying too much when I flashed my waxed kitty. *You* called me back. *You* decided to play. Or maybe your dick did." She glanced down at his crotch. "Is that why you're so angry, Ryan? Something else calling the shots?"

"Stop."

"No, I deserve some straight answers."

"I just told you! What more do you want from me?"

Cass narrowed her eyes. "I want to know why what we do

as consenting adults in the privacy of your bedroom is cause for such a freak out."

"Because it's not just here, okay?"

"What, the call-girl thing? The sex shop? If you're worried about conduct unbecoming, Major, we don't ever have to again. We're the only two people involved here. *We* set the terms."

Hands still tense, he raked his scalp. "Sure, but now Jon knows."

"He's not the paparazzi. You think he'll tell anyone?"

"No."

"So it's just that *someone* knows?"

"Why not? It's not like I go broadcasting this."

Cass curled her fingers against her mouth, her heart pounding too loudly. "Not ever?"

"Once, okay? Once," he spit. "That was a huge disaster. I definitely learned my lesson."

"Who?" Cass couldn't contain her curiosity, not when this had become so intense. He shook his head, which only made her angrier. "I deserve to know, Ryan. This affects both of us and you know it."

He sagged onto the mattress, his shoulders curving forward. With a glance up he said, "Her name was Ashleigh. We dated all through my senior year. I even popped the question, thinking she'd want to make it official before I asked her to wait for me on deployments."

It was Cass's turn to sag. He'd had a fiancée and hadn't even told her. What a fool she'd been to think she knew him.

"We'd played around some," he said. "Stockings. A cheerleader costume at Halloween. When I asked her a few weeks later to wear it again... Shit, Cassandra, she freaked. I tried to explain it. I owed her that after asking her to get married. Nothing calmed her down. 'Women aren't Barbie dolls to help you get off,' she said."

That judgmental bitch. Cass curled her hands into fists, riding a surprising wave of disgust. Sure, it wouldn't work for every woman. But had this Ashleigh really needed to belittle Ryan like he'd done something wrong?

"That's why you didn't tell me," she said quietly.

He lifted his gaze from the floor, his expression weary and defeated. "I thought she loved me. I thought we were going to spend the rest of our lives together—and even that wasn't enough. Do you really think I was going to risk something as new as you and me by opening up about my perversion?"

"Perversion?" She made a face. "Oh, come off it."

"Of course it is."

"Which part doesn't track with your brutish gender, hm?" Ticking off the list on her fingers, she said, "Sex with submissive young women, sex with high-class call girls who claim you're the biggest and best, sex that pushes limits and provides an escape. Just what the hell is so weird about any of that? It sounds like ninety-nine percent of the straight male population."

"Because it's common, Cassandra. It's weird. It's *trashy.*" His slouched pose only accentuated the fit definition of his abs where they rippled in on each other. "You know how I grew up, right?"

"What you've told me."

"There I was, in that sleazy trailer park. It sounds like a stereotype, I know. Some trailer parks are nice. They're a real community, well kept. This wasn't." He shook his head. "You wouldn't believe some of the stuff I saw when I was younger. Drugs. A stabbing. There was this feud between two families that wound up with an arson charge. Every boy knew where you could hide behind a few old fences to watch the prostitutes come out after dark."

Cass's hands shook. She clasped them together, then held as motionless as a rabbit in danger.

"After Coach Dan kicked some sense into me, I worked my ass off. I wanted out of there. Someday I would be a pilot. Do you know what kind of ridicule that much ambition gets in a place like that? So I stopped telling everyone. Just kept my head down, kept focused on my goals."

"Ryan, you've achieved them."

He lifted his chin, meeting her eyes. "It wasn't just about the job. I swore I'd be better than all of that one day. I'd have a nice house, a great wife, people's respect. No one would have to know..."

Cass forced the tight tendons of her neck to relax. She tested him when she concluded, "No one would have to know you're just as unworthy as that trailer trash."

A sigh pushed out from his strong chest. "Busted. Now you've dragged all this playacting shit out of me and there's no going back."

That flickering rage, almost quelled by his pain, flared back to life. "Me? *I* dragged this out? How is this my fault?"

"Just drop it. You've poked at me enough for one night."

"No, I won't. Everything we've done has been straight out of your deepest fantasies, and now I get the blame for it? How is that fair?"

He surged off the bed, his defensive anger like a tidal wave coming in. "It wasn't enough that I think about it all the time. You had to go make it *possible*. Now how the hell can I shove that knowledge back?"

"You don't! You thank the sweet baby Jesus that you finally found a girl who loves it too and wants to play along."

"I don't want you to play along! I want something normal and good."

"And this..." She pointed to the plaid skirt where it lay in a rumpled heap. "This isn't normal or good. I get it."

Cass left him there, her steps nearly blind as she hurried toward the apartment's front door.

"Where are you going?" he called, coming after her. "You can't leave the house in that."

"I can."

"Cass, don't do this."

"Cass? I'm Cass now, huh? All that adorable Cassandra stuff was just part of the All-American act, wasn't it?"

"What act?"

"You! Your whole life is an act."

"Screw that."

"Sure it is! You play dress up every day, *Major* Haverty. People see your uniform first. Then they see that quick smile of yours and, well, who could blame them for not looking any deeper? I did. And look what I found."

"Don't bring my job into this."

"Why not? It's not off limits here. When was the last time you were with a girl who didn't know you as a pilot first, or a varsity quarterback?" His hesitation was answer enough. Cass grabbed her coat and tugged it on. "I caught you off guard, didn't I? Me and my stockings and these fucking pigtails."

He flinched.

"Before you knew it, you'd revealed too much. You showed me just what you liked and just what you needed. It was okay, though, right? Just a weekend. Just a fun fling." Her motions were sharp as she cinched the jacket's waist tie. "It's fine to whore around with a waitress. You probably could've locked that weekend away in a dark corner, only bringing it out to jerk off on special occasions. All nice and private. But the longer we stayed together, the tougher it's been for you to reconcile. So I'll go."

"Don't. Please."

"You don't think I'm staying here, do you, Professor?"

His expression revealed surprise and hurt. She'd lashed out using his shame as a weapon. At that moment she didn't feel like being kind.

"That's not fair," he said. "You liked it too."

"My point exactly, you stubborn asshole." Her voice shook. She couldn't stop herself from venting it all. "I liked it too. I have from the start. I wasn't ashamed, not until about four minutes ago. *You* did that to me. You took the fun and the laughter out of it and turned it into something gross."

Ryan crossed the living room. His face said contrition, but his posture remained painfully tight. Even defiant. He was just going through the motions of placating her.

"I'm asking you not to go. Don't...don't go away angry."

"I'm not one of your subordinates, Major. You don't get to tell me what to do."

"*You* don't get to lead me around by my dick."

"I can. I did. Not anymore."

His nostrils flared. "What are you saying?"

"I'm saying we're done."

"Don't be stupid."

"I'm not," she said, forcing the words out of her constricted throat. "In fact, I'm applying some pretty shrewd logic to the situation. I'm sorry about your ex, Ryan. I am. I'm sorry you didn't trust me enough to tell me about her before now. But I'm even sorrier that she made you think you need to choose between fantasy and reality. So I'm making it easy on you." She nudged her chin back toward the bedroom door. "That outfit is a size six. Keep it anonymous and I'm sure you could find another waitress to fill it out."

"It's not like that!"

Cass held back her tears by force of will. He was ruining something wonderful with every word. She needed to get the hell out. Soon she wouldn't be able to look back on any of their time together without fits of nauseated shame.

"How am I supposed to trust that?" she asked. "You didn't even have enough trust to tell me in the first place."

"Cassandra," he rasped.

"Good luck, Ryan. I hope you figure out that there doesn't need to be a choice. That there might actually be a good woman in this world who can give you everything." She shrugged, her heart breaking. "I just hope you don't realize that it could've been me. I imagine that would hurt like hell."

Chapter Thirty-Five

Lost in the last dregs of sleep, Ryan didn't know what was pounding at his door. He stretched a hand across the bed and found nothing. Cool sheets. No warm body or soft hair. Just like there hadn't been for the past three weeks.

Shit.

The pounding kept up anyway.

He stumbled out of bed, glancing at the green glow of his iPod dock. Six a.m. Who in their right mind would bother him at that hour?

Jon and Leah. Of course.

They stood in the walkway outside his door dressed in workout clothes. Jon leaned against the railing while Leah practically danced. The woman had so much energy she lived life at a full-out sprint.

"Ready to go?" she asked.

For a second Ryan wondered if they'd arranged to meet and he'd just forgotten. He was doing a lot of that lately. His mind had gone to mush. Not surprising, considering that colossal fight with Cassandra took up most of his brain. Then again, he was being actively antisocial.

He scrubbed sleep out of his eyes. "What are you two doing here?"

Leah bounced on the balls of her feet. Her dark ponytail swung around the shoulders of her tank top. "Work out. Come on. Your building has the best gym."

"That's crap and you know it," he said. "Tin Tin's place is ten times nicer, and the gym on base is ten times bigger."

"Fine." Jon crossed his arms. "Truth, Fang?"

"I generally prefer it."

The two traded a doubtful look. Ryan fisted his hand

around the doorknob.

Finally Jon stepped forward. “We wanted to ask why you’ve been such a dick the past couple weeks. We wanted to do it here, where no one else could overhear.”

Leah tried a grin out on him. “Since you won’t go out with us, we figured we didn’t have a choice.”

Christ. That was just what he needed. Obviously they’d sat around discussing him. *Poor broken Fang. What’s wrong with our major?*

That they could’ve discussed his goddamn proclivities was just the icing on the cake.

He set his back teeth together and let them grind. It did nothing to ease the brain-spiking tension locking him down. “Cassandra and I broke up. End of story. Go work out somewhere else. I’ll see you at oh eight hundred.”

He slammed the door and face-planted on the bed. If he could push it all away, he had a chance at another hour of sleep.

After all, it was the only place he still got to see Cassandra.

Even that didn’t keep the idiots at bay. Only a minute later his bedroom door opened. Jon pulled the pillow off his face. The comforter disappeared next.

“Let’s go,” Jon said in an obviously fake-cheery voice. “Up and at ’em, Major. Your chain of command would be very disappointed if they knew you were skipping out on PT.”

He levered to a sitting position. “Why in the name of heaven did I ever give you a key?”

“In case you were ever ‘I’ve fallen and I can’t get up,’” Leah said. “Now where are your workout clothes?”

She pulled open his top drawer, and everything in Ryan went ice cold. “Get your fucking fingers out of my shit,” he growled.

Leah froze, her hands hovering in the air. The only part of her that moved was her head, swiveling to stare at him with huge, wounded eyes.

Ryan didn’t think he’d ever cussed around her, except maybe when he’d been drunk. Cussing *at* her, though? Never.

But that was where he'd shoved Cassandra's plaid skirt and tiny white shirt.

He was up in a flash, slamming the drawer shut. Sharp-edged anger wrenched inside him. At this point, it wasn't even fearing that they'd know what got him hot. They probably were fully aware.

No, the outfit was Cassandra's. Hers. Not for anyone else to even look at.

With hands curled around the edge of the wood, he took a deep breath. "Look, I appreciate your concern. It's best if you just leave. I'm not up to dealing with anyone else right now."

To be honest, he missed Cassandra too damn bad. It was an empty ache in his chest. Every time he picked up his phone, he thought about calling her. Hell, every time he climbed in the cockpit, he thought about her, about how he'd love to recount his day of flying. He thought about *her*. What he'd had. What he'd done. What he'd lost.

She was in his head constantly.

He wanted her back, but that was the easy part. How to line up the pieces in his head… That was practically impossible. Only, the way Cassandra's words still rang in his head made him think he could get his shit together. He *needed* to.

Jon laughed quietly. "We're not really up to dealing with you either. Someone had to try."

"Mind your own business, Tin Tin."

Leah crossed her arms over her chest and glanced at Jon. "Go on. Tell him."

"I don't think so," Jon said. "It's obvious he just wants to ignore it."

"Tell me what?"

"We're going to the exhibit opening tonight."

Ryan tensed. "The hell you are."

Jon scrubbed a hand over his cropped hair. Leah edged around Ryan to stand beside him. Her mouth twisted into an apologetic attempt at a smile. "We are. Both of us. We *like* Cass."

Ryan shook his head in denial, but it wasn't working. They

just kept talking.

"I also happen to like art now and then," Jon said dryly. "Keeps up my old-money cred. So we're going."

"Fuck no, you're not." He was losing control of his mouth, but that wasn't much of a surprise. He'd already lost control of his life. "That's an order."

Leah laughed. "Sorry, boss. You can't order us around on this one." She turned and walked out of the room, Jon following behind her. "So I guess you'll either have to trust we'll behave…or come and make sure of it."

Ryan pinched a hand across his forehead. His head had started to pound.

He'd meant to stay away from the exhibit. Cassandra had settled on her decision. As much as he missed her, he wasn't about to make her big night blow up in her face. Seeing her most recent ex might throw her off her game.

There was no way he could allow those two to go unchecked. He needed to attend, even if only to run herd.

If a small part of him sighed in relief at being able to see Cassandra again… He'd ignore that part.

He'd been ignoring parts of himself for years.

The gallery was packed with people. A steady hum of quiet voices dipped and rose around the room. Wearing the same suit from their call-girl game, Ryan could almost convince himself that staying anonymous was possible.

He'd spotted Cassandra almost as soon as he'd entered.

She looked beautiful. Elegant. Every bit in her element.

A black dress hugged her curves. Her strawberry-blonde hair had been scooped into a twist at the back of her head. With her only ornamentation a black silk cord that dipped under the boat neck of her dress, her pale creamy skin practically glowed.

Or maybe that was her happiness. A soft smile curved her mouth as she talked to the knot of shifting people that constantly surrounded her.

Jon slipped alongside Ryan, holding a glass of champagne.

"If you don't want to actually talk to her, you should probably stop staring at her."

"Stuff it, Tin Tin. I'm not in the mood."

He wanted to talk to her. The problem was how to line up his thoughts—his desires—with his quest for a perfect life. What was perfect other than having everything he wanted? He'd been denying himself for so long that his fantasies never figured in. The intimacy he and Cassandra shared had nothing to do with the world outside the bedroom. That he'd refused them both such a perfect alignment of sex and love was a goddamn disgrace.

I hope you figure out that there doesn't need to be a choice.

She had seen it clearly, with the same open acceptance she'd always shown. Hell, her words had practically slapped him in the face, even though he'd been unprepared to accept their truth.

Disgusted with himself, impatient to talk with her, Ryan faced a large print. The vintage erotic photographs were remarkable. Dramatic. Cassandra had done well to volunteer to make this her first show.

Yeah, they were nudes—but they were more than that too. Frank examinations of the female form in an otherwise stark existence. Placards explained the setting: the famed Storyville, New Orleans prostitution district at the turn of the last century. Some of the women wore masks. On other prints the negatives had been scratched, the women's faces transformed into sharp black amorphous forms.

It wasn't right. No one deserved to have their true selves obliterated out of fear of exposure. Whether it was because of their profession or their choices. Their...appetites. In trying to obliterate that part of himself, he'd done the same to Cassandra. Tried to make her and their playtime anonymous. Safer that way.

Instead he'd made it shameful.

Admitting his fears was more than embarrassing, and yet the pain he'd caused the woman he loved was heartbreaking. Nothing was as important as the magic he and Cassandra had created.

Regret crushed in his chest, turning his lungs to stones. His skin flushed cold. Cassandra hadn't deserved the way he'd treated her. He hadn't deserved the way he'd treated himself either.

That he liked to play games wasn't really what he'd blown it into. It was a choice. A private choice. He could partake or resist. The same could be said for any of his partners. But Cassandra, her laughing and teasing and enthusiasm, had made the experiences mind-blowing. More than fantasy. More than tab A going into slot B, even if slot B was decked out in a costume. She had offered the chance to claim everything he'd ever wanted.

He'd fended off his own doubts by assuming she would judge him like Ashleigh had.

What a coward he'd turned out to be.

He looked away from the prints, seeking her out. Christ, he had to fix this. Even if she refused to take him back—and she'd be totally justified in brushing him off—he needed to apologize.

He spotted her instantly, as if he maintained a constant awareness of where she was. She stood at the far end of the room, laughing with an older man.

Thinking about moving his feet wasn't necessary. They took off on their own, heading for her. The crowds parted around him, then melted into the background until there was only Cassandra. Just like it had always been.

She saw him when he was a few feet away. Her blue eyes widened and her shoulders went stiff. Slim fingers tightened around the stem of her wineglass.

"Ryan," she said, with a tiny incline of her head.

"Cassandra." He wanted to say more. Tell her how much he'd missed her. How badly he wanted her back.

This wasn't the time or the place. He wouldn't ruin her moment.

"Ryan, this is Mr. Hungerford, the gallery owner." She waved a hand toward the older man. It pained him that her eyes begged him to behave. "Mr. Hungerford, this is Major Ryan Haverty."

The two shook, then Ryan shoved his hands in his pockets.

They wanted too badly to reach out for her, to touch her. He didn't have that privilege anymore.

"Mr. Hungerford, you should be very happy with Cassandra. She's put on quite the event."

The older gentleman had a wide smile. "Oh, trust me, I am. Very proud of her choices." He looked back and forth between the two. "If you'll excuse me, I see a patron I should greet."

Cassandra and Ryan stood staring at each other, alone in the middle of the crowd. Reading her eyes was impossible. He couldn't see past his own hurt.

"The exhibit looks like a huge success."

She glanced around. "Yes. We've gotten a great response."

"I'm happy for you."

Finally he was able to read her. The pain that washed over her face and dimmed her smile was impossible to ignore. "Are you?"

"Absolutely."

Being so close to her without touching her was torture. He reached out with one hand and looped his fingers around her wrist. Under that tentative touch, her pulse fluttered wildly. Her throat worked over a swallow. Her gaze dropped to his hand, where they were connected.

He had to cough back the tightness in his chest. "Can I talk to you? Just for a minute."

For a second he thought she'd say yes. Her face was so open. Hopeful. Then she shuttered down.

He had the sudden realization of how shitty it was to be on the receiving end of that reaction. She'd never closed herself off from him. She'd offered him the deepest, most hopeful parts of herself, and he'd brushed her away.

Cassandra pulled her wrist from his grip. A single lock of hair curled around her pixielike jawline. "I can't do this here, Ryan."

His body leaned toward her of its own volition. "You can't do this here, or you can't do this ever?"

She took one step back. Then another. "I really don't know."

Chapter Thirty-Six

"Cass, my little girl."

She turned just in time to be swept into her father's arms. It probably wasn't the most professional thing to do, but her dad wasn't any ordinary patron.

After the brief, tense encounter with Ryan had yanked the air from her lungs, Cass needed a bear hug. Tears borne of too many emotions pricked behind her eyelids. Anxiety, relief, pride…and heartache.

"Thanks, Dad. I needed that."

"I just wanted to let you know that we're leaving."

"So soon?"

Something unreadable flashed across his familiar features. "Your mother has made it impossible to stay any longer."

Cass's spirits plummeted. On top of all the worries about the actual mechanics of the gala opening, she'd also dreaded her parents' reaction to the Bellocq photographs. Though not prudes by any means, they probably hadn't expected vintage erotica. How could she defend her career choice if they looked on her first professional success as smut-peddling?

"I'm sorry to hear that, Dad. I mean, I know the photos are—"

He leaned in with a conspiratorial wink. "Save it, Cassie girl. We're leaving because your mom can't keep her hands off me."

Slapping her mouth shut, she didn't know whether to laugh or groan in embarrassment. At least they weren't ashamed.

Her mom arrived after having fetched her pashmina from the coat check. Together they looked elegant and happy. A twist in the vicinity of her heart made her want to search for Ryan.

Instead she gave her mom a fierce hug. "Thanks for coming. It means the world to me."

"You've really achieved something here, sweetie," her mom said. "I hope your boss appreciates it."

"He does. Mr. Talbert wants me to lead up another exhibit this year, one I'll plan start to finish. He's recommended that I represent the gallery at an exhibition in Florence later this summer."

"Then I'm glad we already had our talk about you and the tours. You belong here. We're both so proud. But we'll let you get back to work." She kissed Cass's cheek, where she whispered, "He hasn't stopped watching you all night."

Cass didn't need to ask who "he" was. The heat along the back of her neck was surely Ryan's steady gaze.

"I don't know what to do."

"Have you heard him out?"

Shaking her head, Cass tried to calm her faltering breath.

Across three long, agonizing weeks, she'd been sure of her course. No matter how many times she revisited their fight, she couldn't find reason to think her expectations were too high. Honesty. Trust. How could they even think of a future if he couldn't give her those two basic necessities?

So she'd managed to keep her mind occupied. Mostly. The bigger achievement was keeping her hand off the phone. For once, calling him would've been the coward's way out. It was up to him now. Ryan had broken something wonderful. They both deserved better.

"Maybe that's where you should start." With one last squeeze, her mom let go. "Then make up your mind."

Cass stood in the middle of the gallery, the best success of her life. She hadn't been this proud of herself since spending her first night alone in Paris. Transatlantic flight at the age of nineteen was nothing compared to seeing this goal realized.

The hollow in her chest would not fill up. It was all she could manage to keep her eyes from wandering, searching the gallery for a handsome fighter pilot who looked as forlorn as she felt.

"Hey, beautiful," said Gilly. She was dressed to the nines in a gorgeous gold linen suit. Only the length of the skirt, which was *really* revealing, suggested she wasn't a businesswoman. "I see you checking out my legs."

"Everyone in this place is checking out your legs."

"Nah, you have them too distracted with all these lovely nekkid ladies." She gave Cass a quick hug. "This is just all so glamorous I could spit."

"Which wouldn't be glamorous at all, so please don't. Besides, there are some incredibly rich patrons here tonight. You wouldn't want to miss your shot at a very special love connection."

"If you could be so good as to point one out?" Her expression shifted, etched with sympathy. "So?"

"So?"

"Is he here?"

"Yes. Lurking around. I said I couldn't talk to him now. He was good and didn't press." Cass shrugged despite how difficult it was. "That's where we're at."

"But he wants to talk."

"Just so you know," Cass said with a slight smile, "if you tell me I should hear him out, you'll be echoing my mother."

"Better your mother than mine." Gilly downed her champagne. "Mine would've married him by now. While being six weeks pregnant."

"My dear Miss Whitman," came Mr. Talbert's voice.

Gilly's eyes went wide. "Oops! Nearly busted. That's my cue to let you work." She gave Cass another quick hug. "Call me? Anything you need."

"I will. Promise. Now go have fun." She nodded toward a man in his early fifties with a full head of silver hair wearing an exquisite charcoal suit. "By the way, that's Mr. Price. Go say hi."

Mr. Talbert smiled as Gilly sauntered directly toward her male target. Then he was back to business. "Stunning job, Cass. Mr. Hungerford is nearly speechless."

"Except when he describes the nuance of shadow over the female form."

"You noticed that too? I keep passing him off to interested patrons." His demeanor seemed a touch looser than usual, as if he'd partaken of one too many glasses of champagne. "He wants to take the staff out for drinks after we're through here, to toast your success. Just across the street at Clockwork. Can you come?"

"I'd be happy to."

"Oh, and these are for you," he said, handing her a beautiful corsage of orchids and baby's breath. "Lisa Moyet had them sent over. She called me this afternoon from her living room, apparently rocking her son to sleep. She's as pleased with how you pulled this off as I am."

Throat thick with emotion, Cass pinned the corsage to her gown's swooping neckline. After emailing and spending hours on the phone with her mentor, she was especially warmed by the idea that Lisa's support hadn't been misplaced.

Never had she imagined scoring such a victory for her first opening. She glanced at the nearest display, offering an appreciative thank-you to the deceased photographer and to his anonymous model lounging naked in a New Orleans doorway. Good thing Lisa hadn't planned on a showing of Brueghel. Cass couldn't imagine the turnout or enthusiasm being quite so overwhelming for Dutch landscapes.

Two hours later, her mouth was sticky from the champagne and too much talking. Ryan, to her surprised dismay, was nowhere to be seen. Jon and Leah had offered their congratulations, both of them pale versions of their usual manic selves. She almost felt sorry for how they were caught between her and Ryan.

That he could leave, giving up on her so easily, stung more than she wanted to admit. She touched the silk cord she'd worn as a necklace and resolved to finally give up the casino chip when she got home. No sense in being sentimental about it anymore.

Struggling for a breath that didn't pinch with disappointment, she helped Mr. Talbert lock up, then walked with him across the street to Clockwork. Trendy but oddly classic, the hip wine bar remained a secret that the tourists had yet to discover. Cass loved its burled wood and brass fixtures, as if a radical Victorian had designed the décor. The crowd was modest by Vegas standards.

"Can I take that wrap for you, ma'am?"

Ryan's voice washed over her, just as his hands smoothed softly down her arms. Closing her eyes, Cass fought the compulsion to turn and fling herself into his embrace. He'd waited. He'd sought her out.

That wasn't the same as making things right.

She owed him the opportunity to do so.

"Mr. Talbert? I'll be over in just a moment."

Her boss waved from where he scooted into Mr. Hungerford's private booth. That was where she belonged, with the people who had made her evening such a success, but she also belonged with Ryan. They belonged together. If only he would admit as much. The old version of herself, so timid and stuck, wouldn't have held out for this long, not when "good enough" remained an option. She was long past thinking of "good enough" as anything but a cop-out.

Unusually dark circles hugged his lower lids. He was just as fit, just as put together as ever, but his fire was missing.

"Now's fine," she said. "If you want to talk."

Without watching to see if Ryan followed, she wove through the wine bar until she stopped in a quiet corridor. Sure it led back toward the restrooms, but she wasn't up for actually sitting with him at a table. She had no guarantee of what he wanted to say, which meant no telling how long they'd need.

Her palms were sweating, so she hid them behind her back and leaned against the wall. Ryan matched her pose. To anyone else, they might have been appraising the Clockwork's bizarre collection of doodads and antique inventions that lined the hallway.

"I miss you," he said simply.

She'd known he was capable of some smooth lines, but the way her heart flipped with those three words reminded her how difficult this conversation would be.

"You didn't call."

"Too scared." He found a strangled laugh. "Seven tours of

duty, and now hundreds of gallons of jet fuel a day, and I couldn't pick up the phone."

He turned, his shoulder braced against the wall. The graceful strength of his body hadn't lost its potency. Cass fixed her gaze to the Windsor knot at his throat.

"You were right," he said softly. "About damn near everything. That fight… I haven't been able to think straight." He shifted his weight. "You got under my skin so damn quick. I blamed you for doing what no one else had managed. You looked deeper and I hadn't been ready for that. I just…didn't know how to trust that we could have it all."

She dared a glance up. Big mistake. His hazel eyes were shadowed with such need, as vulnerable as she'd ever seen. "And the whole Barbie-doll thing? Ryan, I can't do this if some other woman's words are going to haunt you forever."

"Baby, I'm so damn wrapped up in you. The idea of sharing this…this happiness with anyone else just doesn't make sense anymore. No matter what they wore or what role they played—Cassandra, they wouldn't be you." He brushed his knuckles along her cheek. "You said something about not having to choose. About finding a good woman who could give me everything. Tell me I don't have to keep looking."

Closing her eyes, Cass leaned gently into the hand he cupped against her cheek. He was trying. Really trying. She'd seen it in the tight set of his mouth, the clench of his jaw. He had no guarantee that she wouldn't head right back down the hallway toward Mr. Hungerford's table, all without a backward glance. Yet he was humbling himself, opening a vein for the chance they might be together again.

She could give him what he sought, but she had needs too. Needs she was no longer so shy about expressing.

"Ryan, I want our laughter back."

He blinked.

"And not those fake smiles you can force if you need to," she said. "Save those for your COs."

"You can tell the difference?"

"Of course I can tell the difference." She took his hand in both of hers, kissed his knuckles. "If I'm with you, I just want you. No ghosts. No hiding. So tell me now if you can't—"

The end of the sentence never happened. Ryan's kiss was a quick, closed-mouth shocker. He pulled back, looking panicked as if he too had been caught off guard.

Then he chuckled. It was a beautiful sound, wedged somewhere between bashfulness and wicked intent. He flattened his palms along the inward flair of her waist.

"I can." That beautiful mouth was still shaped by his laughter. "Promise."

"So does that mean you want to be my boyfriend?"

"Very much."

Cass grinned. "Good. I don't think I could call you my lover, not with a straight face. I'm not actually French."

"You had me fooled."

"I could've told you I was Cleopatra and you'd have played along."

He leaned in close, touching a kiss to her earlobe. "Only if I got to be Mark Antony."

"Oh, I'd pay money to see that."

Rumbling masculine laughter teased into her body. The glint in his eyes made her shake her head in wonder. None of his embarrassment remained. None of his shame. He was the man she'd met months earlier, who'd drooled after her seamed stockings and twin braids.

She couldn't help but want to reward such a brave step. After three weeks of loneliness, she was desperate for his mouth. Crisscrossing her forearms behind his neck, she stood on tiptoes and feathered three delicate kisses along his lower lip. His arms tightened until she thought he'd crush her corsage.

At the moment, she didn't care.

Relief, happiness, desire and an end to weeks of aching and regret—Cass gave him all of it. Their mouths met, gently at first, as if asking one another if it was really happening. The agonizing was over. He kissed her with all the passion they both deserved, his tongue slicking her bottom lip. With a moan, she opened for him. They nipped and sucked, finding the rhythm of bodies at play.

Ryan's hand slid down to cup her rear. The proof of his need pressed against her hip. He broke the kiss and dipped his forehead to hers. "Baby, you'll be the death of me."

"You'll be smiling when you go."

"Amen."

"Are you going to take me home now? I want to celebrate my night."

"Check please," he said against her mouth.

Cass giggled, then led Ryan back toward where the gallery staff were well into their third bottle of wine.

"Good night, all," she said with a wave. "See you Monday."

They didn't protest, merely lifted their glasses. There may have been a catcall or two.

Outside the bar, Ryan held her hand as they walked down the dark street. "My truck's just up here. I can drive you into work on Monday morning, if you want."

Cass smiled to herself. It was just so normal. Small plans they could make together. She liked the idea that this was only the beginning. "That would be perfect."

"You know, I really liked that guy Bellocq," he said. "He had an eye for beauty."

"That he did."

Ryan stopped her under a streetlamp. "Have you ever considered modeling?"

Laughing, Cass shook her head. "You're nuts. No way."

"No, I'm serious. You have great bone structure." He winked, then reduced the space between them to mere inches. "I'm a photographer. It's my job to notice these things."

Realization hit her first. Then heat. Pure heat. He was doing more than bringing their play back to life. He was offering her *all* of his trust—the first time he'd initiated something from his imagination. Cass felt humbled by the faith he'd put in her. In them.

"I'm flattered," she said, tipping her head. "You really think I have a shot?"

He exhaled the breath he must've been holding. Then it was game on. "Sure, babe. We'd have to take a few test shots, though. Just to make sure. My studio would be perfect."

She pouted. "But, mister, I don't know a thing about modeling."

"Don't worry. I'll tell you exactly what to do."

Epilogue

The casino was loud. Crazy loud. Sitting at a blackjack table on the Bellagio gaming floor, Ryan could barely hear himself think, much less concentrate on his cards. Thankfully, most of the noise was over by the roulette table where someone had gathered quite the crowd. They must be on a winning streak.

Ryan had been on an awesome winning streak lately too. Every time he walked in his front door to find Cassandra waiting there, sometimes with dinner on the table, sometimes with a takeout menu in her hand, he knew he'd hit the jackpot. The nights when she came in late from the gallery and smiled at seeing the food he'd managed not to burn, her smile was another jackpot. One of the huge ones that left a lucky man happy for life.

He hit on fourteen, only to receive a jack. The dealer swept away both cards and chips.

Ryan's fingers tapped on the padded edge of the table without rhythm. His foot bounced wildly. With short jerks, he twitched down the cuffs of the dress uniform Cassandra had asked him to wear.

He was more than nervous. Insanely so.

"Excuse me." A low voice cut through the haze of noise to his right. "Are you alone?"

The tension that had been flying through him slid right out through his toes before he even turned to look. He knew that voice. It was the voice that brought him home every night. "Yep. I'm only in Vegas on leave."

Cassandra was wearing a cream-colored sweater set of all things, along with a pale green skirt that swirled around bare knees. She smiled at him. "I'm on vacation too. From Kansas. I'm a kindergarten teacher there."

"A kindergarten teacher?" The laugh that took him was sudden but not surprising. He and Cassandra did a lot of laughing together.

She nodded as she primly stacked her chips. "That's right. For the last three years."

He managed to get a hold of his smile. "I bet that's rewarding work."

"It sure is." The look she slanted out of the corners of her eyes was all Cassandra, full of minxish humor. "Except when I want to strangle the kids. Or the administration. But that's a job, right? Good parts and bad?"

The dealer flicked out another round of cards. Ryan managed to look down at his. A ten and an eight. He stayed.

She crossed her legs at the ankle. "So you said you're on leave? I can never tell the uniforms apart. Are you in the Navy?"

"Nope. In the Air Force."

She opened her eyes wide. Her lips parted on a quiet gasp. "Ooh. That's so exciting. What do you do in the Air Force? Probably just paperwork, right? My cousin Eric's in the Army and that's all he does. He says it's not nearly as exciting as it seems."

Apparently her character chattered. Babbled, even. Ryan focused on his cards in order to keep from laughing and blowing the act. "I fly fighter jets."

"No way," she breathed. "Are they as fast as they seem?"

He grinned. "Even faster."

The dealer called, and he and Cassandra flipped over their cards. His eighteen lost to the dealer's twenty.

"You're a careful gambler, aren't you?" Cassandra teased.

He broke character for a minute. He couldn't help it. His hand curled over her knee, fingers flirting under the fluffy skirt. "I used up all my luck finding you."

Her expression melted, her eyes going wide and soft. She covered his fingers with hers. "You're a good man, Ryan Haverty."

He leaned over to steal a kiss from her beautiful mouth. "Because of you, baby. If I hadn't found you... I think I would have imploded eventually. Hiding too much of myself."

She stroked a touch down his jaw, then shook her head. "I don't believe that. If you want to tell me more, though, you have my permission."

Christ, she was so perfect for him. Her easygoing acceptance. Her life and energy. Something warm and contented unfurled inside his chest.

"I love you, Cassandra Whitman. You're everything to me."

It seemed only right to tell her there, at the blackjack table. They'd started their adventure at the same damn table. When they'd planned that evening's fun, he'd known instantly where to sit.

Her lips parted. Pink flushed across her cheeks. She hopped off her stool and threw her arms around his neck. "I love you too, Ryan."

The kiss he brushed over her lips started soft. Gentle. Appropriate for such a moment.

As usual, the heat between them flared. Ryan crossed one arm around her back, using his other hand to angle her head and stroke deeper. Her taste went to his head every time.

The dealer cleared her throat. "Will you be in the next hand?"

Cassandra giggled. "Yes, yes, we will." She tugged the black silk cord out from under her pale sweater. At the end was tied a ten-dollar chip.

"Is that what I think it is?" he asked with a laugh.

"You bet." She grinned at him over her shoulder. "The chip from our first night. I kept it as a good-luck charm. But I don't think we need any of those anymore."

She tossed it into play, and Ryan kissed the soft skin behind her ear. "We're making our own luck now."

"Together."

Before the dealer could pass out new cards, she grinned at him again—the wild, reckless grin that made all the blood rush to his cock.

"So," she said breathlessly. "Feel like giving a kindergarten teacher the best vacation of her life?"

Author's Note

The 64th Aggressor Squadron is an active United States Air Force unit assigned to the 57th Adversary Tactics Group, stationed at Nellis Air Force Base in Las Vegas, Nevada. The pilots' objectives are as we've described: to fly as adversaries against allied pilots from around the world, teaching them to better counter enemy tactics. The unit dates back to WWII when it participated in multiple theaters of operation.

Now, the 64th and other "bandits" from the 57th ATG regularly conduct dogfighting simulations in the United States, known as Red Flags, and Maple Flag exercises in conjunction with Canadian Forces. They also add their expertise to the USAF's Weapons School syllabus and travel the country to provide training and test mission support to various units.

All individuals described in this story are fictitious. Research mistakes are entirely our own.

In the meantime, we enjoy assuming that at least one of these dedicated, highly skilled bandits appreciates seamed stockings.

About the Author

Katie Porter is the writing team of Carrie Lofty and Lorelie Brown, who've been friends and critique partners for more than five years. Both are multi-published in historical romance. Carrie has an MA in history, while Lorelie is a US Army veteran. Generally a high-strung masochist, Carrie loves running and weight training, but she has no fear of gross things like dissecting formaldehyde sharks. Her two girls are not appreciative. Lorelie, a laid-back sadist, would rather grin maniacally when Carrie works out. Her three boys love how she screams like a little girl around spiders.

To learn more about the authors who make up Katie, visit www.katieporterbooks.com or follow them on Twitter at @carrielofty and @LorelieBrown.

Zero to kinky in 3...2...1...

Inside Bet

© 2012 Katie Porter

Vegas Top Guns, Book 2

As junior partner of an accounting firm, Heather Morris is at the top of her game. Her straight-laced colleagues wouldn't believe the secrets she hides: her wild teenage past, work-of-art tattoo and nipple ring.

Her orderly life veers off course when she's approached at a wine tasting by an arrogant pretty boy with a dirty mind and a hardcore dangerous profession. She finds herself tempted to step outside her respectable façade for some well-deserved excitement.

Captain Jon "Tin Tin" Carlisle knows women. *Loves* women. One glimpse of the nipple ring under Heather's conservative blazer lights up all his instincts. He's stumbled upon a rare treasure: an exotic beauty with a sexy laugh and a taste for dares.

After a red-hot hour of roulette, their simmering attraction bursts into an exploration of mutual passion that tests even Jon's erotic limits. Soon he craves something he's never desired before. *More.* But for Heather, *more* means trusting, and trusting leads to trouble.

Now Jon must decide if the best sex of his life is worth chancing his heart on a woman who shields hers so well.

Warning: Contains hot power play featuring a fighter pilot who comes from old money but knows all about bringing the dirty. Also: a nipple ring, sex on the hood of a hella sweet sportscar, and one teensy, tiny, wickedly naughty fluid exchange.

CPSIA information can be obtained at www.ICGtesting.com
Printed in the USA
LVOW08s0849110414

381277LV00004B/674/P

9 781619 212459